SLATE DAMNATION

You made me do it

Emery Hale

SLATE DAMNATION

Edited by Sam Boyce
Book Formatting by Derek Murphy @Creativindie
Author Photo by Justyna Makuch
For any information please contact:

emeryhale3@gmail.com

First Edition: October 2022
ISBN Paperback : 9798847661072

10 9 8 7 6 5 4 3 2 1

BOOK 2 IN THE ***OMEGA SERIES***

SLATE DAMNATION

You made me do it

Emery Hale

S L A T E D A M N A T I O N

TRIGGER WARNINGS

-Extreme violence

-Murder

-Mentions of sexual assault (not depicted – a character refers to an incident)

-Torture

Dedicated to the Swann, Orr, Smith, Renwick and Miller family.

Thank you for letting me pursue my passion for writing, rather than pushing me towards being a doctor – cause let's be honest, I'd be rubbish at it and can't add or subtract to save myself.

CHAPTER 1

Pistanthrophobia

The fear of trusting people.

NAOMI JADE

18th of June 2016, 19:36

England, London, Westminster Bridge

With a breath of fire, I observed the godless sight in front of me, only remnants of destruction and nihilism remaining.

I'd had little time to think on the plane, we were all too busy trying to make sense of it all, but I didn't see the point, not anymore. We'd taken care of one minor detail compared to what Trojan had planned.

The Reign Academy was an established source of new agents every year for Trojan.

This barbaric publicity stunt had been decades in the making; part of me knew there was no way we could have known but the other part, the voice raging through my head, was screaming I should have seen it coming. I had gone into this as an investigator, open-minded to every possibility, but as soon as the threat disappeared I'd let my guard down.

Jessica trusted me to unearth the truth. But now – she was dead.

As I stood on the bridge, the evening wind was cool on my cinder-like skin. The air, settling after a downpour, floated around me. It was soft and innocent, yet the sight in front of me made my skin crawl. Could one terrorist organisation do all of this? I feared there was much more to this conspiracy but I had to face facts, and right now I was just staring at shattered glass.

The ferocious flashing of camera shutters blinded me, hordes of reporters clambering on top of each other wanting an exclusive of the biggest story yet. Others stood away from the reporting, live to the news channels, but their eyes flickered back and forth from the scene.

If I forgot the news headlines, I couldn't have known schools around the country had been forced into lockdown. I wouldn't know people were looting the streets and I certainly wouldn't know the death toll, in the last hour, had already reached four thousand.

I was in the eye of the storm but the carnage awaiting just a few feet away scared me enough to keep moving. If I stopped I'd have to face up to the consequences of what I'd failed to investigate.

The police had taped off the bridge for safety, though it wasn't clear from what – the explosion appeared pretty final. The corpses that had been laid out on the concrete earlier had been removed, little yellow evidence cards on the wet tarmac the only sign they were there.

One of them could have been me, reduced to a number on the ground.

The hordes in front of me were as solid as a wall, the road now barely visible. Flashing shutters only giving me glimpses of the next person ahead, all of them battering each other down for the perfect shot of an empty road. How far would those journalists go to uncover the truth?

I could tell them; I could tell them everything.

'Hey!' A rough arm jostled mine as Lily led me away from the deafening crowds. 'We're not here for our close-ups.'

I spotted the team up ahead, all lingering by the steps that led down to the Thames. We were meeting someone who would give us an inside view of what was going on – after all, this wasn't our jurisdiction.

Lily walked ahead, pulling her hood closer, but every so often she glanced back at me – there was something ruggish about her, without the flair I was used to. On the plane she was the quietest, which surprised me; it was as if the churning fire I'd come to know had vanished. It was primal the way she prowled towards the team, like a tiger ready to strike, eyes alert as though she could see every miniscule detail all at once.

Our footsteps were drowned out by others running to the scene of the crime, but I focused on Kayson; he'd been the one to drag me out of the bathroom on the plane, not my finest moment.

Over the last couple of months I'd learned one of his jobs was to keep Quinn safe, and now I was seeing it in action: he stayed tight against Quinn's back as she frantically tapped away at her laptop, looking incredibly small on the large steps, Kayson's denim jacket wrapped snugly around her and secured with a rucksack.

Everyone had stripped on the plane, so while the team talked strategy I was still trying to fix my knickers. We didn't know who we were meeting but he'd get us inside MI5, or so we'd been told. I'd managed to slink away to the bathroom for a moment – it was a place, however small, where I could let the numbness I'd allowed to carry me melt away, even if it was just for a moment.

The knowledge that these guys were free and able to do as they pleased should have comforted me, but now it was a constant reminder of why we were here in the first place.

'ETA twenty seconds.' The words slipped from Grace's full lips with ease, her slender fingers tapping on her earpiece as she headed down the stone steps.

The cold and bossy façade I'd grown accustomed to over the last few months had disappeared, now replaced with cool, calm and collected. It was almost as if she was trying to embody Jess.

We all descended down to the riverside, camera clicks and shutter flashes fading into the background, replaced with the whirring of helicopters. The wind was cold but I enjoyed the sharp brittleness of it, biting at my fingers and face.

The way we walked looked intentional; Grace leading the way, her head whipping back every few seconds to make sure we were following. Kayson stayed by Quinn's side, an arm hovering at her back while his eyes scanned the area like a machine. Lily slipped back, pushing me ahead as if protecting me from behind.

As we approached the banks of the river, anticipation clenched my heart. All we knew was that the man from MI5 was a trusted associate of Nicola's and that they'd worked closely for many years. My personal grievances with her aside, she wouldn't put us in a vulnerable position, not after losing James and Jess.

The river sloshed against the wall, the peculiar smell anything but pleasant. I've always wondered how deep it was; if I jumped from the bridge would I break my legs or go under? Either option curiously brought relief to my mind – this could all be over within a matter of seconds. I wouldn't have to ignore the retching inside of me or the rawness of my throat that sharpened with every breath.

If I hadn't gotten involved Jess might still be alive.

The vile water was tempting, the little voice in the back of my head begging me to jump. Anything could be waiting there, ready to drag me under.

A sudden nudge on my back jolted me from my thoughts. It was Lily who now wore an unreadable expression, only saying one thing.

'Don't.'

Did she know what I was thinking? How could she possibly know? Had she ever been in my position? She mentioned this team had come from military backgrounds, so she'd probably dealt with death. When she witnessed someone die did she ever let those merciless thoughts in? Did she let them rub rabid? Had she ever let them win?

I pushed forward, trying to reel my thoughts away from the water. We were meeting someone who could help us;, I had to appear professional. I had to look like I knew what I was doing. I had to pretend that my best friend hadn't died two hours ago – what the hell was I doing?

On Grace's orders we were to stick to our codenames because she wanted our identities kept out of it. So as far as this man knew, I was just another agent looking for the answers everybody craved; how the fuck did this happen?

The team came to a stop about halfway down the small passage, Kayson leaning against the wall. There wasn't an ounce of panic on Grace's face, she looked like she had everything under control. By the way she turned to me and smiled, the perfect lie was almost believable.

It was only after that it occurred to me: death never gets any easier, no matter how many you've witnessed. You just get better at hiding the pain.

Working as a medic in the Academy of all places meant Grace must have seen a lot of death – how did she get through it?

'Do we know this guy's name?' Kayson asked roughly.

'No.' Grace replied quietly.

I wanted to get through to Quinn and explain my feelings but her glassy eyes were cast down to the ground, the laptop she'd carried now slung away in her rucksack. I didn't have time to ponder what she might be thinking as a sultry bass voice spoke.

'Nightingale, you're certainly not what I was expecting.'

A man stood ahead, tall in stature, the dead-set look in his eyes as subtle as concrete. The sunlight warming his cool umber skin. His thick eyebrows almost accenting his face as he gazed around the team, pausing at me momentarily before returning to Grace.

'Nicola told me you had dark hair but I thought you'd be older,' he commented. He had a similar accent to Nicola's but this was deeper and, if I were honest, a little sexy.

As Grace subtly observed the man so did I; he had no blemishes or scars from what I could see, his long navy coat covering most of his arms. It was a stark contrast to us, who all looked ready to hit the pub. He was clean-shaven, not a single speck of stubble in sight.

'Likewise,' Grace said, with her usual elegance.

'Do I get to know your name?' he asked.

'For someone who's meant to be the senior agent, you ask a lot of questions.'

'God, you're just like A Branch,' the man muttered, but with the shake of his head he moved on. 'My name is Saul Jackson, I've been the one in correspondence with Nicola.'

'We got that much,' Kayson stated, like he'd already grown a hatred towards the man.

Saul didn't seem impressed but continued. 'We don't exactly have an itinerary, but with the country in crisis I've had to compromise.' His formal shoes clicked as he took a few steps down the path. 'Follow me, I'll brief you at Thames House.'

'No.' The words shot out before I could stop them.

The night James arrived at Reign, he'd said he was worried Trojan had infiltrated Thames House. There was no way I was going in there, and from the way everyone was passing skittish glances to one another, they didn't want to either.

The man stopped, turning curiously on his heel. I assumed he would try to analyse me, like the others had done when I first arrived but he didn't, his eyes stayed perfectly level with mine.

'Why not?'

'Can we just go somewhere else?'

'You are?'

'The Carrier of this team,' Grace cut in, promptly standing at my side, giving a brief nod as if she were taking my concerns into account – she better had, we shared the same one! 'Of all the places we want to go that is not one of them, but like you, I am willing to compromise.'

'Compromise?' I echoed.

'Yes,' Grace replied, but she wasn't looking at me anymore. 'We'll go in the side door, nothing fancy.'

Why the hell was Grace agreeing to this? For all we knew we could be walking straight into a trap with no protection or backup. It could be the Reign Academy all over again.

'That's reserved,' Saul stated, seeming amused at Grace's challenge. 'We'll go through the main doors.'

'Mr Jackson, if the Carrier has concerns for this team's safety then you will take them into account.'

Saul clicked his tongue, as if he was holding back. Did we have a high standing here? If we didn't, I don't know how Grace got away speaking to him like that. Since the team that Jessica worked with left her behind, I thought the rest of the services viewed us as bottom feeders. Maybe Grace just had that poise about her.

The long pause from him only seemed to irritate her.

'We're all equals in this team; my Carrier's concerns are mine. If you won't take it from her then take it from me as Team Lead.'

'Not by choice I hear – your last one got careless.'

Instantly my blood began to boil – what the hell did he just say? How dare he! He didn't know the first thing that happened. Jess wasn't dead two hours and that was all he had to say? No sympathy at all. Jessica didn't get careless, the team abandoned her.

I got that we were here to understand how this happened but I couldn't push aside the urge to jump back on the plane.

'And yet, here I am,' Grace retorted, surprisingly pleasant.

We'd only just arrived and this guy was already pushing my buttons.

However, Grace was always one step ahead and far more composed than me.

'Now, we'll go into Thames House but through the side door. We will comply with the security scans but due to the secrecy of our visit we do not have formal identification. If we need to present such documents then I'm afraid that was your department. It's hardly our fault if you forgot the appropriate paperwork.'

'Ma'am,' Saul tried, attempting the polite approach, 'I believe it best that we take the more public entrance. Our agents use that door and I would rather follow protocol.'

'Your so-called protocol hardly stopped the entirety of the United Kingdom falling into catastrophe. Northern Ireland has gone dark, England's Prime Minister's head was on a spike and the First Minister of Wales is missing,' Grace stated, looking tired of his antics. 'I assume we're taking a car?'

Saul looked ready to choke on his own tongue.

'You have no right to talk about national security.'

'I don't? Tell me, is Scotland still standing?'

'Yes but in the past –'

'Then where is the car?' she asked calmly.

Saul bit his lip before lifting a slender finger, pointing up the set of steps we'd just come down.

‘It’s a silver BMW. Your whole team won’t fit, we’ll have to do two trips.’

‘No need,’ Grace said dismissively, motioning to Lily and Kayson. ‘My Runners are going to do some groundwork, they’ll catch up with us later.’

Without another glance, the pair slipped away. Lily took the lead, but her movements weren’t agile or precise; if anything they were slow as she blended into the crowds above. Kayson on the other hand held himself proud, then a split second later slammed into Saul’s shoulders sending him stumbling back, Kayson only giving him a small wink in return. Did they know each other?

I knew this was the plan, we’d discussed it on the plane, but I wasn’t entirely sure what they were going to do. I’d slipped away to the bathroom at that point.

Just as Kayson started climbing the steps, Saul spat, ‘I can’t authorise this.’

‘Well, it’s a good thing there’s no need,’ Grace said, flipping her hair over her shoulder, heading towards the steps herself. ‘Now, I know the country is in crisis, Mr Jackson, and your itinerary has flown out the window but I like to be punctual, so if you would hurry up.’

As Lily went left and Kayson right, assurance sat in my stomach. Even though I hadn’t the faintest clue what ‘groundwork’ meant I knew they’d be on the ball. It wasn’t just me that wanted to get the job done and go home.

The excitement to do any sort of field work had left me; I just wanted to help people. If I stayed by Grace's side we'd get to the bottom of this. It was the best place for me, it wasn't the time to run around playing pretend.

I wasn't the biggest fan of going into Thames House, but if Grace compromised then she must have seen an opportunity. Besides, it would be good to see inside one of the most coveted buildings within British security. Who knows what they had on the Reign Academy?

I'd taken my phone from the plane and as it sat at the bottom of my hoodie pocket, it hit me that maybe I could film something. Would that be possible? I could always try.

Before Saul could move I grabbed Quinn's arm, pulling her with me, her little feet shuffling on the ground as she tried to keep up. There was no way I was waiting for Saul.

'What are you doing?' she whispered.

'Trying to be mysterious, come on,' I whispered back.

Quinn let out a little yelp as I dragged her up the stairs and rather roughly into the silver car that waited for us at the pavement. As I slid in, I made sure to sandwich myself in between Grace and Quinn; we had to appear as one unit. That and there wasn't a chance in hell I was sitting next to Saul – if he said one more thing about Jess I'd probably hit him. Bet that wasn't anywhere in Grace's etiquette code.

The car was sleek with black leather seats that were surprisingly comfortable. There weren't any compartments with hidden IDs though, guess they did things differently here.

Saul slipped in just as Quinn pulled her rucksack to her chest, sitting opposite us, tapping the closed partition behind him.

'Now, I need to know,' Saul started as the car pulled away from the kerb, 'what kind of agents am I dealing with?'

'Nicola should have briefed you, you're really not good at the admin side of your job.' Grace told him, her gaze fixed out the window.

'You can't speak to me like that, I'm your superior, Nightingale.' Saul snapped, but Grace didn't even flinch.

'Oh no, are you going to run to Nicola and tell her that you can't handle three young adults?' she asked. 'I feel like that would reflect badly on you rather than us. You're what, twenty-six?'

'Twenty-four.'

'Well, like they always say, the job ages you.'

Grace was being a little harsh, he didn't look that terrible, I mean – no, stop it.

'Quinn, can you give Nicola a brief update before we arrive?' Grace asked turning to her with a soft smile.

Quinn seemed grateful for something to do, reaching for her bag without hesitation, until Saul jumped in.

‘We’ll be arriving any minute. We can call Nicola when we’re in Thames House.’

Quinn paused, her fingers gripping the edge of the bag, eyes flitting between the pair. I had a feeling any sort of decision-making was going to be a battle, both sitting a little straighter and staring each other down.

‘I believe my Techie can send a quick update, she’s good at her job.’

‘Techie?’ Saul asked, trying out the word. ‘You know, I tried to understand your ways, but I don’t get it.’

‘Our ways?’ Grace echoed. ‘Mr Jackson, our nations are neighbours. You don’t need to understand it, we won’t be here for long.’

Grace gave a brief nod to Quinn who whipped out her laptop, opening the lid. I didn’t peek at what she was doing, as I realised Saul was staring at me.

‘Something wrong?’ I asked, silently begging him to say something that would warrant a punch to his perfect nose.

‘Nothing.’

‘It’s clearly something.’

‘You must have been close to your Team Lead,’ he commented. ‘You’ve been glaring daggers at me ever since I mentioned her.’

I was? With everything going on I hadn’t been paying much attention to my face. Perhaps I expected him to show a little bit of sympathy. I wasn’t asking for grand gestures or a card, but maybe a little bit of perspective. We’d all lost someone – I’d lost my best friend, and all he could muster was some snarky remark.

'She didn't get careless.' I tried to keep my voice clear, but a warm palm on my thigh told me to stop.

Grace threw me a look as if to say 'stop talking' and immediately I wanted to scream. Why couldn't I defend her? I wasn't going to let him defame her name like this.

'No, but she did get herself killed,' Saul retorted, and if it weren't for Grace I would have flown out my seat. 'The whole country has been devastated by these attacks, I won't apologise for being realistic.'

Grace's hand squeezed tighter but her gaze went to the window, as if she trusted me not to launch myself at Saul but not enough to let go. At the same time, the calming sound of the keyboard clicking slowed as his words hit Quinn.

I wished I could smack the bastard in the face – how did he get away with talking to people like this? It wasn't fair, he didn't know the first thing about Jessica or me.

To distract myself from him I tried to focus on Quinn's typing, but by the way her lips clamped shut and eyebrows furrowed I knew she was in the same boat as me. She was the quiet type but I knew there was a storm brewing inside. If Lily were here Saul would be pinned to the floor of this car. Now, I wouldn't say I'd have been clapping her on, but I wouldn't have helped the man in a hurry.

Grace was definitely the silent yet conquering type, she knew when to act and when not to. Even though Nicola trusted him, my own trust was waning. If he was the best man England could offer, then God help us.

Saul was right on one matter, though: the car journey was short. It was if it were just down the street, which in hindsight, it was. As Saul pressed the button to talk to the driver, he let him know we would be going through the side door, and out of the corner of my eye I saw Grace let slip a small victorious smile.

As the car pulled to a stop, Saul was the first one out, holding the door open. I caught Quinn rolling her eyes and wondered if it was bad that I wanted to see what would happen if she let him have it. The thought of seeing her lose it on the guy brought me a sadistic feeling of enjoyment.

I slipped out, pulling my clothes tighter around me, the air now incessantly pricking my skin. Grace got out like a complete lady, zipping her parka up fully as she stared at the sight ahead of her. It looked like a simple alleyway, but as Grace led us closer, I saw that a door was practically embedded into the wall. In all honesty I didn't think a box of dynamite could make a dent: it was pure metal and the lock at the side didn't exactly look like you could pick it with a hairpin.

The three of us walked single file; Quinn at my back, her quiet yet frantic breathing hitting the nape of my neck, her stare practically burning holes into the back of my skull, or rather Grace's. She was the most poised and collected of us all as Saul sauntered to the door.

Wasn't she a little nervous? I doubted she'd been here before. Had Quinn?

Saul banged his fist on the door and as soon as his hand left it, a latch sharply scraped open, the loud clanking of a lock following as the door opened. As he stepped inside, Grace motioned for us to follow, even though the voice in my head was begging me not to.

I'd stepped foot into Reign uninvited a year ago, now I was walking into one of the securest buildings in the country and I was still, utterly, shitting myself.

As we entered, I realised the place was a lot smaller than I'd thought. The room was dark, only lit by small lights in the ceiling. It was a little cramped for my liking, as if they had backed us into a wall. I spotted four pairs of beady eyes focused on us – by the way they were dressed they had to be guards, guns tethered to their belts. Did the agents who worked for MI5 get this warm welcome every morning too? To one side of us was a booth, the glass front reaching the ceiling. One guard stood behind it, his face resembling melted wax.

I knew the world was going to shit but there was no need to act like we'd pressed the detonator.

'Identification?' one of the guards asked, his voice gruff.

Saul reached into his jacket pocket and handed a stack of papers to the man in the booth. Grace didn't say anything but she kept an eye on his every move. He reached into his pocket again, pulling his wallet out and handing over what I assumed was an ID card.

As I watched the guard check everything over, three more armed guards came towards us and I felt myself stumble back into Quinn. Crap.

Come on Naomi, keep it together.

'I need your personal belongings in here,' the man said, holding out a grey tray towards Quinn. I assumed it was because out of the three of us, she was the only one with the bag, but he soon turned to us. 'Anything – phones, electronics, pieces of paper – has to go through here.' He motioned behind him to what looked like an airport security scanner. 'Take your shoes off as well.'

Oh god, I didn't have anything illegal on me, did I? Oh get a grip, it wasn't the airport. No, this was a security room for Thames House and the security guys here had guns! Maybe it wasn't the best idea to try and film, they probably had sensors that could detect cameras.

Quinn slipped her laptop in the tray delicately, as well as a phone she had stashed in her pocket along with some earphones. The man handed her another tray so she could put her rucksack in it as well as her flesh-coloured earpiece. She kept quiet while doing this, throwing small glances to Grace, who only nodded encouragingly as they both moved to take off their shoes.

A plastic tray was jutted under my nose and I practically flung my phone and earpiece in, trying to remember if I had anything else on me. I didn't think I did – when we left the dorm house it was essentials only, and since Quinn was our mobile tech department she had everything.

I thought it would have raised suspicion when we threw in the earpieces, but that must have been normal around here.

A metal wand like they had at the airports was whipped out from the guard's side and immediately waved over us. As Grace was forced to take her jacket off I worried they'd be snapping on the gloves for a full body cavity search. I hoped not, I hadn't had time to shave.

'Is this necessary?' I asked the guard, but he didn't even look at me.

'Absolutely.' Saul answered as the latch snapped open, the papers and ID card being returned to him.

I shook my head, resisting the urge to roll my eyes and making a start on my shoes. Of course I understood why this was happening, but given what had just occurred, couldn't we skip the formalities and start figuring out the bigger issues here?

Despite the room being dark, it felt quite warm as my socks touched the smooth floor. I wondered what was going through Grace's mind as they scanned her; she remained motionless, her eyes solely fixed on Saul. She'd been promoted to Team Lead, something Jess and I joked she'd always wanted. I wasn't the best at reading people but I knew the way she talked to Saul, someone of superior status, wasn't from a lack of care but from a position of power. Belief in her own status, no matter what anyone else said.

Perhaps, even when all the odds were against her, she believed in herself. She believed we could fix this, right?

The trays were put through what looked like an X-ray scanner and unconsciously my knee began to bounce. I always hated this bit. I felt like a criminal, even though the worst thing I'd ever done was steal a Murray Mint from my grannie – oh, and break into a top-secret government institution which trained assassins that one time.

Once they'd gone through, one of the guards banged on the wall behind him before passing our belongings back to us. As soon as I saw Saul's eyes drift down to my feet I'd never moved faster to shove on my shoes; turns out when changing, I'd grabbed a pair of Quinn's pink, strawberry-covered socks. Not exactly the attire of a serious agent.

Just ahead, a door slid open and the guards moved aside, the light from an apparent corridor flooding the room. I didn't make a move, watching what Grace would do first, but she didn't get a chance as Saul took the lead.

'I don't like him.' I muttered, coming up behind Grace.

'As long as you don't punch him, we'll be fine,' she said, throwing me a side glance.

I turned to her, a little confused – was she talking about the incident in the car? In my opinion, it was completely justified.

'You heard what he – Saul was completely out of line.'

'Like I said,' she repeated. 'Don't punch him and we'll be fine.'

With that she took off after him, not looking back.

Quinn came to my side, both hands clutching the straps of her rucksack.

‘You distract the guards, I’ll throw a few right hooks.’ she whispered with a smirk.

‘You heard Grace.’

‘Hey, I didn’t always listen to Jess.’ Immediately that mischievous smile drooped to a sad one. ‘Sure, she gives orders, doesn’t mean we can’t have some wiggle room.’

‘We don’t have all day to stand about!’ Grace’s sharp voice shouted back to us.

Quinn tensed a little. ‘Although we should probably follow that one.’

‘Yeah, probably.’ I nodded quickly but couldn’t help the smile on my face.

Even though I’d been with this team for some time now, every day I was learning new things about them. I’d always thought Quinn would want to stick to the rules, but it hit me a few weeks back that, if anything, she was most rebellious of them all. She was the one to send my mum the videos after all.

The sadness that lingered within was pushed to the back, just like Jessica used to, and now I saw why. There was work to do and the clock was ticking.

CHAPTER 2

Philophobia

The fear of being in love.

GRACE ASPIN

18th of June 2016, 19:54

England, London, Thames House

Saul led the charge, his head held high and formal shoes clicking on the marble-tiled floor. For someone who was my superior, he certainly was compensating a lot.

The inside of Thames House was what I expected, resembling the Academy in some aspects; the floor, the tall ceilings, and the walls of tension that swooped through the air ready to knock you down. No one that passed bothered to look our way, too immersed in the documents they carried, the phone at their ear or the person next to them.

To say I was surprised by agent Saul Jackson was an understatement. Of course he held rank over me and my team but when it came to preparation, it was apparent he hardly knew a thing. The unnecessary interrogation at the riverbank wasted time, he should have known from Nicola's briefing that we were to meet and immediately split off. It would also have saved us from any rogue agents listening in. To say I trusted Saul would be a complete lie: even though Nicola worked with him there were many things wrong with the picture. The only people I trusted were my team and, to an extent, the woman who'd sent Jessica to her death.

I was on the ward handling a blood bag when David got the call. Everything moved in slow motion but I knew it wasn't good news. Before I could stop it, my hand clenched and the bag burst. I didn't care – my mind had already concluded the fate of Jessica-Grace Winters.

Ever since they remodelled the institute I had a feeling information might slip out, and especially after what happened, it was inevitable. Although, as we walked through one of the most secure buildings in the country, no one seemed to care. I didn't care about the politics of it all, we were sent here purely to gather information. It wasn't relevant that trust was thin – we had a job to complete.

I made sure that Quinn and Naomi were behind me at all times; I didn't want them wandering off. Despite Naomi's lack of experience, she was a vital part of this team. If there were any sort of downtime I'd have to check in with her. Getting thrown in at the deep end was never easy.

After trailing down various corridors and up at least five flights of stairs all bustling with people, Saul opened the door to a briefing room.

I unzipped my jacket; the heat in there was stifling. I sat a few chairs down from the head of the table, since I presumed Mr Superior would want to sit there – not that the seating plan mattered when someone's head had been put on the Queen's gates a few hours ago.

Quinn and Naomi shuffled in together, not bothering to thank Saul for holding the door as they sat beside me. The table was short and rectangular, an intercom placed in the middle as well as a bowl of real fruit. A few cabinets were dotted around the room, containing some of the first spy cameras and comm devices. Thankfully the security downstairs hadn't confiscated ours, so Lily and Kayson's voices rang in my ear occasionally, updating me on what they'd found; civilian casualties on the streets as well as the chatter and rumours going round. We needed to be on top of this. Trojan had always been one step ahead, and I wanted to change that.

Saul closed the door with a slam, taking a seat at the head of the table.

'Firstly, to get it on the table, you're not to involve yourselves with other agents or missions, you're authorised to be here for two days, including today. There's a lot we need to get done around London, let's not waste time.'

'Thought you said we didn't have an itinerary.' Naomi stated smartly.

My jaw clenched; her little comments weren't helping matters.

'What she means to say,' I cut in. 'Is that we were under the impression we had free jurisdiction down here.'

'Are you mad?' Saul snapped. 'After everything that's come out of the Academy you expect us to let you do whatever you want?'

'What exactly is it that you've heard?' I asked, trying my best not to react to his outburst.

'That some of the students were brought into Trojan by Daniel Harkness, as well as bringing some of the faculty into the terrorist cell itself.'

'Well I can assure you, Mr Jackson, it was a fairly small number.' I lied, a small smile softly pressing on my lips. 'That's why you were so against my two Runners, I take it?'

'You're lucky I'm overseeing this and that Nicola has vouched for you all,' he said, like we should be grateful. 'We need to find out what went wrong and for some reason, I've been saddled with your team to figure it out.'

'Well then, let's get to it.' I told him, trying my best not to take offence.

He had to be the type of man that worked alone, because anyone with common sense would have taken him down a step or two by now. His so-called 'people skills' needed work.

'We have to consider first, Mr Jackson, that some of your agents may be corrupt.' I said, trying to get the hardest thing for him to comprehend out of the way, given his ghastly expression.

'None of the agents I run are corrupt, Nightingale. All agents go through rigorous training regimes, the surveillance training alone last months, followed by a year on probation. If there were any indications of such corruption, it would have been identified.'

'Don't you have an anti-corruption department?' Naomi asked. It was then I noticed Quinn taking out her laptop once again, good girl.

'An anti-corruption department?' Saul repeated. 'You've been watching too much TV.'

'So, just an HR Department then?'

'B Branch.' Saul corrected, shaking his head in disgust. 'My agents are not corrupt.'

'They get paid to spy on people . . .' Naomi trailed off like her point was obvious.

To be fair to the girl, she was right. One way of turning an agent was to bribe them with cash, something we knew Trojan had a lot of. A thought sparked in my mind so I quickly stood up, darting to Quinn's computer and getting it down.

Jessica's mother was an investor in Reign. Find her, find a money trail, find a source.

'What are you doing?' Saul asked, irritated.

'Writing a quick note for my team to look into later.'

'Anything you write down that is vital to this investigation needs to be made known.'

'Yes well, it's about Jessica-Grace Winters who you called careless and by the sounds of it, reckless and irresponsible.'

'Now –'

'No.' I cut him off sharply; he needed to understand this from our perspective. 'Jessica died just over two hours ago. Do you want to know the reason?'

'It doesn't matter.'

'It was because the team she was working with abandoned her, they left her to die.' As my words lingered in the air, Saul began to shift uncomfortably. 'Now I don't know about you, but I've never heard of someone from MI5 or MI6 doing that simply because they didn't fully trust someone.'

'I take it she knew the risks.' Saul said, trying to defend himself.

'She did – and unlike you, Saul, she appreciated human life. Yes, the country is in crisis so let's move on quickly but before we do I will make one thing clear. My best friend is dead because of your agents. Try telling me an entire team didn't listen to Nicola Ramos,' I challenged, feeling the fire on my brow. 'Tell me with a straight face that there isn't doubt in your mind.'

He hesitated.

'I can't.'

'Good, then we can move on.' I said, taking in a breath. I shouldn't have let my emotions get the better of me but I was close to smacking some sense into that man. 'I assume we'll be doing groundwork at the different sites of the explosions.'

'We've already gone over this. It's bad enough your two Runners are out there, I cannot allow you three to go alone. You don't have the freedom to walk around.'

'We're British citizens.' Naomi stated.

'You're assassins.'

'Who are British citizens.' Quinn added again. 'I should have brought my passport and flown economy, would have been easier than sitting through this pointless briefing, in which you've not actually told us what we're doing.'

This was all getting a little antsy for my liking. My outburst wouldn't have helped, I had to fix this.

'I have a better idea of how we could go about this. My Techie can stay here at Thames House as insurance, the Carrier and I will go with you and my Runners can continue their jobs, they're probably on their way to the crater of Downing Street right now,' I said, glancing down at my watch.

'I will?' Quinn asked, a little confused, but then soon caught on. 'Yes, I will.'

'We're not leaving her here.' Naomi said, turning to me.

'Come now,' I started. 'Mr Jackson is well aware of our skillset if a hair is out of place by the time we get back. Besides, the only time she'll leave this room is for a glass of water or the toilet. Which I assume you have proper signage for?'

Saul looked a little startled at the question, even mesmerised at the utter randomness of the subject.

'We don't have signs all around the building.'

'My Techie doesn't know her way around, she'll have to ask someone for directions,' I said, nodding in Quinn's direction. 'Unless she's not permitted to speak to anyone or use the facilities?'

Saul rubbed his face, completely irritated. I had to work extra hard to keep my smile down

'Yes, she can ask where the bathroom and the canteen are, nothing more.'

'Excellent. Now, shall we go?' I asked standing up, bringing Naomi with me.

Saul followed suit, pointing a finger at me.

'I need to arrange things first. Unlike your team Nightingale, certain motions have to be activated before we can simply leave. You three stay here and don't break anything for the love of God.' He ordered, promptly leaving the room, the door shutting with a slam.

'That'll be the door shut.' Quinn muttered with a smirk.

'I'm not comfortable leaving her here.' Naomi said, crossing her arms.

Without hesitation I reached down my jeans, pulling my thong strap back and retrieving a small black bugging device. Naomi's eyes widened.

'Oh relax, it wasn't touching anything.' I said, handing the device over to Quinn.

'There's no bugs, recording devices or cameras in here.' Quinn confirmed, looking at her computer screen and I smiled.

'See, not just a note taker, she's good at her job.'

Naomi's hands flew up in surrender. 'Hold up, how did you sneak that in?' she asked. 'What about all the security?'

'I designed a lining for her underwear in second year,' Quinn told her. 'Not just hers of course but it acts as a damper and doesn't get picked up on a bug search.'

I placed a hand on Naomi's arm. 'Quinn is going to stay here, gather some intel on the inner workings of Thames House for us and plant a bug on someone important. She has two opportunities to leave the room, one for water to find the target, the other for the toilet, to plant the bug on the target.'

'Who's the target?' Naomi asked.

'Don't know yet,' Quinn said, closing her laptop. 'I'll find that out when I see them. I'll try and put it on the Minister of Defence if he's in the building.'

'Isn't all of that my job?' Naomi asked, perplexed.

I nodded. 'Yes, but Naomi, everyone always overlooks the one with the computer so we're going to use that to our advantage. See if Quinn's been paying attention in class.'

'Are you sure you're going to be OK?' Naomi looked back to Quinn who nodded, casually leaning back in her chair. 'What if something happens?'

'It won't,' I tell Naomi with a firm nod. 'Everyone is far too busy to care. Now remember, Quinn, no one knows your name until I say so, use one of your aliases if absolutely necessary.'

‘Yes ma’am,’ Quinn said cheekily. ‘I’ll keep you updated on important matters and while you’re gone I’ll call Nicola.’

‘Using?’

‘My phone that’s attached to my dad’s server so it can’t be traced,’ she said, sounding like a child getting instructions from her mother. ‘I’ll add your phone onto it later tonight, Naomi. Don’t worry, no one knows you’re here except your mum and I doubt she’d blab to anyone important.’

‘Right, that’s that sorted then,’ I replied, seeing Quinn’s smile. Unfortunately, I had a feeling it wouldn’t last for long.

With everything going on, a smile was the highest thing I could aim for. Jessica was dead, point blank – no two ways about it. Two hours later we were working and the grief had to be put aside. We’d done it once before, with Willow.

‘We’re about a mile out from Downing Street.’ Kayson’s voice rang through our ears. ‘It’s Mean Streets out here.’

‘Has anyone attacked you?’ Quinn asked, opening another tab on her laptop, Kayson and Lily’s channels pulled to the front.

‘No but it ain’t pretty,’ Kayson replied.

‘On my route there are cars on fire,’ Lily reported. ‘Protesters, you name it, even some guy proclaiming it’s the end of days, but he could’ve just been drunk. What about you guys?’

‘We’re heading out with Saul, don’t know where. Is it possible for one of you to divert back to the House of Commons?’ I asked. ‘We need to know who’s going in and out of the building that isn’t rubble.’

‘I’ve got it,’ Lily said.

Screams and bellowed voices broke out from the wavelengths on Kayson’s channel.

‘I’ve got guys marching towards Downing Street, I’ll keep back, sounds like the police are heading this way.’

‘No close contact,’ I ordered.

‘Yes ma’am.’

With that the channels became background noise and I turned to Naomi. ‘I want you to get close to Saul,’ I told her. ‘But first call your mum and ask her to monitor the news for us. We need an outsider’s perspective. If any more gets out about the Academy, we’re finished.’

‘I’m not getting close to Saul,’ she stated.

‘You won’t be, for at least five more minutes. Now go call your mum,’ I said, pushing her gently and handing her Quinn’s phone. ‘Don’t use yours, just in case.’

She let out a heavy sigh but complied, walking to the other side of the room, and I left her some privacy.

We were fucked but not completely, which gave me hope.

A vibrating sound came from the pocket of my jacket, and my head snapped over. Who was that? I knew Quinn had added my phone to the server so the call was safe but no one had that number except David – had something happened?

I grabbed the thing, bringing it to my ear.

'What's wrong?'

'I'm asking her for a divorce,' were the first words to slip through, his once smooth voice now spiking fear within me.

'I'm sorry?' I asked, unsure if I heard it right.

'I can't do it anymore, Grace, this whole thing has put it into perspective. I'm asking her for a divorce. You're the person I want to be with. It doesn't matter what anyone else thinks, I want people to know that . . .please.'

What? No – that wasn't our arrangement. I slowly edged my way to the corner of the room, my nails picking away at the lining of my pockets.

'Don't do this now,' I told him, trying to keep my voice level. 'You can't do this to me now.'

'I have to, my life is miserable with her Grace, you know it as well as I do.'

My next words came out as a mere whisper.

'I thought this was just sex.'

'We both know it was more than that.'

It couldn't be more than that – of course if it were more, I wouldn't exactly decline. Maybe I would at first, it was hardly appropriate, he was my mentor. Oh, get a grip, Grace.

I'd known Dr McKay ever since I first came to the Academy; he'd helped me study on my breaks in between classes, going over everything from anatomy to surgical procedures to labelling blood samples. He was the person I could rely on when Dr Williams was in a bad mood because something or other had stopped working. He was the person who'd bring a projector into one of the private rooms to watch films after hours.

He'd faked my blood results more than once. He'd even promised we could run away together once he got the money in an offshore account. I didn't think he was serious until I saw the account details. I'd even stayed at his house when that bitch of a wife was on holiday – wait, bitch wasn't the appropriate term, she was a lying cunt.

Had our relationship bloomed into something more? I had a team to lead, could I commit to this?

CHAPTER 3

Akrasia

Lack of self-control.

NAOMI JADE

'I'm not getting close to Saul,' I stated.

I didn't care if it was my job, there was no way I would willingly spend more time with that man. He was insufferable.

'You won't be, for at least five more minutes. Now go and call your mum,' Grace told me, handing Quinn's phone over. 'Don't use yours, just in case.'

I pulled up the dial pad and typed in my mum's number. She wasn't going to be the biggest fan of this idea. I could tell her I didn't fly into a disaster zone but that was a blatant lie and given what I was asking her to do, she'd never buy it.

With a deep breath of self-encouragement, I pressed call and, like always, my mum was the first to speak.

'What in God's name do you think you're doing?' she yelled down the phone.

'Mum, just because you went to church a few times as a kid doesn't mean you can just chuck his name around,' I said, trying to lighten the mood.

'Naomi Jade, you answer me right now!' OK, not the best time to crack jokes.

'OK, OK, I'm safe but I can't tell you where I am.'

'I know where you are, it's pretty bleedin obvious given your recent track record. Do you have any idea how dangerous this is?'

'Mum, calm down.' As soon as the words left my mouth, I wished I could take them back.

'When you wanted to help your friend I said yes because you were an adult – I gave you freedom to do as you pleased even though it was extremely dangerous. Now the situation has gotten worse and I'm telling you, as your mother, to come home.'

'You know I can't do that. I called because I need you to do something for me.'

'Do something for you?' she repeated. 'She wants me to do something for her, Charles!'

'Don't bring Dad into this,' I groaned.

'You want me to do something for you, I'll do something – I'll get on a plane and drag you home by the ear.'

'Mum you can't do that, they've probably shut everything down.'

'Then I will drive.'

'Mum, the entire country has gone into lockdown.'

'Then I will walk!' she announced.

The scary thing is, my mother would actually do that.

'No, Mum, listen,' I shot out before she made a grab for the hiking gear. 'I need you to stay at home and watch the news. If they let any more information about the Academy into the public, or any rumours start to spread, we're screwed. Speak to your journalist contacts as well, see if they know of any rumours or anything with facts and figures around it.'

'You're worried about that right now?' she asked. 'Sweetheart, I believe that is the least of your issues. You're in a literal crater!'

'Technically I'm in a briefing room,' I added, but shook my head; she wouldn't have appreciated that. 'The be-all and end-all of it is that we need these people to trust us, and if news gets out of what the Academy really did, then I wouldn't be surprised if they arrested us on the spot.'

'Who needs to trust you?' she asked.

'It doesn't matter.'

'If I am committing espionage, which is punishable by law might I add, I need to know details.'

'You're an investigative journalist mum, you basically do this for a living already.'

'That is not the point,' she said, I could practically see the finger she was raising to prove that it wasn't the point.

‘All I need you to do is watch the news and if you see anything important, text me on this number – not my phone, it’s not safe to use yet,’ I said, exasperated.

‘What counts as important?’ she asked.

‘Anything to do with the Academy, politics or just, ya know, world ending news.’

‘Tell Naomi to speak with that Prime Minister!’ I heard my dad shout in the background. ‘Tell her to speak with those politicians too – tell her to tell them that I’m not paying any more tax!’

‘Oh, shut it you, go and cut the grass,’ Mum nagged.

‘I’ve been out there all afternoon, it’s a beautiful day, where do you think I’ve been?’

‘Well go and paint the fence.’

‘It doesn’t need another coat!’

‘There’s more of my coats on the hallway hanger than coats of paint on that fence!’ Mum grumbled. ‘Fine, I will do this but promise me one thing. You’ll be back soon.’

‘We’re only authorised to be here today and tomorrow.’

‘You’d better come and see me.’

‘I’ll try, OK?’

The briefing room door swung open and Saul stepped in, already looking unimpressed.

‘We need to leave now,’ he stated.

'Who's that?' Mum asked.

'Gotta go, keep me updated,' I said, hanging up – it was better to apologise later.

I handed the phone back to Quinn, hoping my mum could speak to some of her contacts so we could get more ground on this situation.

'We have a short window, let's move,' Saul said.

Despite his demands I stayed where I was, awaiting instructions from Grace but she didn't say anything. I glanced over and for the first time, every ounce of composure had shattered, her lips trembling and skin now grey.

'Nightingale?' I asked, concerned, quickly snapping her from her trance-like state.

Grace coughed, tucking her phone into her jeans pocket.

'Sorry, right, let's go,' she said, heading for the door.

Quinn and I exchanged looks, had she seen it too? Who'd been on the phone with her? The only person I could think of was Nicola. I refrained from questioning her about it though – London was already falling apart, I'd rather wait to hear home was crumbling down too.

'You sure you'll be OK?' I asked Quinn before I left.

'Course,' she replied, opening her laptop. 'Might grab some water in a bit.'

I smiled, heading out. We had a plan, and it also told me something else: Grace trusted the people here as much as I did. Especially after pulling a bugging device from her panties. If Quinn could plant it on someone important we'd get all the information we needed.

I followed after Grace, keeping to her side – not close like I would Quinn, but close enough. The way she'd let her façade slip seconds ago contradicted what I'd thought: she didn't have everything under control, and something back home had gone horribly wrong.

* * *

After being subjected to a car ride filled with chatter between Saul and Grace, we'd pulled up outside one of the tallest buildings I'd ever seen. I didn't bother to listen to any of the chat, it was like they were speaking in code. Saul wanted to take us into his office so we could have a look into some personal records he kept on file, which could give us a start on figuring out the corrupt officers. The sooner we took down Trojan's defences, the better.

I couldn't help but wonder: in what world was I qualified to deal with this? This team was meant to react to catastrophes, to observe and report. This team had been torn apart and yet we were still standing. How? It certainly wasn't because of me. Sure, Grace had given me a job to do but I was heavily inclined to ignore the order. I didn't know how to get close to someone and find out everything they knew – that's a spy's job.

Instead of getting out the car the pair in front of me were caught up in their conversation, but further down the street I caught a glimpse of a woman.

She was barely visible, covered from head to toe in white dust and cradling something in her arms. Men in uniform surrounded her, moving her out of sight and I had to hold back the urge to run after her. She must have been close to one of the explosions. I hoped to God if there was a child in her arms, they were alive.

'My Carrier will take care of that for you.' Grace's words snapped me from my thoughts – crap, I should have been paying attention. 'She's aware of the details.'

Details? What details? Did she mean what we spoke about on the plane? Because to be fair to myself I did hide out in the bathroom for the better part of the briefing.

'I don't need details, I need an explanation of how Daniel Harkness was able to convert these agents.'

Oh, now this was something I could give him at least two essays on – I'm not saying they'd be structured or any good, but I could talk at length on this.

'Simple psychology, really,' I answered shortly, my fingers clenching the door-handle. I'd been holding onto this rant for some time. 'They set rules and when those rules were broken, they'd punish them. If punishments like waterboarding and starvation weren't enough, they held leverage over their heads: family, friends and loved ones. They made sure that any agent Harkness planned on converting cut ties with the outside world. It's like a cult.'

Saul was taken aback by my blunt tone but I was done being passive. I didn't care what Grace said, I'd get close to him on my terms.

'That wouldn't work,' Saul said. 'I mean it happens, but it's unlikely.'

'I can't believe you – you're wrong, I've seen it happen first hand,' I shot back.

'Naomi,' Grace said sharply.

In a split second we'd clocked what she'd revealed: my name. Crap.

A victorious smirk reigned on Saul's lips.

'Naomi. It suits you.' He pushed my hand out of the way, opening the door, stepping out but purposefully turning back to me. 'If we can grab agents straight from the source, we might get closer to finding out who did this.'

Grace's face had dropped, disappointment brooding quietly on her brows. She couldn't have messed up that badly, right? I mean, Saul already knew I was in the country and there were a lot of Naomi's across the nation. Besides, wasn't it just preferable that they only knew codenames?

Suddenly, one of the building's long glass doors opened and a woman stood there, dressed formally in office wear and a purple hijab wrapped neatly around her head.

'Saul, the acting Prime Minister is here. We need you.'

'Ruta, I'm not in office today I'm just dropping by –'

'He wants them too,' she said pointedly, motioning to me and Grace.

Grace bolted to Saul's side, a glare alight in her eyes and for once I understood why. We were meant to be here in secret but at a single glance, a complete stranger knew who we were. How did the Prime Minister even know we were coming? How were we even on his agenda given his boss was decapitated?

'Are you kidding?' Grace asked.

'Let's not do this on the street,' Saul said, his hands raised in surrender.

I was on Grace's side: if he had told people we were coming, then who else knew? Trojan?

'You have one of our own in Thames House and you've neglected to tell us that the whole building knows we're here?' she asked. 'We are walking targets.'

'All the more reason to get off the street,' Saul repeated, his voice challenging Grace's.

She shook her head bitterly, turning on her heel, whispering something to Ruta before disappearing inside.

'You know, for someone in the secret service you're not that good at keeping secrets,' I muttered.

I went after Grace, making sure to keep at a power walk, since her speed earlier practically had me jogging. I passed Ruta, who gave me a warm smile as she held the door open for me.

'Thank you,' I said. Even though the world was crumbling to shit, manners didn't cost anything.

She nodded in return, holding the door open for Saul before following after us.

The building we walked into was one I'd seen a hundred times on TV; it was modern with white floors and grey walls, the windows and doors all made of glass, with four silver lifts straight ahead. There was a matt grey reception desk ahead of us but the four people manning it were manic, their fingers locked in a death match with the phones. Creepily, their eyes followed us as we walked across the reception.

Grace soon slowed down, waiting for me to catch up. Even though I tried to start off with a smile, a glower was dead set in her face.

'I'd probably have let my name slip at some point,' I told her quietly. 'It's no biggie. You let the name slip, Saul told people we were coming – I see it as draw.'

'Naomi, there's a difference between a simple name and exposing an entire team. The Prime Minister shouldn't even be aware we're here. Now, he wants an audience.'

'Isn't that a good thing? Instead of having to infiltrate the meetings we're already invited to them.'

'We're too exposed here,' she muttered with a shake of her head.

Why did I have the feeling we were going to have to get used to that?

'Give me a rundown – the short version,' I heard Saul ask Ruta.

'The country has gone into a state of lockdown. All four nations have closed their borders. Airports have grounded all flights, no one is getting in or out. All pupils have been kept in school for their own safety. The Pentagon has been trying to get through ever since the incident but we've been sending them to voicemail,' Ruta informed him, tapping at something on her tablet.

'Why?'

'I think we should get to the bottom of this before we blab to the Americans. They'll send the warships and I don't know about you, but I don't fancy spending the next six months explaining that to the Palace and House of Lords. Mossad have also been in touch, they want to know if this is something they should be worried about,' Ruta said.

'And should they?' Saul asked.

'I told them nicely to leave us alone, let us sort it out ourselves,' she told him. 'Also Alexander Buchanan has been brought in as acting Prime Minister and the politicians are kicking up a fuss. For the general public, those living within a five-mile radius of any incident sites have been evacuated to hotels. The NHS is struggling, public transport has been shut down, so essential workers aren't able to get in. Most of the hospitals are playing catch-up and there have been reports of surgical procedures carried out in the backs of ambulances, due to the overflow of patients.'

'Ruta!' a lady from reception yelled, her hand pressed over the phone. 'It's Clayton, he won't take no for an answer.'

'This, this is why I will never work for the CIA,' Ruta said bitterly before marching over to the desk. 'Can never mind their own bloody business.'

Grace and I came to a stop in the middle of the lobby, watching as Ruta took the call, and from her tone shift, put on her polite phone voice. Saul, however, kept going, straight over to the lifts and pressed the button.

'That's Ruta – as you can tell, she keeps this place spinning,' Saul said. 'What are you waiting for, an invitation? We're staying for five minutes and then excusing ourselves.'

As we stepped into the lift I had another bad feeling: either this was going to be the most awkward lift ride ever, or by Grace's hand there'd be one less of us when we got out.

As soon as the doors closed in front of us, the words flew like wildfire from Grace.

'How could you do this?'

'Nightingale, please – Nicola should have told you this could happen.'

'We are walking targets for Harkness – my best bet says he knew we would come here and now your corrupt officers will've informed him.'

'I didn't plan for you to be exposed either – Nicola's superiors must have told Alexander. Considering I only found out I was babysitting you all of ten minutes after the city went tits up, I didn't exactly have time to text the group chat,' Saul replied sarcastically.

'You should have kept control of this,' Grace warned. 'We're here to try and figure out what happened, not sit in a politicians' meeting and hope answers appear.'

‘Look,’ Saul snapped, seemingly having had enough of Grace, and for a moment she actually appeared startled. ‘Apart from grabbing those files from my office there is no plan. I didn’t know Alexander knew about you until Ruta opened that door. I know this wasn’t what you were trained for, and you’d rather go about shooting people like trained monkeys but the answers we need might be in this room.’

‘Hey!’ I shouted, but apparently Grace’s philosophy had faster reflexes than my words as she smacked him across the face.

Oh no. Guess the no-hitting rule was out the window.

It didn’t take Saul long to retaliate, his fist raising, going for Grace.

‘OK – Hey! Hey! Stop!’ I shouted, wedging myself in between the pair, trying my best to push them apart. ‘This is a very small lift.’

Considering he called us trained monkeys and cold-hearted killers, I was surprised it was only a slap. She’d been so keen on keeping me from hurling a fist that I hadn’t thought she’d want to get hers in there too. Saul was stuck with us now – and yes, maybe she shouldn’t have hit him. Although the longer I thought about it, the more his earlier comments rang in my ears.

Could I throw a quick swing before the lift opened?

As the heavy steel doors parted, Grace was the first one out, following behind a trail of people dressed in suits. Guess that’s where we were heading.

‘You’re not making this easy on yourself,’ I told Saul, going after Grace.

We weren't exactly dressed for a meeting – I certainly wasn't, it was more of a popping to the shops sort of look. How I wish that were true. The men and women in suits didn't even glance back as they entered the large room ahead. It had two big double doors, with tables all set out in a rectangle, and the windows locked down with what I guessed where thick metal shutters. As everyone started to file behind chairs I spotted the one man at the head of the table, illuminated by the light beaming down on him.

He wore a solemn expression, his knuckles white as he squeezed his hands tighter. His navy suit was wrinkled, as if he'd rushed to put it on, his stubble untidy, like he hadn't shaved that morning, but his hair was neat – he'd at least put a comb through it.

'Please, take a seat.' His voice was clear and assertive but the man barely looked up from his hands.

I didn't follow politics but I recognised his face. This had to be the deputy Prime Minister – it was probably just Prime Minister now.

Grace and I stayed close to the walls but Saul took a seat, reaching for a glass of water. I knew there were steel shutters on the windows but I stared at the wooden door we'd just come through and anxiety riddled through me as I realised just how breakable it was.

I followed Grace's lead, clasping my hands behind my back.

'It's a great tragedy that's occurred today,' Alexander started. 'I can imagine we've all lost those close to us: colleagues, friends, family.'

At that a younger man from down the table let out a small whimper. He barely looked twenty-five, had he lost someone in the explosion?

'What we need to do is figure out the how, fix it, and then get back to regaining this country,' the Prime Minister said.

'With all due respect,' Saul interrupted. 'This isn't the House of Lords or a campaign.'

'Who are you?' he asked.

'Saul Jackson, I'll be speaking for the security services. I believe that the best course of action is to devolve more power to the security sector. We can focus on finding out the why and how while you focus on damage control. The public are running scared, we've had to evacuate everyone within a five-mile radius.'

'And how much is that going to cost?' A voice spoke from the other side of the table. 'You want more power – how exactly did you prevent any of this from happening in the first place? Isn't that A Branch's job?'

I didn't know who to watch: the broken Prime Minister, the angry heads around the table or the poor young man, clearly out of his depth, holding a hand over his mouth to quieten the sobs.

'Devolved powers are exactly what we don't want: we gave Scotland more freedom and somehow they came out untouched.' Another voice sounded.

Hold up? How were we suddenly the bad guys?

'I'm afraid I can't –'

'Saul, don't spout that bullshit. The First Minister must have known the bloody country came out of this without a scratch. Speaking of which, where is she? Right, hiding in that stupid doomsday bunker.'

'Or we managed to stop it instead of arguing about it,' I thought with a bitter laugh, fiddling with a thread on my top.

There was no winning here: this team had managed to stop an attack and now we were the enemy. I wasn't expecting a balloons and a 'well done', but come on. I mean we did stop quite a few people from dying, a card would have been nice.

Wasn't there anyone from Scotland down here to represent us? Didn't we have an MSP or something?

Only when I felt the stares of the entire room fixed on me did I look up. What? Saul shook his head, clearly irritated. I didn't – wait.

'Was I talking out loud?' I whispered to Grace.

'Yes.'

Well fuck.

'Please excuse us,' Saul apologised. 'These are agents from the Scottish branch.'

'Since you're from Scotland, perhaps you'll have some insight.' Alexander spoke up. 'And before you give me some corporate answer, we heard the agent perfectly clearly. You managed to stop the attack?' His eyes now seeking mine.

I wasn't speaking out loud again, not when everyone in the room looked ready to bash me over the head twelve times. Thankfully, Grace took the initiative and pushed past the nerves that were rattling through me.

'Yes, we stopped the attack. There was a bomb that was going to Holyrood, most likely designed to activate today.'

'Why weren't we aware of this?' Alexander asked, but he wasn't talking to Grace, he was talking to Saul. 'Forget the rest of the attacks – you knew of one that was stopped. Why weren't we informed?'

'The entire operation was overseen by the Reign Academy, sir. We don't have jurisdiction there. It was hard enough to get one of our own involved.'

The room suddenly filled with air that would chill a dead man, every head turning in our direction. I think that was the political way of throwing us under the bus. If they were aware 'a few' people had been turned to Trojan's side, then did they suspect us? Better not tell them that every single student there was trained for them, who knows what that would start.

'You're the Omega Team?' Alexander asked, and it was then I realised he was the only one who wasn't looking at us in sheer terror. 'I thought there'd be more of you.'

'We're not here for long, sir,' Grace answered. 'My two Runners are getting some groundwork done and my Techie is stationed at Thames House. We were sent by Nicola Ramos, to get some idea of the situation down here. Although I was under the impression you wanted to see us, sir?'

'Yes,' he said, nodding. 'I apologise, I thought I'd have time to speak to you this evening but I don't. I'll arrange a time when I have your entire team present.'

'Alex, they're assassins,' a man said ludicrously. He sat by the Prime Minister's side, his eyes bulging and head shaking. 'You can't be serious. We need real agents here.'

Wait, what? I thought everyone was under the impression the Reign Academy was training agents, Not assassins. Even Grace threw me a look but I softly shrugged my shoulders.

'They stopped an attack,' Alexander said, defending us. 'Besides, I believe it's up to them to accept.'

'Accept what?' Saul asked.

'Figure out what went wrong within our security system, then perhaps I'll tell you,' Alexander said standing up. 'The United Kingdom is apparently one of the leaders in advanced weaponry, and we have a gruelling training process for our agents, so once you've made a few phone calls, you can explain to me how this happened. Now, get out,' he said, placing his hands on the desk. 'Don't come back until you have some real answers for me. I want to see results, not more excuses. If the Scots were able to stop these attacks then so should we.'

Saul stood promptly but I didn't need to see his face to know he was either offended or mortified. My guess was the former. Maybe now he understood what it was like being spoken to as if you were nothing. To be fair,

Alexander did have a point: if our team had managed to intercept a bomb then why hadn't a team in England? Wouldn't they have come across intel that would have led them to this? Oh! Look at me, using fancy words like intel, talking like a proper agent! Oh for crying out loud, Naomi calm down, you're just pretending.

Saul, now looking rather humiliated, quickly headed for the door, but just as we went to follow, Alexander called out to us.

'Not you two, I need a way to contact you,' he said.

I looked to Grace uncertainly – I couldn't just give the Prime Minister of Great Britain my phone number, could I? I could already imagine the look on my mum's face if she ever saw his name pop up on my phone.

'Yes,' Grace answered smoothly, walking elegantly over to him, grabbing for a notepad and pen. 'This is the number my Techie uses – if you want live updates, she's the best person to call.'

'Thank you,' Alexander said gratefully, before motioning to the door. 'Where's the other one? You only mentioned five, including yourself. I was under the impression there were six.'

'Indisposed,' Grace answered quietly, pulling away from the table.

'Indisposed,' one of the politicians sneered. 'Doing what? Getting her nails done?'

'She's dead, sir. Now if you'd excuse us, we have work to do.' She then turned to Alexander. 'Give that number a call when you want to arrange a meeting. Best do it soon.'

With that Grace left with her head held high and a swing in her hips. An awkward silence fell over the meeting, the once proud politicians now shamefacedly flicking through their papers, anything to avoid meeting Grace's eye. How could they just sit there acting like we were the ones who screwed up? Sure, we weren't perfect. There was an institution sat in the heart our capital which was the literal definition of corruption – but from that, somehow we were able to stop a bomb. What exactly had they done?

'Did you want to say something?' Alexander asked me, but it wasn't condescending, there was a genuine look on his face. 'I think a lot of us have forgotten that this is a democracy. Please.' He gestured to me, and all of a sudden, it felt as if a candle was being held to my face.

Sure. I'd think about what I wanted to say but I'd never say it out loud. Around this table were probably some of the most powerful people in the country. This wasn't like the Academy, but if I did speak against them, would anything happen? Would relationship between the secret services and politicians crumble? Maybe there were more factors at play here than I realised.

'Uh . . .' I trailed off, a little unsure, but then something Jessica once said came to mind. 'Just one thing, the next time you look down at agents like us, remember who it is that got you the intel to make decisions with. Not all of us have the luxury of sitting round a table. Not all of us have the luxury of security. We weren't the ones who fucked up but don't worry, we're going to find out which one of you did – sir.'

Then just like Grace, who was standing at the door, I held my head high and left.

My fingers dug into my palms as the tall doors closed behind us, should I have said anything else? Should I have kept quiet? Dear God, did I just swear at the emergency cabinet?

'Did that really just happen?' I asked aloud.

'If you're referring to the part where you basically told their entitled arses to get to fuck?' Grace asked. 'Then yes.'

'Should I go back and apologise?' I asked her, even though I really didn't want to.

'Absolutely not.' Saul's voice sounded from ahead. He stood waiting for us at the lifts, a collection of files in his hand. 'Now, before they try to pull us into any more meetings, let's have a look at Downing Street. Your Runners were heading there, yes?'

* * *

I had expectations of what Downing Street might look like: filled with rubble, the ground crunching with glass, perhaps the Number Ten plaque tucked away under a rock. What I hadn't expected was the street to be a crater – only a little bit of the building remained, and even then the walls were stained black.

I'd only ever seen Downing Street on the news before, with its long black gates and dark brick walls. Now only remnants of those bricks littered the ground. Most of the roof had been completely obliterated, some tiles pivoting over the edge.

As I stepped out the car there was something else I hadn't expected: the street was completely empty. I knew that people had been evacuated but I thought reporters would be breaking down the barriers. The only sounds I could hear were the soft whispers of the wind and the smack of our own shoes.

'Nightingale, I made it through and picked up Blackbird, ETA five minutes.' Kayson's voice rang through the earpiece and I jumped, forgetting the thing was in my ear. I'd never get used to this.

'If we wanted to keep your identity as hidden as possible I thought this would be a good place to start. We don't need a team from Scotland being photographed by reporters.'

'Why aren't there any here?' I asked.

What happened to all the political journalists? Shouldn't they be among the first people on the scene?

'It's been designated a red zone. Anyone seen photographing or reporting on anything within the area will be prosecuted. Not even helicopters can fly over anymore. Until we find out how this happened, we don't need the media spreading stories based on rumours. We're trying to get red zones authorised all over the city but it's going to take time.'

'Prosecuted?' Grace asked. 'What happened to freedom of speech?'

'What happened to this country?' he retorted, before descending into the pit below.

The air felt a little thicker here, like the dust had just begun to settle. Was anyone standing here when the bomb went off? The street outside Number Ten was a public one, were any bystanders killed? How many people worked in Downing Street? How many people were inside the building?

Carefully, I headed down after Saul, minding my footing as the dirt squelched beneath my feet like a paste – I had to throw my arms out to keep my balance. I hadn't noticed how deep the crater was until I reached the bottom; it was at least three times the size of me. I'd have to crawl up the sides to get back out.

'Survivors?' I asked Saul, but he only shook his head.

'Not sure,' he answered. 'Many of those near the front when the explosion went off were killed instantly, those at the back are either in hospital or died on site. I've not got any reports yet, everyone's a little busy.'

Even though it chilled me to know there may not be any survivors, I was more scared I'd eventually step on an arm or leg buried beneath the dirt.

'Do we have any idea where the explosion originated from?' I heard Grace ask from above, strands of her dark hair flowing over the top.

'I've heard it could be from the cabinet room but I couldn't say for sure, need to wait for the report.'

Now we had to wait and see – we were stuck playing a waiting game in the middle of a war. This had to be a declaration of one, right?

'You're from Reign, heard they were developing all sorts there, did you see anything that could create this?' Saul asked me, his fingers picking at the ground.

'The Academy dealt with guns and people, not bombs,' I told him.

Over the last few months I'd rifled through every inch of that institute, the only thing that could cause an explosion was a couple of hand grenades.

Even though all I thought we'd be able to see was dirt, dirt and more dirt down here, something gold glinted against one of the crater's walls. A sudden ring sounded around the crater, and Saul darted to answer the phone, so I reached out to grab whatever was glinting. Surprisingly, it wasn't a door handle, it was a cat collar. Huh, weird.

'Daphne.' I read the name aloud, mainly talking to myself. The last Prime Minister must have had a cat.

I thought Grace would have come down into the crater with us but when I turned to look over the top, she was gone.

'You OK up there?' I shouted up.

'Fine!' her voice shouted down but she didn't show her face. What was she doing?

I scrambled back over to the edge of the pit, clawing my nails and fingers into the dirt, the toes of my shoes disappearing as I wedged them inside, trying to get a grip to pull myself up. Thankfully, the rain had made the dirt more solid so it wasn't crumbling under my feet. Just as I peered over the ridge of the crater, I realised Grace was in a heated discussion with two very solemn-looking Runners. Lily and Kayson held themselves tall, arms crossed and lips pressed tightly together.

'Unbelievable.'

Just as the words left Lily's lips I felt a light tap on my ankle. Saul stood there, his hands locked together.

'Give me your foot, I'll push you up.'

I'd already started to pull my foot out of the dirt, my trainers stained brown, when a hand shot towards me from above. Kayson didn't hesitate, grabbing my arm and hauling me out. I was surprised he didn't need any help but he lifted me with one hand. Well . . . he was certainly strong. Been doing those pull-ups I presume. Despite the jacket he was wearing his shirt was pulled taught and – no stop it.

I was about to turn and thank Saul for the gesture but Kayson's hand slipped to the small of my back, urging me away from the man. Tingles running up my back as his arm slung around my shoulder, pulling me close.

'I know this isn't where you want to be,' he said softly, breathlessly.

'Don't think this is where any of us want to be,' I told him, slipping the collar I'd found into my jacket pocket. 'We were pulled into a meeting with Alexander Buchanan.'

He nodded.

'Grace told us everything.'

'He wants a meeting with us, don't know what for and somehow, he knew we were here.'

‘I wouldn’t worry too much,’ he said, messily running his hand through my hair, tugging a little.

A giggle escaped my lips as I jokingly threw his hand from my head, trying to sort my hair so it wasn’t a riot. Being in Kayson’s embrace now was different, the butterflies from before had disappeared, as had the constant panic about what he was thinking of me. Honestly, I was just glad to have him at my side.

‘Alexander’s a politician, probably wants to talk legislation or something,’ he said.

‘Ronan!’ Saul’s deep voice bellowed from behind us.

Kayson halted, his eyebrows raising and tongue clicking as he turned back. Please tell me this wasn’t going to be a repeat of the first time I met Chris.

‘Yes?’

‘What did you find?’ Saul asked, smacking his hands together, small flecks of dirt bouncing off.

‘Nightingale was given a full report, she can tell you later.’

‘I need to know information as and when it is available, I don’t work to your schedule.’

‘And we don’t work for you,’ Kayson snarked.

‘Let’s get back to Thames House,’ I added quickly. ‘Pilot is there, we shouldn’t keep her waiting. We can all squish in the back.’ I was praying Kayson wouldn’t suggest I sit on his lap.

‘Mr what’s-your-name, we sent the info to Pilot already,’ Lily said, leaning against the car. ‘We should head back there.’

‘Nightingale, I told your team –’

‘If you keep speaking to them like that all you’re going to get are snarky remarks. I know we’re younger but treat us with some respect. We work differently to you. Thames House is a fortress, yes? Then the information will still be there when we get back, unless you don’t trust the people in your office anymore?’ Grace snapped.

Saul went to reply when his phone started ringing again. He jutted a finger out. ‘Get in the car, I’ll deal with you later.’

Lily burst out laughing, grabbing the door and jumping inside.

‘Come on guys, think Mum’s on her period.’ She smirked and the comment had clearly made its mark; Saul’s eyes may as well have had pointy daggers coming out of them.

‘Seriously?’ Grace muttered.

‘Don’t take the high ground with me. I insulted him, you slapped the guy.’

‘Just move.’

CHAPTER 4

Atelophobia

The fear of not being good enough.

GRACE ASPIN

It was pertinent that the rest of my team were brought up to speed with current events, as well as everything we'd discussed in the meeting with Alexander. The ride back was certainly a tense one, Saul solely focused on his phone while Kayson glared daggers into the back of his head. I didn't understand why he had such an innate hatred towards the man, he barely knew him. Yes, I'd slapped him but that was because I knew he was a selfish asshole. Lily, however, was full of the chat, going on about scared-shitless tourists while poor Quinn and Naomi were squished like sardines in the back.

Lily Chan was one of the people I trusted with my life, even when I didn't fully understand her. She didn't seem at all upset about what had happened, even though a serious tone flickered in her voice now and again. That's why as we sat around the table in Thames House, I was surprised by her comment after Saul and I had given the team a more detailed rundown of what happened.

'So after that really long and boring verbal PowerPoint, in short terms, we're positively fucked?' Lily asked, sitting back in her chair.

'Essentially,' I answered.

'Fabulous, just wanted to double check.'

'So we need to be more careful down here,' Kayson said. 'No problem, we can blend in.'

'It's Trojan we're talking about. Our profiles are in the system, they'll know everything down to Quinn's bra size,' Lily remarked.

'They don't have Naomi's,' I said, looking over to her. 'All Harkness has is a visual profile. She's the Carrier, let's get her in disguise and she can go into more public areas.'

'You've seen the streets, Grace,' Kayson said. 'They're mental, she can't go out there without cover.'

'Why don't Trojan have Naomi's profile?' Saul asked.

'She's an undercover agent under Nicola Ramos, her file in the Academy was a fake one,' I said smoothly.

RING.

RING.

RING.

Quinn scrambled to pick her phone up from the end of the table.

‘It’s the Prime Minister,’ she announced, throwing the mobile in my direction and I caught it with a snap of my hands, answering the blasted thing.

‘The Prime Minister is on the line,’ a man’s voice said.

‘Yes, thank you, put him through.’

‘Hello?’ Alexander said. ‘Who am I speaking with?’

‘Sir, this is the Team Lead of the Omega Team,’ I told him. It may have been a secure line, but I wasn’t going to give anymore away.

‘Excellent,’ he replied, but I didn’t hear anything else he said, since Saul was frantically waving his arms, motioning to put it on speaker. With a roll of my eyes, I complied. ‘I apologise for the brashness of my invitation.’

‘It’s not a problem at all, sir,’ I told him, placing the phone on the table.

‘Is your entire team there?’

No, I wanted to reply.

There were a few empty chairs around the table and I kept imagining Jessica sitting in one of them, leaning forward casually like she always did, fingers drumming on the table. She didn’t say anything, she just stared right at me.

God, why did you call her back so soon?

‘Yes,’ I said, coughing a little.

‘Good. Now the proposition I wanted to put to you earlier isn’t exactly something that is, shall we say, common practice.’

‘Go on.’

‘Now I don’t know a lot about the Reign Institute, but I have had a chance to look at your files. Your skillset is very impressive.’

I shot a look to Quinn who immediately went to her laptop, trying to find the answer the question I had silently asked: how did he have access to our files?

‘How are we able to help, sir?’ I asked.

‘Considering my predecessor was taken out, I need protection. The SAS are busy pulling the strings behind the scenes and frankly, I don’t trust my own security team. I want yours.’

‘I’m not sure I understand,’ I told him honestly – we weren’t a team for hire.

‘I want your team to become my personal security, especially the one called Blackbird. I would use her name but all information apart from your training has been redacted. There’s another emergency cabinet meeting tomorrow but it’s a much larger party and I can’t go in unaided. The last thing we need is another attack.’

Quinn shuffled to my side, spinning the laptop round. The files she found weren’t long but it was the first time I’d ever seen my own file, as well as the girls’. Most personal information had been redacted apart from age, gender and skillset. As Quinn went further down the page we came to Lily’s, and from her list of skills I could see why Alexander wanted her – she was a machine.

When we reached the bottom, we saw finally who’d sent the file. Nicola Ramos.

I had to establish what the protocol was with her over the phone; I thought we were meant to be here in secret but if not, who else had access to this? Even if she was ordered by her superiors, she could have warned us.

I looked to Quinn, whispering, 'Find out who else has access to this,' before turning back to the call with the Prime Minister. 'Sir with all due respect, our team are here for observational purposes only.'

'Yes, well I've thought about that. The rest of my party don't trust you but I do. Once you've informed your superior, I want you there first thing tomorrow. The public are panicking, they're losing faith, so I need you to restore it. It's not a campaign trail, but as acting Prime Minister, I need to try and gain their trust. Show that we can rebuild this country through stability and honour.'

'Are you sure that's the best thing to do?' I asked. 'Leaving any secure location you're in is a high risk.'

'That's why I need you. Your team has carried out many operations successfully according to the file, and we both have a common enemy. Until I've rooted out the bad apples in my cabinet and security team, I want you. Give me a call first thing tomorrow.'

Just as I was about to reply, the dial tone droned through the phone.

'Do we actually have to do as he says?' Naomi asked me, echoing my own thoughts.

'Unfortunately, yes,' Saul answered. 'Congratulations, you've got yourself a job.'

‘At least this way we might stand a better chance of understanding what’s going on,’ Quinn offered softly. ‘Since we’re mostly in the dark.’

At that I nearly let a sigh slip – that probably meant she hadn’t been able to plant the bug on anyone. Damn it, Quinn. I’d have to talk to her about that later.

‘I’m not doing it,’ Kayson said pointedly.

I turned to Lily. ‘He asked for you specifically.’

She held up a finger.

‘Before you ask, no Grace, I don’t know why. I haven’t met the bastard and I don’t want to. None of us even want to be here.’

‘We may not have a choice,’ I told her. ‘Quinn’s right, this is how we figure out what’s going on.’

‘Leave that to Mr Fancy Pants over there.’ Lily pointed to Saul. ‘It’s his security team that’s a mess. They have the whole of MI5, MI6 and MI-whatever at their disposal. We’re here to get ground on the situation and report back. I’m not being someone’s private security team.’

This was going well.

‘How long, theoretically, can it take?’ I asked. ‘This way we get intel as soon as it comes in.’

Kayson flew out of his seat, kicking his chair out.

‘You’re not getting it. We don’t want to do this and I don’t think you can run a security team without any Runners, Aspin,’ he spat before heading for the door.

‘Yeah, I don’t think you can either,’ Lily agreed, heading out after him, letting the door swing shut behind them.

Jessica would have known what to say.

I could practically feel Saul’s eyes burning into the side of my head.

‘Aren’t you going to do something?’

‘You’re welcome to try and stop them,’ I said, motioning to the door before slumping in my seat.

Maybe this wasn’t a good idea. To be fair to myself, I hadn’t agreed, merely entertained the idea.

Lily was right, none of us wanted to be here. I would much rather have gotten on a plane and never come back. Let the world fix itself. But Alexander wanted us, which could be a chance to prove that we could be trusted, prove that we weren’t the bad guys.

David kept slipping into my mind – how I wished I could be wrapped in his arms. In truth, he wouldn’t have been any help but I wanted him there – not as a strategist but for comfort. He always knew what to say to make the worry slip from my mind. He would trickle his fingers up and down my bare back, the other hand on my neck. Goosebumps chilled through me just thinking about it. My phone was on the private server so I could call him, not to talk about the divorce – just him. I wanted to know what he was doing, what he was wearing, how his day was going.

‘Saul, there was a phone call for you in your office while you were out,’ Quinn said softly.

Instead of being grateful for the tip, Saul took the defence. 'Why were you in my office?'

'I was passing by your office, I know when a phone is ringing.'

'Well it'll have been ringing off the hook all day.'

'They said they'd call back before seven, it sounded urgent.'

'So you were in my office.'

'They left a voicemail.'

Even though this wasn't funny at all, I had to hold back a laugh at the pair's little exchange. Of course she was in his office, but if I were to go and check the security cameras I'm sure I wouldn't see any sign of Quinn.

Saul shook his head, rising from the table and heading for the door.

'Be ready with your team to leave in ten minutes, I'll take you to the safe house you'll be staying in.' With that he turned and left, letting the door swing shut behind him.

'Did someone really leave him a voicemail?' Naomi asked.

'Yip,' Quinn said, then she went quiet, going back to her laptop.

Was she not going to share with the rest of the class? I thought she'd at least tell me what went wrong with planting the bug now Saul was gone but she didn't, she just sat there staring at the screen.

'Quinn, tell me what happened with the –'

'Oh yeah, the summer holiday. Mum decided not to go, she cancelled the flights with everything going on.'

The summer holiday? I took a step closer to Quinn trying to eye what she had typed on her computer and when I did, I tried to imagine David's arms around me but even that didn't make me feel better.

SOMEONE'S LISTENING.

'Oh yes, I remember you saying about that, show us the flights again would you?' I asked. 'Was thinking of booking a getaway after all of this is over.'

At least this would give her some more to type. Naomi, instead of appearing clueless like always, stared over Quinn's shoulder. Good, she was catching on. Even though Naomi was in the know that Quinn's mum wasn't upset about the cancelled family holiday, that didn't stop her eyes bulging as she read the screen.

DON'T KNOW HOW OR WHERE BUT SOMEONE BUGGED THE ROOM WHILE I WAS OUT.

SOMEONE KNOWS WE'RE HERE.

This was exactly what I was afraid of.

Maybe now Saul would take our concerns into account. Or was he the one to order the bug plant?

'Now I see the prices maybe not,' I muttered, shaking my head. 'Can you see if there's anything more local?'

Of course this wasn't a disaster but it was a setback, and I hadn't anticipated it since everyone here appeared too busy to care about us. The Reign Institute was supposed to be independent, unaided and under the highest level of secrecy, but perhaps it wasn't as secretive as I thought. I'll mention to Quinn to look into this more tonight.

As Quinn got to work searching for the source of the bugs I watched over her shoulder, hands pressing on my hips. Windows shot up all over the desktop, lines of code streaming down them. Although I didn't bother trying to understand it, I focused on Quinn's expression, which didn't give me one ounce of confidence. Her fingers kept tapping but it didn't appear like she was getting anywhere.

Seeing a notepad on one of the cabinets I reached for it, as well as a pen from the table, scribbling frantically before showing Quinn.

IS IT JUST AUDIO OR ARE THERE CAMERAS?

She pointed to the first one.

'Right well, let me know if you find anything,' I said to Quinn, darting to the nearest cabinet.

I ran my fingers over the smooth surface, checking the edges and inside the drawers, making sure to be as quiet as possible. If someone was listening they didn't need to know we were onto them. I guessed by now Quinn would have checked the cameras to see who had come in and out of the room but given her bewildered expression, I had a feeling the people we were dealing with were slightly more strategic.

I heard a small clink from the other side of the room. Turning, I saw Naomi had opened one of the cabinets and was looking inside. I threw my hands up, waving frantically – that was probably a priceless security artefact.

Her head snapped over and I mouthed 'no', but she pointed to MI6's first ever spy cam with a hopeful nod, which I soon crushed with the shake of my head.

Loud footsteps clicked outside the room along with the low tones of Saul's voice. What happened to ten minutes? We both sped back to the table but soon realised Naomi had left the cabinet door open, so she sprinted back. I was going to have to give her a lesson about not touching things that she doesn't know how to work. It was a cabinet, how difficult was it?

'Close it,' Quinn whispered, her eyes now focused solely on Naomi.

'I'm trying,' Naomi whispered back. She pushed it gently at first, but after another failed attempt whacked it shut, shattering the glass of the door.

We were here to observe, keep the peace, gain their trust and now we're smashing cabinets. Splendid. Saul's voice outside paused for a moment and even though breaking something wasn't exactly treason, it didn't look good.

In a split second, Naomi flung off her jacket, throwing it over the glass on the floor and standing tall in front of the now three-sided cabinet.

The door to the room sprung open, Saul leaning in. 'What was that?' he asked, looking at me.

'My brain shattering from your stupidity,' I told him, making sure to keep his attention on me. 'We've been out in the open too long, we need to get to the safe house. I hope it's all arranged?' I asked, giving him a look before heading out of the room and luckily, he followed.

Well our nations weren't best friends to begin with and now Naomi might have broken a priceless artefact then thrown a jacket over it.

I could hear the scuffling of Quinn and Naomi and decided to keep Saul distracted with some light conversation.

'I do have some organisational skills,' Saul told me pointedly.

'I beg to differ but carry on,' I said in retort.

'It's been decided that I'll stay in the safe house with you. Considering you're vital assets now, you need protection.'

'With all due respect, Mr Jackson,' Quinn's voice piped up from behind, 'your branch's safe houses aren't really safe. I mean they have control panels to fry anyone's brain, but they're either near main roads or in the middle of nowhere.'

'Your point?'

'They're either easily accessible or not at all, which poses a problem for us if we had to make a break for it.'

'You're never happy are you?' Saul asked. 'You're lucky you're even getting a safe house with everything going on.'

Quinn did have a point, but wherever we stayed was never going to be safe, and it was somewhere to put our heads for the night. It was also a far better option than sleeping on the streets.

Saul led us down the same corridor we'd arrived by but started heading towards the main entrance, where a standard reception desk sat with no one manning it, the phones' incessant blaring echoing around the halls.

I caught the figures of Kayson and Lily both leaning on the entrance door ahead but as soon as they saw us, they turned their backs.

For goodness' sake, did Runners have to be so stubborn? It was just an idea.

I made sure to speed up, walking a good bit ahead so I could speak to Dumb and Dumber first. Although right now, it looked like they were pretending they couldn't see me. Sorry, Runners weren't stubborn, they were childish.

'What happened to professionalism?' I asked.

'We'll act professional when you stop taking jobs without even asking us,' Lily spat back.

'I didn't agree to anything.' I let my voice slip but reined it back in. 'If you don't want to do it we won't, but you need to consider what we'll lose out on if we refuse.'

'Yes, because I really want to drag the Prime Minister's ass about,' Kayson said. 'It would be the highlight of my week. In case you've forgotten –'

'I've not forgotten,' I snapped, shutting him down. 'If Trojan are here, being beside the most powerful man in Britain is a good call.'

'Jessica would have at least –'

'No, Jessica would have said yes straight away, then told you the score.' I stopped dead, eyeing up the pair of them. 'I get it, you're upset and there will be plenty of time for that when we get back to the safe house, so can you two please pretend to be a part of this team until I can convince Saul to leave?'

The pair sighed, exchanging looks with each other, and as we glanced over to Quinn and Naomi getting in the car, I added, 'You might hate me right now but let's be honest with ourselves, Jess wouldn't know what to do either.'

'You're wrong,' Kayson said.

'No, she's not,' Lily admitted, shoving her hands in her pockets. 'Jessica didn't know what she was doing half the time, she just pretended like she did cause it made us feel better.'

It was something the team and I had become used to over the years: whenever there was a crisis, or punishments being dealt out, Jessica always had a plan. It may have been a fruitless one but it gave us something to focus on. If she was here right now, she'd know exactly what to say to turn things around.

I could admit to myself that I had no idea what I was doing. Imagining Jessica sitting at that table only made me think of what she said to me in confidence, the night Naomi made a run for it and we'd become victims to Trojan's drugs.

'Look at me, we'll get through this,' she'd said, through the shadows licking her skin.

I'd reached out a hand across the empty space between the beds and she grasped it so tight.

'We're not even going to know who we are. I felt it earlier, I'm losing myself,' I'd said.

'Where's that faith of yours?' she asked. 'We're going to make it through this, just maybe in a way you won't expect.'

Naomi and Kayson certainly weren't my idea of salvation and yet, here I stood. I knew I had to keep Jess in the back of my mind: if I kept her attitude and outlook then we'd get through this. We had to.

Even though Kayson looked worlds away from accepting this bargain, Lily nodded, in a way that told me she wasn't happy but was willing to play along.

'Let's go,' I said, heading to the car.

'God, I need a bottle of wine, can we pick up some on the way?' Lily asked.

* * *

Quinn was right, this didn't look very safe. The house we pulled up to was at the back of a small estate, all the lights were on but as we got out the car I spotted two men just randomly walking around. They were dressed as civilians but it was obvious from their beady eyes and stature, they were security.

'In you go,' Saul said, his long legs making him taller than Lily.

'Don't you have the key?' I asked.

'The door's been unlocked by our security team . . .' He trailed off, looking to his watch. 'Two minutes ago.'

'Wow,' Lily drawled, 'I feel safer already.'

‘They just run things differently down here,’ Naomi tried.

‘Yeah, differently and unsafely,’ Lily said. ‘I’ll go check the house for any serial killers that may have snuck in while your lame-ass security waltzed about pretending to be cool.’ She headed towards the house and with a thud kicked the door in, sending it crashing against the wall. ‘Yoo-hoo! Mummy’s home!’

Saul turned to me but I didn’t get a chance to comment before Kayson marched ahead, taking Naomi with him.

‘Just be glad it’s not your face,’ he snarked.

Naomi attempted to apologise but was practically dragged away by Kayson’s firm grip.

‘It’s been a long day,’ I said, trying to appease Saul.

Lily was just upset I would let her stop at the church or shop on the way back.

I looped my arm in Quinn’s and headed inside – it was getting chilly so I didn’t want to hang around all night. The house was quite lovely; the hallway wallpaper really accentuated the security panel on the wall. A flight of stairs sat dead ahead while the doors to my left and right led to various rooms. I believe I heard Lily clattering around in the kitchen – probably looking for something to drink.

‘Gracie,’ Quinn said gently, her hand clenching mine. ‘I couldn’t find anyone to place the bug on, all the important people were in meetings or had left the building.’

'It's OK, these things happen. Have you still got it?' I asked and she nodded. 'Good, then we can use it for something else.'

It was a little irritating that she'd failed but like I said, these things happened. Just as I turned however, Quinn said, 'I can't do another meeting.'

It was only then I realised the poor girl was falling apart: cheeks flushed, eyes like glass and body trembling like a flower in a storm. Earlier, I'd put it down to exhaustion but it was far more than that. When Willow died, Lily told me she'd held Quinn for hours, that she'd never heard a cry like it. In this moment, Quinn was teetering on the edge of a thin blade and I didn't know what to do.

What would Jessica say?

'Quinn, I know it's difficult,' I started, but as soon as the words slipped from my lips, her little face dropped. 'It'll be a quick one, everyone needs to know what to do tomorrow.'

'You can tell me in the morning, please,' she protested.

'There won't be time, we'll be heading straight out,' I told her firmly, but it didn't seem to make things any better.

Without another word, she ripped her hand from mine and shot off. OK, perhaps that wasn't the best way to handle it. The way she looked at me was unlike anything I'd ever seen from her. I understood she was tired but we were all going through the same grief.

I went to call after her but stopped, seeing her coat disappear behind the wall. I shouldn't baby her – Jessica had shouted multiple times, even made her cry. This was just a setback. Quinn was strong, she'd be fine.

Saul slipped past me, a grin on his face.

'What?' I asked.

'For a Team Lead you don't appear to be that good at leading, didn't your predecessor teach you anything?'

'She taught me to smack anyone who disrespected me,' I replied. 'But I believe you and I already covered that.'

I kept my head high following after Quinn, making sure the small heels of my boots sounded off the floor. I headed straight for the kitchen; Lily and Kayson were passing a half-empty bottle of what I presume was rum between them, while Quinn pretended to be busy on her laptop.

'Really?' I asked, pointing to the bottle.

'You wouldn't stop at the shop or the church,' Kayson remarked.

Oh, for crying out loud.

I heard Saul behind me and moved to let him through. The kitchen was a little cramped so I had to push myself back against the cheap laminate counter.

'You really are living up to the Scottish stereotype aren't you?' Saul mocked. 'Drinking on the job.'

'And you're really living up to yours but when I want to come off as a condescending asshole, I make sure to wear higher-waisted trousers,' Lily snapped back.

'The plan of action for tomorrow?' I cut in before a full-on argument broke out.

'Given Alexander wants you to be his new security team –'

'Which we've not agreed to,' Lily added.

'The Emergency Cabinet as well as different branches of government will be attending tomorrow. Alexander's private security will be with him as he travels there but once he's in the building they'll step back, and you become the primary team.'

'Dance monkey, dance,' Quinn muttered quietly from across the kitchen.

'Saul, we're here to observe and report,' Kayson stated. 'How many times do we need to say it?'

'You don't have much of a choice. It's a chance to see who's really in charge.'

'In charge?' I echoed.

'Trojan. If you think this government is corrupted as it is, then the big players will presumably be there tomorrow.'

I could get Quinn to compile a list of everyone and check their backgrounds. They'd probably all appear squeaky clean, but we just had to scratch the surface.

'Excellent.' I clasped my hands. 'Saul, I'll see you tomorrow, we'll be ready to leave for seven.'

He paused. 'I'm staying here.'

'No you're not,' I told him. 'You don't trust us and we don't trust you. I believe it's better we go our separate ways now.'

'Nightingale, this safe house was given to you on the condition I'd be here to supervise.'

'Well, we won't tell if you won't.'

Saul stood in silence for a moment before scoffing and marching out, the door slamming shut behind him. I had a feeling he was as keen to be rid of us as we were of him.

'Now Quinn, I need you to –'

'No.'

A stillness fell around the room. Only Naomi, leaning against the back wall, appeared confused as Lily, Kayson and I exchanged looks. Quinn had never refused an order – ever.

'Quinn, I need you to do a few background checks before tomorrow,' I tried again.

She slammed the lid of her laptop shut and tucked it under her arm, heading for the door. I didn't try to say anything and neither did she, but something changed in that moment. Something snapped. She whipped round, jabbing a finger in my direction.

‘I thought you would be different but you’re not,’ she spat in my face. ‘I thought you would at least care about what happened. You criticised Jess all the time for moving on too quickly and pretending things didn’t happen.’

‘No I didn’t.’

‘Stop denying it!’ she yelled, and I nearly stepped back.

‘Quinn, it’s OK,’ Lily said softly, it didn’t seem to make a difference.

I expected tears to be brimming in her eyes but there was nothing except anger.

‘You’re such a hypocrite. The first night Naomi stayed you went into Jessica’s room and told her how wrong she was for letting her stay, told her she was wrong for moving on from Willow so fast. That it wasn’t right, it wasn’t decent.’

‘How do you know that?’ I asked.

‘Don’t even get me started on what you said about Naomi in the command room, you said she was dangerous, that she would get us all killed.’

‘I never said that.’

Lily stepped forward.

‘Quinn it’s been a long day, come on, we’ll head upstairs, we can talk –’

‘No!’ she yelled. ‘No, I’m sick and tired of this. Jessica is dead and the only people who seem to care are the ones who don’t lead this team. You wanted Team Lead from the beginning but Harkness picked Jess and you resented her for it ever since. Now you've got the job and guess what? You're not any better at it than she was!'

'Quinn, you don't know what you're talking about,' I warned.

She laughed. 'So when Jessica died and you stood up at the back of the room doing nothing, you didn't mean it when you said that she might still be alive if it wasn't for Naomi.'

'OK, stop now.' Kayson walked towards her, reaching out an arm.

'Don't touch me.' She recoiled. 'You know I'm right. You were all there when she said it.'

'Did you?' Naomi asked, her voice deeper.

When Quinn brought it up, I hardly remembered saying it. Perhaps I did – OK yes, I did, but I didn't mean it. Jessica had just died and it slipped out. Why she was using this against me I didn't know. Was it because she was hurting?

'Yes,' I answered solemnly. 'But I didn't mean it.'

'It's not like you're wrong,' she replied.

'No, Naomi, I didn't mean it.'

There was no way we could have known if Jess would still be alive or not; there was no way of knowing if Kayson's plan would have worked without her. I was angry beyond belief, I didn't mean anything by what I said, it was in the heat of the moment, wasn't I allowed some indiscretions?

'I rest my case,' Quinn stated, stomping away up the stairs.

Lily muttered something under her breath before roughly barging past me, my hand flying to my forehead. This was exactly what I wanted to avoid, this was the time we were meant to work together but so far, all I'd managed to do was drive us apart.

'I'm going for a walk,' Naomi announced.

'I'll come with you,' Kayson said, but Naomi was already halfway out the kitchen.

'On my own.'

A few seconds later the door slamming once more reverberated through the house. Well, at least she'd be safer than the rest of us out there, no one cared who she was. She was a nobody and for once it was going to play in her favour. That's the difference between me and her, people knew who I was; important people with power who could destroy my life in a flash, and that was only including the people back home. What I would give to be a nobody.

'Did you know Quinn was going to say that?' I asked.

'Is that seriously your concern right now?' Kayson scoffed, taking another gulp of the rum. 'Your reputation?'

'No it's not, I just don't know where that all came from.'

'Take a look in the mirror, maybe you'll figure it out.'

I bit my tongue, holding back any further remarks. This was a mess. I could admit that – just not out loud. I wasn't a hypocrite – OK maybe I was, but I didn't need to admit it. Yes, I was trying to be like Jess, but only because the way she led this team worked, and I thought if I acted the same then I'd get the same results. Besides this was . . . we could . . . why couldn't I do this? Warmth flushed through my cheeks, my fingers falling over my eyes as I tried to hide the inevitable. Why couldn't I be strong like her? I'd never seen Jess cry, ever.

A sob broke from my lips and that's when the shaking started.

'Come here,' Kayson said, this time his voice soft instead of stern.

'No, please,' I begged – if he came any closer I'd never stop crying.

'Grace,' he tried.

'Please.'

Large strong arms wrapped around me. I tried to push them away but his hold was firm, strong.

'It's OK,' he said, his hands supporting my back.

It was then I let my guard down, my whole body shivering, pins and needles spiking up my arms as I let out the first cry, clenching the material of his shirt. My soaked eyelashes pressing into his chest, wishing the world could just disappear.

'I can't do this,' I admitted.

'Yes you can,' Kayson told me. 'You just need to lead this team like you would, not like Jessica.'

'But her way worked.'

'Because she's Jess.'

'She was stronger than me.'

'No, she was just better at repressing every ounce of emotion.'

At that we both laughed, pulling away from each other. Even though it wasn't something to laugh at, we did anyway.

'I can't believe I cried in front of you,' I muttered.

'Oh, I know,' Kayson said, mocking disbelief. 'I'm revelling in it.'

'A leader should be strong. They shouldn't need reassurance, they should know what they're doing, even when they don't.'

'Again, you're thinking like Jess,' Kayson told me. 'You are strong and asking for help isn't a bad thing.'

'Why are you being so nice?' I asked. 'A minute ago you hated me.'

'Well, you were crying, I'm not a dick.' He smirked and we both turned to the window, gazing out at the sunset. 'After everything we've all been through, I think we should just be decent with one another. No more hiding things or going behind each other's backs. Just plain honesty.'

'You think that's how we'll survive this?'

'I think that's how we'll stay together.'

This sunset was a peculiar one: against the cold sky it looked like the city in the distance was on fire, the clouds now smoke from the desolate remains. A blaze at its heart, churning away liked something damned had risen.

He was right, maybe all you could be is decent, a decent human being amongst the anarchy.

'I should go and apologise to Quinn,' I said.

'I'll come with you,' Kayson said. I was waiting for him to make a joke but his face was one of sincerity.

As we headed up the stairs I wondered what I was going to say and how I was going to say it. Quinn was probably bawling her eyes out so I had to keep it simple, soft and gentle. She always said I gave good hugs, so maybe I could do one of those. This house probably didn't have any hot chocolate or green tea but there should be something around here.

Kayson pointed to the first door on the left, the only one slightly ajar. Knowing Lily, she was probably trash-talking me but I didn't mind – if it made Quinn smile it was worth it. Maybe if I admitted acting like Jess was a bad idea then she'd forgive me.

I went to grasp the handle but stopped after hearing a rather strange sound. Kayson mirrored my expression as we peeked through the gap in the door. The blubbering sight of Quinn I'd expected was far from the truth; Lily's hands sat at the button of Quinn's jeans while their lips crashed together. From this angle it was hard to tell but I believe there was tongue.

The pair of us slowly edged away from the door, heading back down the stairs.

'We should come back later,' I whispered.

'I can't believe it,' Kayson admitted.

'What?'

'Quinn and Lily, those two, together.'

'Do you have a problem with it?' I paused, a hand falling to my hip.

'No, just – Quinn didn't strike me as Lily's type.'

‘Anything qualifies as Lily’s type as long as it has a vagina.’ I smirked, walking back to the kitchen.

‘Grace, I’m horrified, I’ve never heard you speak so vulgar,’ Kayson mockingly joked.

‘Don’t tell the nuns at my convent,’ I threw back.

Kayson was right, I shouldn’t lead like Jessica, I should loosen up and figure things out my own way. That started by letting Quinn and Lily forget about everything for one night. If I was Jess I would have walked in, awkwardly stood there and made them stop while I told them what the plan was for tomorrow but I’m not her, I’m me.

Maybe it was a good thing those two were getting it on, might make them more vibrant tomorrow.

CHAPTER 5

Lassulus

Worn out, exhausted.

NAOMI JADE

Was this all my fault?

Sure, Grace said she didn't mean it but there had to be some truth behind her words. It was like a tidal wave had washed over me but this time I wasn't numb, it was like grains of sand were scratching at my skin. I didn't even know where I was going. I just had to keep walking.

Shoving my hands into my pockets, I let my fingers fiddle with the thin material. Jessica died this afternoon – when she got back from her mission with MI6 we were meant to go out for lunch. There was this little place in Glasgow that had just opened up – I thought we could go together.

A lot of the Reign students protested against keeping the Academy a secret. A lot of them wanted to tell their families what was going on but Nicola had convinced them not to, much to my annoyance. She said that she had to get everything in order while the school was being remodelled, that everyone would get a fair chance to speak in court, however steps had to be taken before then to avoid pure anarchy. In Nicola's defence, I could see her point now. If it had gotten out, parents and agents from around the world would have rained down hell; couple that with terrorist attacks and a new Prime Minister, and I think a civil war might have broken out.

How was it fair though? Jackie was murdered for speaking out, where was the justice for her? Where was the justice for Willow or Jessica? I vowed then that they'd never be forgotten.

'What the hell are you playing at?' Saul called from across the street, breaking me from my storming thoughts. 'Get back inside.'

He was standing by the car we'd arrived in, laptop resting on the roof and phone in hand. Even though it felt like I'd walked a mile, I'd really only walked halfway down the street.

'I needed fresh air.'

'There's a garden.'

'Do you get off on making people feel like shit or is that just a personality trait?' I snapped. 'Yes, the world is going to shit but can you just be understanding for one goddammed minute?'

At my words he closed the laptop, slipping it away in the car before almost cautiously making his way over. Pushing his hands in his pockets, he let out a sigh.

'I apologise, I've never really had the luxury to linger on the past.'

'You're not lingering though, you're just a twat.'

He laughed heartily. 'Fine, I'm a twat.'

'What were you doing anyway?' I asked. 'Thought you would have left already.'

His smile was almost charming, though it wasn't anything like Kayson's.

'Like Nicola, I run many teams. I was waiting to get their reports before I headed home.'

'Did you lose any of them?'

'Fortunately, no.'

Was it wrong for me to hate him because of that? He'd gotten off easy, surely he cared about the agents he ran. Would he be as torn up as the rest of us if he'd lost someone? Why wasn't he in agony like me? Agony was something I'd always thought was physical, but it wasn't. Every breath I took was one that Jessica didn't – every breath reminded me that she was no longer here. Every breath slipped in raw and left like a whisper: it wasn't heavy but it could have brought me to my knees.

'Did you see any signs of these attacks?' I asked. I couldn't break down in front of him.

'After the one from Holyrood we took extensive measures to detect such things, but nothing was picked up. Anything that was turned out to be false.'

‘You told the Prime Minister you didn’t know.’

‘No,’ he corrected me. ‘I said the facts. In those meetings they don’t care about what you did, they care about how you’re going to solve the problems at hand. Even if I did tell them, they would have just seen it as more excuses, more examples of how we failed as a security team.’

Saul looked a little sombre after that. He did seem to be under a lot of pressure but so was everyone. Besides he should be celebrating – all of the teams he ran were still alive.

‘We all failed,’ I told him. ‘I thought the threat was over. I should have kept digging.’

‘Was there any evidence that there would be any more attacks?’ he asked.

‘I don’t know, I never checked.’

‘Well, there was the whole thing with Daniel Harkness,’ Saul said. ‘I also hear the entire system at Reign has changed. Presumably, that would keep you busy?’

Despite what I thought about Nicola, she’d been great in the remodel of the Academy. Once the school was cleared and the prison level sealed off, she’d sat down with all the faculty, saying they could either help or go to prison. The faculty, as far as I was aware, were now constantly monitored by Nicola and one of her teams. Grace had shown us a picture she’d taken of the new curriculum – it looked good. There was everything from hand-to-hand combat, to language classes, to driving lessons and more.

I'd also been allowed to train with the team and Kayson. I went there three days a week for training, then on the weekends, I studied from books and case files that Jessica and Grace had compiled for me. I wasn't an expert, but I surely knew more about the world I'd been so blindly walking through before.

'Yeah, it did,' I said.

'How old are you?'

'Eighteen, nineteen in a few months.'

'So, you're still a kid.'

'You're calling me a child now?'

'No,' he said adamantly. 'You just . . . you don't have the same experience. The built-in paranoia. My security team unlocked the house for you all practically as we drove up, and your team were scared that somehow in that time, Trojan or a criminal had broken in.'

'I'll get the hang of it.'

'Please, push it away as long as you can,' he said, which made me pause. 'It's nice to finally meet an agent who isn't constantly looking over their shoulder. You even hold yourself differently.'

I wanted to tell him I wasn't an agent and I was practically still reading the how-to guide.

'Well, like you said, you don't understand us Reign lot,' I replied.

'I'd like to.' This time his voice was soft, any hint of the malice from before fading away. 'If you'd let me.'

'It's not really my call.' I shrugged. 'Nightingale is in charge.'

'Naomi,' he mused, staring right at me. 'I've had the displeasure of meeting many people in this industry but I've never met anyone like you.'

Seriously? What kind of line was that?

'I'm sure there's plenty of people like me,' I told him dismissively.

'Suit yourself,' he said as I turned, ready to keep walking, 'but I've never met someone who'd speak to the Prime Minister and Emergency Cabinet like that.'

'Oh, please.'

'Really, I haven't.'

At that I paused. Surely someone had to have shouted in their faces at some point? Even then I didn't shout – I just stated the facts, then proceeded to blame and swear at them. I probably could have worded it better.

'Reign trains assassins – they're tough,' I told him.

'I'm starting to see that,' he commented, motioning back to the house. 'You should head inside.'

Even though it was the last thing I wanted to do, perhaps it wasn't the smartest decision to linger out here. There was no need to take unnecessary risks.

With a heavy sigh I turned back towards the house. What awaited me inside? I couldn't bring myself to look Kayson in the eye – did he think like Grace? For so long I worried what the team thought of me, if they saw me as an outsider. What if now they only saw me as the reason Jessica died?

'Are you alright?'

Saul's words struck me as odd, as I was no longer facing him. It hadn't occurred to me that my arms had slipped around my waist.

'Fine,' I replied but my lips trembled.

What if they hated me? Grace was always the one to speak up – what if she was just voicing the opinions of the team? She'd said I was a liability and now there was a body to prove it.

'I'll see you tomorrow,' I added, darting back inside.

If I'd stayed I'd have burst into tears and I couldn't do that, not in front of him. I had to appear strong. To him I was a Reign agent; they didn't show weakness so neither could I.

I closed the door with a quiet click, the murmurs of Kayson and Grace floating through from the kitchen but I didn't listen, nor did I intend to join them. I needed sleep. If my mum texted through any updates Quinn would know about it, so there was no point phoning her to ask.

Should I walk up to Grace and ask her what the whole story was to put my mind at ease? Yes. Was I going to? No.

The thought of being around anyone right now just made the rigid hole in my chest tighten. I needed to think things through on my own. As I ascended the stairs, my fingers gripped the banister. At some point I'd have to accept that yes, perhaps I was the reason Jessica died but if I hadn't gotten involved, she'd probably have ended up dead anyway.

Walking around without any thoughts or feelings, with another man's words falling from your lips like a disease was no way to live.

By that point you'd be better off dead.

CHAPTER 6

Pseudologist

Liar.

GRACE ASPIN

The rattling chains were as cold as the hollow wind chilling my bones. The thick leather cuffs that bound my wrists together were tight but not tight enough to bruise. He never left a scar or mark – that was reserved for the rest of my team.

I'd been in Daniel Harkness's office before but this time it felt smaller than usual. The tail ends of my chains were wrapped underneath his desk as I sat there, like a dog. I couldn't remember how long I'd been there, it had to be reaching the third hour at least.

The only reason he'd done this was because I'd asked too many questions.

Why didn't we know of the enemy agents? Who were they? Surely Trojan wouldn't target a single team for a few bits of info?

I'd fashioned a pin from my hair grip, but I couldn't tear my eyes away from the door as I shoved it into the lock. I'd done this many times before but for some reason, this hairpin had become exceptionally tricky to work with.

Or it could have been because my hands were shaking so hard and my heartbeat was thudding in my chest. My hair fell in front of my face as I focused on the lock, passing the first few pins inside when I heard the lock release on the door.

I threw the pin away but it was too late, there he stood and he knew everything.

'What are you doing?' he asked, his voice eerily calm as he closed the door.

'I'm sorry.' The words escaped me. 'I didn't mean it.'

'I had one rule, Grace.' His footsteps thudding on the dull carpet as he stalked towards me.

My back hit the thick wooden ridge of his desk. Even though I'd been trained to get out of hostile situations, even though I knew countless ways to debilitate a man, I found myself completely incapacitated.

The wickedness in his eyes made me want to run and scream, my chest heaving. Why couldn't I move?

He reached out – his hand coiled around my throat like a serpent, then rested there, patiently waiting. Then it slipped to my chin, his fingers crushing my cheeks. His other hand grabbed me hard, yanked me round and slammed my head into the desk with a sickening crack. I knew immediately that my hair would hide the bruise.

I cried out but he didn't care.

'Please.'

'One fucking rule!' he roared. His breath lingered at my ear, searing and vile. 'It's your fault.'

'No it's not.'

'You left me with no choice.'

'I didn't know it would happen.'

'Why don't I show you?' he asked. 'Why don't I show you what you caused.'

'No.' The words shot out as his hands went for the leather cuffs, the key from his pockets jammed into the lock. 'No, please.'

The leather fell from my wrists but before I could run, his hands clamped my hair and shirt.

'Stop!' I screamed, but then the door opened and his callous hands dragged me into the hall.

I cried but nothing stopped him.

I tried to stand, my feet scrambling for grip along the floor but all I could see was the ceiling. My heels cracked against the stairs as he took me down two, three at a time. His fistful of my shirt practically lifted me off the ground and before long I knew where he was taking me. The morgue.

Except it wasn't a morgue, it was a hallway where they dumped the bodies because the freezer was full. He was taking me to Willow.

'Stop, please, I don't want to see this!' I shrieked but he didn't listen.

Soon enough he tossed me to the ground, the concreate smacking against my arms and I saw the long black plastic at my side. He couldn't make me! I wouldn't do this.

'Open it,' he ordered. 'Open the bag.'

'I can't,' I said, a sob rising in my throat, the shiny zip swinging, almost daring me.

'Grace, open the bag.'

I knew he wouldn't let me leave so I reached for it, gripping the small zip with my fingers, and pulled.

'Pull it open so you can see her face.'

I shifted to my knees, holding a breath. My fingers inched under the plastic, the material rubbing. As I pulled it apart I saw her face, small, slender and pale as paper. Her dirty blonde hair lifelessly ruggish, dirt marking her face. The bullet that had found its home in her cranium had been removed and the hole stitched up but I could still see it. Her lips were as small as before but behind them hid a scream, one loud enough to make the ground shake.

'You caused that,' Harkness told me.

'No I didn't.'

His vile breath lingered by my ear once more.

'You're the one that failed, Grace, you let it slip that Willow had her hands on my files. You knew she was onto me and yet . . . you gave her up.'

'You were going to kill me if I didn't.' I tried to reason with myself. 'I didn't have a choice.'

His hand grasped the back of my neck once more, forcing me closer to Willow, my face inches from hers.

'Look at her!' My nose was almost touching Willow's, and I couldn't hold it in any longer. I screamed, thrashing against his grip. 'You had a choice and you gave her up – now I had to put her in her place. You're pathetic.'

'I didn't do this, you're the one who ordered the hit, you're the one that killed her!'

'I wouldn't have had to if it wasn't for you.'

It was then I saw, dead ahead, Jessica lying on the ground. She was wearing what I'd seen her in many times, black clothes and boots, with the small addition of a gold-plated ring hanging on a chain around her neck. But now, she was choking on her own blood. Her hands shaking and eyes pleading for my help as I stared at her bullet-ridden body.

'Jess.' My voice left me.

She'd been in a park when she was shot, I wondered what it looked like. I imagined that there would be so much blood it would soak into the ground, the grass cutting into her skin.

‘You did this.’ The voice whispered but this time it wasn’t Harkness, it was Jessica. ‘You could have saved me. You could have saved Willow but you gave her up when she started digging up dirt. You dug our graves.’

The blood on the floor reached my fingers, then like a wave lapped at my knees. It soaked my jeans, each lap bringing more and more – it was never-ending. I couldn’t do this, I couldn’t lead this team.

‘You knew all along that we were working for Trojan – Lily said you didn’t seem that shocked when you found out. You knew the entire time and you didn’t say a word.’ Her face sat unnervingly at my side.

‘He would have killed me,’ I said.

Then he returned.

‘You know I’d never do that, I need you,’ he said, his voice sickly as his fingers ran through my hair.

It was disgusting.

‘He killed Willow,’ Jess said.

‘I didn’t know – Jess, please, you’ve got to believe me. I didn’t know he would do it.’ My voice trembling, begging.

‘Yes, you did,’ Harkness said.

‘I didn’t,’ I pleaded, the tears rolling down, snot dripping from my nose. ‘I didn’t – I was scared, I didn’t know what to do.’ Her blood had now soaked my jeans and socks, dripping down my arms, settling in the cracks of my nails. ‘Help me.’

‘You’re beyond help,’ she said.

‘You’re all mine, my little Gracie,’ he said.

‘You’re going to kill them.’

‘You’ll survive, my little Gracie always survives.’

‘You don’t even care!’

‘You don’t need anyone else, I’ll protect you.’

‘He’ll let you rot!’

‘I’m your salvation!’

‘You really want to die by his hand!’

‘I’ll protect you!’

‘Grace!’

I threw myself from the bed, ripping the covers off, tumbling to the floor. The morning sun streamed through the windows as my nails clenched the floor. I shot up, checking every inch of my skin but I was clean, there was no blood – why could I still feel it lathered on my skin?

I tried to tell myself it was just a nightmare but not all of it was fiction.

The secret had been haunting me ever since I saw Willow in that body bag. she’d told me she’d found a file of Harkness’s – something to do with a money trail. She told me that there was something sinister going on behind closed doors, that she was going to dig deeper to see where it led. The next day Daniel had called me into his office, demanding to know where it was. Willow had used my pass to get into the restricted files unit. I told him so myself, that she was just curious and it wasn’t her fault. I told him she was going to put it back.

No one could ever know.

KNOCK.

KNOCK.

KNOCK.

The door swung open and Kayson walked in, looking rather refreshed as he leaned against the doorframe.

'You alright?' he asked.

'Fine,' I said but then looked at the state I was in.

The pillows had been thrown from the bed, the duvet was hanging off the side and I probably didn't appear that well-rested. 'Bad dream.'

'Need coffee?'

'Please.'

As he headed downstairs I stood there, frozen. What if he found out? What if they all did?

What if my family found out what I'd done – not just this, but everything the Academy had forced me through? As far as they were aware, I was training to be a doctor. If my mother and father found out what I had done, they'd disown me. Not like they hadn't practically done that already but they'd make it public back home.

My family was something I used to hold dear to my heart but after their actions all those years ago, I discovered the importance of chosen family. They were the ones who trusted and believed me, confided in me.

But if anyone did find out I'd wish for Daniel Harkness, who'd pummel me into oblivion, and the pathetic thing was, I'd let him.

* * *

Everything was a whirlwind that morning after everyone had jumped on the bandwagon. We knew we didn't have much of a choice either way but the sooner we got in, the sooner we could leave. We grabbed the artillery we needed from the safe house and away we went.

'This meeting includes anyone who's anyone. Naomi is going to be the one next to the Prime Minister.' A fact I knew she wasn't happy about. 'The rest of us will take our positions around the building, which you're already aware of.'

'What if hostiles engage?' Kayson asked Saul as the car pulled up outside the main building. It was large, the once-white walls now stained and gritty.

'For the most part it's politicians,' Saul said next to him. 'They'll either say something controversial or try and get you to support their party, while belittling everyone else. If an attack does happen, assume regular protocols. Get the Prime Minister out of there.'

Before we left that morning the six of us had stood around the cramped kitchen table, the blueprints of the building laid out plainly. I kept eying Naomi but she wouldn't meet my gaze. The reason she was next to the

PM was because the rest of us would be scouring the building. Saul would be in the room with her as well as some other general security so she'd be safe.

I had to talk to her after this was over, straighten things out.

As we got out the car Quinn lingered by Lily's side, a little closer than usual, which I smirked at but didn't comment on. The cool morning breeze hit my face and I wished I could linger out here a little bit longer but Saul was already ushering us through the back door. We entered in single file, the tight corridor brushing against my shoulder from time to time. Small lights flooded every inch of the place but the floors were littered with dust like they hadn't been cleaned for months.

'We use this time to identify who we need to follow.' I said. 'It's our only time here, let's make it count. Quinn, you're with Saul and Naomi; Lily and Kayson, you're taking the floors, and I'll move from room to room like we discussed.'

'I'll grab the master list from reception,' Kayson said, his voice echoing from behind.

'Once you have it send it over to me,' Quinn said softly. 'By the time we get settled, anyone that's not meant to be there will stick out like a sore thumb.'

'Naomi, I want you to start the conversation with Alexander, keep him occupied, any questions you can't answer just give them some corporate crap,' Saul said, turning his head back to her.

'Yeah, cause I'm the best person to talk legislation at them,' Naomi muttered sarcastically.

I slipped to the side, letting Lily walk ahead, taking Naomi's hand behind me as we walked. I couldn't wait until later – she needed to know I had her back, needed to know that what I'd said in the heat of the moment was just that.

'I asked you to be here for a reason.' My voice was quiet but the corridor was small enough to carry the sound clearly. 'I trust you. Completely.'

'Thank you,' she replied, her hand squeezing mine before I let go.

What I'd said in the command room was selfish, driven by emotion and completely false. Naomi wasn't to blame for this, I was, and I'd spend the rest of my life trying to atone for it.

'Saul, any sign of trouble you raise the alarm,' I said to him as we approached the end of the corridor.

'It's a politicians' meeting,' he scoffed.

'Yes and these terrorists bring guns. Saul, you're taking point of my Carrier and Techie, anything – and I mean anything – looks wrong, you pull them out.'

'We don't need a babysitter,' Quinn's little voice called.

'I'm not taking any chances. We are not risking anyone else,' I stated, our footsteps cracking on the floor. 'Lily, Kayson, same goes for you. First sign of –'

‘It all going tits up we run like hell and don’t look back.’ Lily cut me off but there was a smirk in her voice.

Five assassins, a barely trained civilian and a MI6 agent walk into a room filled with politicians and the Prime Minister of Great Britain – it sounded like the start of a terrible joke.

We ascended a nearby stairwell and of course were greeted by building security who were a little suspicious of us at first but after Saul handed over the paperwork, they smiled through gritted teeth and let us through.

With a brief nod to everyone and the green light from Quinn for comms, we split up. Saul, Naomi, Quinn and I entered the main room; it was large but filled to the brim with people, constantly darting about. I spotted Alexander in the corner, his hand slicing through the air as he spoke to the woman in front of him.

I recognised some of the people from yesterday but tried my best not to draw their attention, slipping over to the wall. If you were silent and on the side-lines, you were practically invisible.

‘I thought it would be more . . . meeting-like.’ Naomi’s breathy voice whispered through my comm, as she slowly made her way over to the PM.

‘Please, this is politics,’ I said, keeping a polite smile on my face.

Quinn tapped my wrist and I looked back just in time to see her sit down at one of the smaller desks, blending right in.

I observed as Naomi slid over, inserting herself in between Alexander and the team surrounding him. She had a smile on her face and as soon as he saw her, he shook her hand. Before I knew it Naomi was involved in the conversation – perhaps those media training lessons with Kayson were helpful after all.

'Who's that?' I asked, nodding my head to the woman in front of Naomi.

'Lillian Montague, she's one of Alexander's inner circle.'

'What does she do?'

'She oversees Government-run institutes, as well as Thames House.'

'Interesting.'

Government-run institutes – didn't that mean she'd know about the Reign Academy? That must have been how Alexander knew and had access to us. She was on the taller side, with blonde hair and an air of wisdom about her.

'Put her name on the list.' I said, pressing my earpiece, the clatter of Quinn's keyboard churning in the background.

If Quinn could get some information on her, then we could find out exactly what she knew. Did she know what Harkness did or was she mislead just like us?

'I don't think she's someone you need,' Saul said, a little confused.

'It won't hurt to look,' I told him in return.

'Someone's pass has bounced.' Kayson's voice tore into my ear. 'The name on the pass is Umesh Acharya but according to the records, he was fired six months ago for threatening the Prime Minister – murder, blackmail, you name it.'

‘Quinn, pull up his profile, I need a visual,’ I ordered.

Saul busied himself with the people passing by, either joining in on their conversation or diverting them away from me as I spoke.

‘Sending it to Saul’s phone now,’ Quinn told us.

Saul slipped me his phone from his jacket pocket, my eyes immediately drawn to the man.

‘Ronan, have you got a visual on your end?’ I asked.

‘Yes.’

‘Sweep the building, find him. He’s probably going to attack the PM, and I’d rather not have a repeat of what happened to the last one.’

My head snapped to Saul and he nodded, quickly making his way over to Naomi.

I slinked around the outskirts of the room, trying to catch sight of Umesh but to no avail. If he left six months before because he’d threatened the last Prime Minister, then I’d safely assume he didn’t come back for the end-of-the-country party.

The room was loud, every person there trying to be louder than the one next to them, giving me the opportunity to speak freely, which was a blessing.

‘Report?’ I asked.

‘Ronan is taking the lower levels, I’m heading up,’ Lily replied. ‘Any sign of him in your area?’

‘Negative,’ I said. ‘Checking the surrounding rooms now.’

Since Saul was covering Naomi and Quinn I headed out of the meeting room and into the corridor, making sure to check the rooms at either side, but there was no one. Well, aside from a few security members and some men in uniform.

'We have the footage from the entrance,' Quinn said. 'The man who used the pass is the same person, it's Umesh.'

'If he's infiltrated the building then he could have changed by now,' Lily said.

'Nightingale, what do you want to do?' Quinn asked.

'Get the PM out now. If Umesh is harmless then the meeting can resume later, but –' I started, but a crackle cut through the comm and someone else continued.

'Now the Prime Minister is the most powerful man in Britain.' A familiar voice tore through my ear, reverberating into my bones. 'But I don't think it's him you should be worried about.'

Daniel Harkness.

'Did you really think we wouldn't know the pass would bounce?' he asked. 'You know I don't like loose ends.'

This wasn't a ploy to get the Prime Minister, it was a trap for us: Harkness knew we'd split up to cover the building.

'Everyone get out!' I screamed.

SCREECH.

A high-pitched wail tore through my ear and I ripped the damn thing out, that was just like Brora.

I turned on my heel and ran back to the meeting room, seeing Naomi nursing her ear, Saul trying to appease the pair in front of him. I motioned urgently to him – we had to leave immediately. He grabbed Naomi's arm, ushering the room security to surround the PM. Quinn shoved her laptop under her arm and ran to my side as my own wrapped around her, keeping her close.

I took in a breath, trying to calm mind my mind but it was impossible. I had to get Harkness out of my head – how did he always manage to wrangle his way back in? The mere thought that we were in the same building made my skin crawl.

Using Saul's phone I tried to call the front desk, but for some reason the phone service was gone.

'Have you lost signal?' Quinn asked.

'That's what Lillian was just saying. The Wi-Fi has gone down too, thought it had something to do with MI5,' Saul said.

'They can do that?' Naomi asked.

'MI5 can turn off mobile reception whenever –'

'Not the time for a history lesson. Our comms are out, we're putting the PM in more danger by being here,' I ordered Saul, gently pushing Quinn towards him. 'I told you we were too exposed and this was a terrible idea.'

Honestly, I didn't really care about the PM, there were countless security here and none of them looked like their eardrums had just exploded, unlike mine, which felt ready to roll out of my ear.

'We can help,' Quinn tried.

'This isn't an attack on the Prime Minister, this is an attack on us,' I told her.

'I'll alert the building security team and get him out of here just in case,' Saul said, before leading the way down the corridor.

Quinn and Naomi both threw me looks but I shook my head. I needed to find the others. There was no phone service and our comms had been knocked out – my best bet was to head up. Perhaps I'd find Lily. I knew that their response was to get out of there, but if Harkness had teams on the upper floors, I wasn't going to leave her on her own.

Naomi and Quinn had Saul, they'd be safe.

It was then I heard the clanking of the meeting room doors shut, three burly men moving to stand in front. They were the ones who'd let us in earlier, I was sure. Then more approached from behind – well, at least this security team was fast.

However, as I moved for the stairs the air in the room stilled, with everyone's eyes targeted on me. Then I noticed that with every step I took, they moved one step closer. Were they trying to keep the Prime Minister safe or were they with Harkness?

‘I need you to come with me, we’ll get you somewhere safe,’ a brute of a man said. He was bald, stocky but well-built.

‘I’m not a member of the cabinet, I’m here with MI6,’ I said.

‘Like I said, you need to come with me.’

I was about to protest when the man broke out the handcuffs, thrusting them towards me, his hand gripping my shoulder. These were Harkness’s men. Out of sheer instinct I spun, grabbing his hand and jabbing my knee into his groin.

Well, that certainly wasn’t going to help matters.

I threw the cuffs aside, sprinting towards the fire escape, ready to jump out feet-first when two more men came at me. I threw a leg out, kicking one of them hard with the heel of my boot, throwing a fist towards the other. One of them snatched my hand but I thrust my elbow into his ribs – then, like a spear, drove it into his eye socket. Flinging myself from their loosened hold, I threw open the fire-escape doors and ran.

Alarms started blaring, voices started yelling but the anxiety that raged through me was just as loud. How could I be so stupid? This entire thing wasn’t for us to find the key players, it was so Harkness could get back his precious team. I knew we were too exposed here.

Saul would keep Naomi and Quinn under wraps. I just had to hope there wasn’t a welcoming party waiting for them outside.

We were running blind without comms or service, I had no way to contact anyone, and with Kayson on the lower floors my best bet was to go up. He was more than capable of taking care of himself.

I took the metal stairs three at a time, yells from the 'security team' below chasing my heels but I didn't intend to slow down. The climb seemed to go on forever and I felt every single step burning my thighs but I didn't give in.

I took the steps four at a time when I could, thankful for my longer legs, managing to put some distance between me and my attackers.

BANG.

THUD.

BANG.

The sounds echoed from above – I didn't know what floor Lily was on but I had a feeling she might be somewhere amongst that racket.

I pushed harder and faster, hearing the thunder of footsteps on the grate below. I only stopped when, at a window, Lily tumbled into sight, letting off a few rounds, her form perfect.

With a heavy fist, I thumped the window.

'Open the window!' I shouted, already hearing Harkness's men getting closer.

Without hesitation she manoeuvred, shooting the window. I threw myself back, arms shielding my face as the spray of glass tore at my shirt. When the bullets stopped I stepped back, kicking through the large panel and slipping inside.

'You know that's not what I meant,' I said.

'There's no pleasing you is there?'

I caught the gun as she threw it towards me, slipping it into the back of my jeans. This level was at least eight floors up and I commended myself on ascending it so quickly, before taking in the room. Clear plastic film covered most of the desks, dust-sheets discarded on the floor.

'There's more coming, five at least,' I told Lily, pressing my back against the wall.

'Oh joy,' she muttered. 'Two idiots came after me when the alarms started going off . . . so this was a trap?'

'You heard Harkness. Think he's still listening?'

'Quinn would have cut the channel,' Lily muttered. 'I hate it when you're paranoid.'

'Why?'

'Cause you're usually right. It's irritating.'

The thundering rattle of men shook the rickety steps from outside. We had seconds.

'They're most likely here to kill us so if you wouldn't mind?' I asked.

As the pair of us backed up, one by one the security team barrelled inside, but Lily didn't seem fazed.

'Give me a few minutes and then I'll join you,' she said, cracking her neck.

'We need them alive.'

'I'll try my hardest.'

I turned on my heel, not looking back, the thuds and smacks of fists being thrown ringing in my ears. As I made my way through the room, looking for a way back down, I worried we were too late. How far had Harkness planned this? How long had he been watching us? Or was it just a stroke of luck he found us?

'How's it going?' I shouted to Lily.

'One of them is a tad stubborn!' she yelled back breathlessly.

I turned the corner, my hand ghosting against the gun at my back as a quiet shuffle across the room caught my attention. A man's head poked out, his arms raised in surrender.

'Don't shoot!' he yelled. 'My name's Umesh.'

The man of the hour was hiding up here, of all places? He was dressed formally in a suit, his hair slicked back and a silver pen in his hand.

'What are you doing here?' I asked.

'You're smart, figure it out. You're Grace Aspin, the leader of the Omega Team. I know Daniel Harkness, he talks about you all the time.'

I snatched the gun from my waistband, my finger resting on the trigger.

'You're one of them?'

'No, yes – well, not really.'

'Does Harkness want us dead?'

‘Dead?’ Umesh asked, breaking into a hearty laugh. ‘He doesn’t want you dead, he wants you by his side. Reign failed but he still needs you, you can join him.’

‘As if I ever would.’

‘That’s a shame but no matter, he’ll pay me generously when I bring you in.’

CLICK.

The whistling of a dart shot straight at me. I flung my body back, bending my knees, the white ceiling now showcasing the weapon as it flew above me in its little cylinder. Once I heard the clink on the glass behind me, I shot up.

‘A dart pen?’ I asked. ‘Seriously?’

BAM.

A thug in tactical gear was thrown into the room, his hands flailing on the floor, moving erratically to get back up. Lily emerged from round the corner, sporting a split lip, bleeding nose, and a challenging grin on her lips. She slipped a gun from her second holster, firing seven shots, none of them hitting him.

How could she miss? He was so close.

Lily sprinted towards him throwing a leg out, kicking him square in the chest, sending him stumbling back. He crashed through the bullet-infested glass and out the window.

‘The window – you threw him out the window?’ I asked.

'You said to take care of it.'

CHAPTER 7

Novaturient

Seeking powerful change in one's life, behaviour, or situation.

NAOMI JADE

'The getaway van is just round the corner, we need to move. Alexander's security team have been alerted, as have the agents in the area. There's nothing else we can do.' Saul was pleading with me but I had half a mind to run back inside.

Anything could be happening and I was stuck out here.

Sirens blared and tyres squealed on the tarmac as we turned the corner. That was probably more security but whose side they were on remained a mystery. Harkness had found us – maybe Grace had a point being so uptight about everything.

'We can help,' I told him. 'If Harkness is here we need to get them out of there.'

'Have you forgotten who your friends are?' Saul asked. 'Besides, don't you have to follow the Team Lead's orders?'

'I think there's some wiggle room,' I said, turning sharply to Quinn. 'How soon can you get the comm units back up?'

Quinn had her laptop resting in her arm as we power-walked down the street, the other hand tapping away on the keyboard.

'It'll take about ten minutes, someone's blocking from me the other side. It's different to Brora, they've redesigned the algorithm.'

'Is there a chance that Harkness could get access to it?' I asked.

'I've cut the channels so he can't hear us but honestly, I don't know,' she admitted quietly.

BANG.

A body crashed onto the car beside us, shattering the windshield, a man all in black rolling off the bonnet and cracking his nose on the ground, blood spurting everywhere – he was just unconscious right?

'Time to go,' Quinn said.

Was it raining men? I scoured the building and about halfway up a large window pane had completely shattered. A bullet case rolled over to my shoe but from what I could see through all the blood, there wasn't a bullet hole in him. Lily was sweeping the upper floors looking for Umesh so it could have been her.

Did Lily throw someone out the window?

'What happened?' Saul wondered aloud, but his brain seemed to pick up the pace faster than mine. 'Did one of your team –'

'I find it best not to look,' Quinn said simply.

As we hauled ourselves round another corner, I whispered to Quinn, 'They can't arrest us for that, right?'

'They can't prove anything,' she told me, stopping at the van. 'Saul, get in the van.'

'Your teammate just threw someone from the window,' he said.

'It's gravity, what can you do?' she asked in return, getting in the van herself.

Even though I couldn't see anything or anyone, I could still picture the man on the road, his eyes open wide and blood pouring into his nose from his mouth. Lily must have been left with no choice, she wouldn't just murder someone – he was probably trying to kill her.

'Naomi, get in,' Saul demanded.

I jumped in, sliding down to the cold wooden floor, fumbling with my fingers. I hated feeling like this, the person who needed to be rescued. Sure, I couldn't have done much, but I could have helped Grace.

Like you helped me? I imagined Jess would say.

Pain sliced like a knife in my heart as I pushed the thought away. She wouldn't say that to me. This was – I just needed to get out of here.

The driver's door swung open and Kayson dived in, still dressed in that black suit and tie, the comm unit dangling on his shoulder.

'Situation report,' he demanded.

'It was a trap to either kill you or capture you. I'm sorry, I should have been more vigilant about security but I didn't have time –'

'I don't know how we could have made it any clearer, five guys just tried to take me out,' Kayson nearly roared.

Five of them? Was he OK? He didn't look hurt, I couldn't see any blood. I wanted to reach for him but stopped, hearing Quinn.

'Three minutes till comms are back online,' she said, her eyes fixed on her screen.

'No point in using them. Go offline,' Kayson told her. 'Any news from the others?'

'One of your team threw a guy from an eighth-storey window.'

'Did you see them do it?' Kayson prodded. Saul remained silent. 'Then we're fine.'

The side door slid open and a man I didn't recognise in handcuffs was thrown in. Lily followed, her eyes fixed on him. I heard Grace up front in the passenger seat with Kayson, her dark brown hair now shoved up in a bun.

'Drive.'

The entire journey Saul was on the phone to Nicola, his face set in a permanent frown. Lily told me the guy in handcuffs was Umesh and that he probably set this whole thing up with Harkness so he could bring the team in. She also mentioned something about the money he would get for doing so.

The shock that flooded my system before, in Reign, when I found out that humans in their eyes were nothing but collateral damage didn't match this – if anything this was worse. Umesh, Harkness and whoever were willing to buy the agents they trained back. Was I one of them? Grace said they only had a visual profile of me, should I dye my hair? I could probably get coloured contacts from somewhere.

Out of everywhere, the one place I didn't expect to end up was an airstrip. After the call ended with Nicola, Saul had ordered Kayson to take us there. We were to return home immediately while MI6 dealt with the situation, as apparently it was no longer safe. I was inclined to agree.

A small grey jet sat waiting for us on the airstrip, people in high-vis jackets and helmets running about faster than I could keep a track of.

As soon as the van stopped, Saul shouted, 'Out! Everybody out! Head for the jet!'

We all sprung from the van, Lily dragging Umesh in tow, but Saul grabbed his arm.

'He stays here for questioning, I'll deal with it personally,' he said to us, the engines of the jet roaring to life. 'Now go, get out of here.'

'Wait, that's it?' I asked as the winds started to pick up. 'What about you?'

'Orders from you know who,' he said, motioning to the phone he'd made the call from.

Kayson's arms hooked around my waist, pulling me round, tugging hard until I started running up the ramp of the jet. He clambered in after, extending a hand to Lily and pulling her in. Quinn tried to pull me to a seat but I watched as Grace lingered with Saul, handing him a black phone and a handshake before joining us on the jet.

He had two phones? Well, he did run a lot of agents.

The ramp door shut with a clank and we all strapped ourselves in. It wasn't exactly a commercial flight; the thing had been stripped of plush seats, with only bare metal on the floor. The only seats were against the walls and they were industrial strength.

'So Harkness wants you back?' I asked.

'Looks that way.'

'What if he gets the better of us next time? What if he takes one of you, all of you?'

'He'll have to answer to me first,' Grace said, with grit in her voice. 'What happened to Willow, what happened to Jessica and James, won't happen to us. We'll make him pay and if we go out swinging, let's make a spectacle.'

'I'll make sure to bring the fireworks,' Lily smirked.

Kayson and Quinn laughed, but I couldn't bring myself to. They were all willing to die to avenge their friends but I didn't know if I was. Maybe I was in the beginning but now I'd seen their world and it terrified me. I'd never thought I was the type to go out with a bang but perhaps that was the best way.

I'd thrown the idea of settling down months ago but was I ready for this? My friends were ready to die for what they believed in, was I?

* * *

'After everything, I thought you would at least have had the common sense not to do that. Of all the things you could do, you arrested an ex-politician and then murdered a man.'

'He fell.'

'Chan, do not test me, you pushed him out of that window. I can guarantee the bullet casings on the ground match your gun.'

'How do you know it was me who fired it?'

'Lily sit down!' Nicola shouted, a finger pointing to the chair.

Now, I was unsure if I was willing to die but I was fully supportive of the world imploding right now, if it wanted to, please?

We were in the lower levels of Reign, the rooms once used to waterboard and torture this team now converted into meeting rooms, all separated by blinds and soundproof glass. Nicola had sent a driver to pick us up from the airstrip in Edinburgh – we didn't even get time to change, she looked ready to drag us all in by the ear when we arrived.

Grace was sitting at the metallic table, one leg crossed over the other. She'd already been the centre of attention for a good hour and it wasn't pretty.

'I don't understand why you're so angry. He was probably Trojan, he tried to kill me so I took him out,' Lily said, plopping down in one of the not-so-comfy chairs.

'Intel suggests he wasn't. The five men chasing Grace were Trojan, the sixth – who came from the stairwell, as you so painstakingly pointed out earlier – was part of building security. He was clean.'

Oh fuck.

'He can't have been, he was trying to kill me,' Lily said.

'Did you see a gun?'

'You don't need one.'

'Did you see it?'

'. . . No.'

'Was he using any defensive strategies that were intending to kill.'

'No.'

'You murdered an innocent man.' Nicola sighed heavily, already seeming exhausted.

'No one's innocent, you know that – before long he would have been turned to Trojan. Besides, you're missing the bigger picture. Harkness was there but you don't seem to give a fuck!'

That was when Nicola paused, her hand falling from her head. She sat up a little straighter, pressing her lips together.

'He's made you all in his image, hasn't he?' Nicola said, and the room fell deathly quiet. 'Did you even check any of the security team? Did you even check if anyone else's comms had been cut?'

'It was only ours they cut,' Quinn said. 'Harkness was targeting us.'

'Then shouldn't you have all left the building instead of sending it into complete lockdown?' Nicola asked pointedly.

'I don't know if you noticed but we tried that,' Lily snarked.

'One more word and I'll have you removed,' Nicola snapped.

Lily scoffed.

'Out,' Nicola demanded.

'What?'

'Get out, I'll speak to you later.'

'What did I do?'

'You're not cooperating and your attitude is terrible. I don't particularly care what you do or how you do it, just get out of my sight.'

Lily's chair battered into the glass as her boot cracked into its legs. Fire churned in her face as she trudged out the room.

'Quinn, what happened to the communication channel? I thought we'd fixed it?' Nicola asked, ignoring Lily's outburst.

'It's a new sort of algorithm, I've never seen anything like it.'

'Find Thompson, see if you can work on cracking it, this can't happen again.'

'Yes ma'am,' she said, ducking out of the room.

It was only Grace, Kayson and me left with her now. Kayson was the quietest, which surprised me – I'd expected him to lash out and defend Lily but he didn't. He'd stayed perfectly quiet, his hands pressed against the glass wall. He looked tired but didn't rub at his eyes or shuffle, he was perfectly still.

'Ma'am can I request to do this debriefing later?' he asked, his eyes cast to the ground.

'No you may not,' she said. 'Your entire team is being removed from active duty until we can assess you individually.'

'Assess?' I asked. 'What for?'

'Naomi, you'll go into training with the junior years so this doesn't apply to you,' she told me, before turning back to Grace and Kayson. 'What happened in London cannot be allowed to happen again. You're to remain here in Scotland for the foreseeable future to protect yourselves as well as the country.'

Hold the bus, what? No offence but come on, I was fine training with the team.

'What about the Prime Minister? He wants us by his side?' Grace said. 'The whole country is in crisis and you're worried about us?'

'Grace, you and your team are to remain in the dorm houses at all times unless you're attending classes.'

'What about Naomi?' Kayson asked.

'She's going to be moved to another team.'

'What?' I asked, unable to even contemplate the idea. 'No, I don't want another team.'

'She's staying with us,' Grace said, coming to my side. 'I don't trust anyone else.'

'And I don't trust your team not to murder anyone. This isn't the Reign Institute where you can kill anyone and everyone. This team is now run by me and I won't stand by and watch this happen a second time.'

There was no way in hell I was going to another team. Join a bunch of strangers? No thank you.

'Naomi, you'll be sleeping in dorm house number five,' Nicola told me, handing a key over the table. 'Until I can find a more suitable team for you.'

I took it but that didn't mean I planned on using it.

'More suitable?' Kayson scoffed.

'Mr Ashford, would you rather we continue this conversation in private or would you rather do it in front of her?'

'Anything he can say to you he can say to me,' I said but the silence that followed confused me; Kayson's mouth had clamped shut. 'Kayson?'

'Naomi, I suggest you get moving. I have to move this to another room,' Nicola said.

What couldn't he say in front of me? Surely he trusted me enough? If he did trust me then what was the issue? A more suitable team, what did that mean? Was there something Nicola left out? Yes, they were assassins but that wasn't breaking news.

'I don't know where I'm going,' I tried, stalling.

'I'll take her,' Grace said, a hand slipping to my back. 'Unless I'm not allowed to go on a walk?'

Nicola contemplated it for a moment before she sighed, giving in.

'Make it quick. Mr Ashford, with me,' she ordered, leaving the room in a hurry.

Just as Kayson passed me his hand squeezed mine briefly, his rough fingers grazing my skin, goosebumps running up my arms as his warmth left my side.

'Come on,' Grace said, pushing the small of my back in the opposite direction.

As we walked down the corridor we came to another door to the left, marked 'Stairs'.

'Grace, I'm not leaving the Omega Team,' I told her as she made her way up. 'I'll cuff myself to the radiator and swallow the key or I'll lock myself to the doors like those people do to trees. I'll go on a hunger strike.'

'Nicola isn't going to be happy,' Grace said.

'I don't care if she's going to have a canary!' I exclaimed. 'I'm not leaving you guys.'

'Even after what I said?' she asked, turning to me and stopping dead.

'Like you said, you didn't mean it,' I told her. 'People say things they don't mean in the heat of the moment. Sure I feel guilty. but there wasn't anything I could have done to stop it.'

I felt sick for saying it but deep down, I knew it wasn't my fault. Jessica had left for that mission without a care in the world and a smile on her lips. There was nothing to suggest anything would go wrong.

'You're different now, you know that?' she asked, walking down to meet me. 'The girl I met would have rolled over and proclaimed it was all her fault. Thrown herself a pity party.'

‘Took a leaf out of Jessica’s book – look at the facts, emotions don’t change anything,’ I said to her and she let out a small laugh.

‘I like it, just don’t lean on it too much,’ she told me, and instantly I knew why.

Jessica was amazing but there was part of her that was pure machine. She’d been raised in the life and I understood that, I just wished we’d had more time.

‘Are you taking me to another team?’ I asked.

‘Please,’ she scoffed. ‘I know the security camera layout like the back of my hand. Like I’d ever give my Carrier up.’

‘Wasn’t much of a Carrier though, was I?’ I asked.

‘You told the British Government to go fuck themselves, that’s the Carrier I want.’

It took a while but I managed to get back to the dorm house without being spotted, mostly sticking to the back gardens and jumping over fences. It also involved a lot of confused looks, begging someone called Eve not to blab and fake-promising a date with someone called Rory.

When I snuck in through the back door I was expecting someone to be there but the house was silent. I guessed everyone had their own jobs to do, but Nicola hadn’t said anything about Jessica, so she must be in her room – no, she wasn’t in her room.

I thought I had this through my head but evidently I hadn’t. Nicola hadn’t even mentioned her but she kept slipping into my mind. If I forgot the last few days I could imagine she was upstairs listening to music or practising a song for her next performance.

Even though I'd regret it I headed up to her room, slowly at first, teetering in the doorway and tiptoeing through like she'd be back any second. The room didn't look too different from last time; it was the same colour, the same military level of clean and even had the smell of her perfume. The duffle bag that was stuffed under her desk was still there and out of sheer curiosity I pulled on the handle.

I smirked at the contents: the first shirt was one I'd seen Chris wear the last time he was here. The bag wasn't for Jessica's laundry, it was spare clothes for him. I shoved the bag back under the desk, but paused – had anyone told him?

Jessica's mobile sat on the desk, almost begging me to call him. Should I be the one to do it? I didn't want to ask Nicola about it, she'd probably bite my head off.

Jessica would want him to know.

Just as I reached for the phone, a voice spoke from behind.

'Naomi, don't.' Despite it being Kayson, I nearly jumped out of my skin, a hand going to my fluttering chest.

'Jesus.' I muttered. 'Don't do that.'

'Sorry,' he apologised. 'But that's not a good idea.'

I turned. 'You don't know what I was going to do.'

'You were going to break the news to Chris.' He sat carefully on the bed, a purposeful look in his eyes. 'Nicola has either done it already or she's going to.'

'Jessica would want him to know.'

'Nicola told me he's in deep in Budapest right now.'

'It's just a job! He'd want to know she's dead!' I exclaimed. 'She's dead, but Nicola doesn't seem to give two shits!'

'Her funeral is next week,' Kayson said. 'That's what Nicola pulled me and Grace out for. She's arranged the whole thing, invited who she could.'

What? She'd already arranged it? What happened to her being too busy or the cold-hearted talk? Was that all just a façade? Even so, I knew there was more to the story than that. If it was just funeral arrangements then why couldn't I be there? What was Kayson hiding?

'She asked me to look for any photos we had of her or any songs she liked,' Kayson said.

'And through all of it she wanted me in a different team?'

'Apparently, she thought it'd be an easier transition after the funeral.'

'That's a load of bullshit.'

'That's what I said.' He headed over to the one of the wardrobes, pulling the door open. 'Now, I'm sure there's some pictures in here.'

He reached to the top shelf, pulling down an old battered brown box. As he opened the lid my brows furrowed, confused – I'd never realised Jess was so sentimental. Our old school tie sat at the top as well as the white leaver's shirt with all different coloured pens scrawled on it. As Kayson tugged it out, underneath lay photos scattered all over the box. Some were of her and me from high school, while others were of her and the girls. There weren't any of her and Chris, which surprised me, but what was even more mind-boggling was the polaroid at the bottom of the box, labelled 'mum and dad'. I took that one out, looking it over. The man in the picture must have been her father, they had the same eyes and lips, while Jessica took her other features from Charlotte. They pair looked happy in the photo, what happened?

'I never met her dad,' I said aloud. 'I only met her mum once.'

'You know the story.'

'Yeah, the cover one.'

'They're the same,' Kayson said. 'He left when Jess was a toddler I think. She doesn't remember him and from what she told me, never wanted to.'

'Has Nicola invited them?'

'If it were up to me no, but yeah, she has,' he said. 'They won't show.'

I plucked a photo from underneath, the blue edge sticking out. It was a picture of the original Omega team: Jessica, Grace, Lily, Quinn and Willow. They were sitting on the living room couch and genuinely looked happy.

'I took this picture,' Kayson muttered but there was something different about his voice; it was thin, warbly.

I looked up to see tears staining his cheeks as he stared intently at the photo. He took in a deep breath, wiping his mouth, but as his eyes flickered to the ceiling more tears fell like stars, glistening in the light.

‘I’d always thought she’d be one of the last ones to go,’ he admitted.

I flung my arms around him as tight as I could, his body shaking against mine. His fingers gripped the edges of my top, his eyes buried in my shoulder. I’d never seen him cry and I hated it, I just wanted to make it stop, make everything better. I wanted Jessica to jump from a hiding place and yell ‘surprise!’ and for a few moments I waited, bracing myself for the horror but it never came. Jessica didn’t appear and Kayson’s tears didn’t stop.

‘I think we all did,’ I said to him.

He pulled back, wiping away the stray tears with his hand, sniffling.

‘Sorry.’

‘For what?’ I asked. ‘Crying? Kayson, you’re allowed to do that. Jessica – she meant a lot to all of us, it’s normal.’

Even though I’d said it, I hadn’t cried yet. I’d thought I would have but no tears came. I was dry as a bone and I didn’t know why.

‘Where do you think I got these scars from?’ he said, pointing to the three thin lines of his forehead, as he sheepishly pulled away.

‘Harkness?’

‘Doesn’t matter where, it’s just hard, you know? Especially with this place.’

‘Well, it’s different now, things have changed. Maybe after the funeral Nicola can find a grief counsellor for us, speaking to someone will help.’

‘Could you come with me?’ he asked, and a breath caught in my throat.

‘Of course, if you think that would help.’

We all needed to talk to someone after this – with everything going on it was a surprise I hadn’t run to the nearest shrink with clearance and retched my darkest thoughts.

‘Do you remember that day I came to your door?’ he asked, swiftly changing the subject.

‘It’s kind of hard to forget.’ I smiled gently.

‘When I said you dropped your phone at the train station, that was a lie.’ Of course it was. ‘Jessica texted me before training, told me to keep an eye on you. I was in town myself, so once I had your profile I followed you. It’s called a brush-past: I bumped into you, took your phone from your bag then changed clothes before I showed up.’

Well at least I knew I wasn’t completely incompetent when it came to keeping a track of my phone. An assassin had snatched it from my bag, not that I minded.

‘So?’ I asked.

‘So?’ he repeated mockingly. ‘I just told you I stole your phone so –’

‘Jessica could keep me safe.’

‘And look where you’ve ended up,’ he muttered.

This time my arm slipped around his shoulders, my fingers rubbing smooth circles on his bare skin.

‘Right here,’ I said. ‘And I wouldn’t want to be anywhere else.’

As Kayson was unravelling beside me I was quickly discovering he was a complicated man: a gentleman, an arsehole – aggressive, protective, but underneath all that he cared for his friends. I knew he'd moved here with his dad when he was small but he barely talked about him – perhaps his own team, as well as this one, were the closest thing he had to a family?

Even as carnage rained from the sister country in the south, for a moment I was glad to be here. In one room, tucked away from the rest of the world where I could forget about Trojan, where I could forget about the death toll and the bodies that lay motionless on the ground. In this room only one thing mattered: Jess. It was here I could mourn her. It was my safe place as it was Kayson's and I'd be damned if anyone tried to take it from us. I didn't check my phone and I didn't check the news – this room was free from the oblivion that encased the sky. I felt guilty for shunning the innocent, felt horrible pushing them aside but in that brief second within an even briefer minute, it was all I could do.

That night everyone slowly trickled in, quiet as mice. Some went to their rooms while others lingered in the kitchen. Even after Kayson left I surrounded myself with Jessica's things, her shirts, her shoes. I even spent a good portion going through her desk, nothing too interesting to the wandering eye but to me, it was a piece of the jigsaw that was her life. The sheet music from Chicago was tucked neatly at the back of one of the drawers, with her handwriting scribbled all over it, some notes highlighted in blue, some in green. On top of her desk I found her perfume. It was in a little glass bottle in a language I couldn't understand but I smiled nevertheless. It reminded me of her. I wondered if Nicola would let me keep it; when Willow died I remembered seeing a few of her things in Quinn's room so you must be allowed to keep something. I found an old-style MP3 at the back of the drawer, it had everything from heavy metal to Broadway to emo.

It wasn't her stuff anymore though was it? It was just stuff. She'd never come back for it.

How fast would Nicola replace her? She wanted me to transition to a different team after the funeral – did that mean she was bringing a new Team Lead in or another Second in Command? Whoever it was, I didn't think Grace would thank her for it. Would the newbie redecorate in here? Even though the walls were basic and the photos clichéd, I couldn't see it any other way. This was Jessica's room and if someone painted over it, it would just feel wrong.

Grace was the only one who could lead this team. I didn't trust anyone else.

CHAPTER 8

Parva, sic ibis ad astra

Little one, thus you shall go to the stars.

GRACE ASPIN

Even though it was nearing ten o'clock, I couldn't bring myself to go to bed. The thought of sleep haunted me. I could still feel the cold wet blood lapping against my knees and her cold eyes picking away at me.

Jessica and I often spoke about matters outwith the team. It wasn't idle-chit chat I'm sorry to say; some childish part of me wished we could have been like that around one another. Our relationship was professional yet personal at the same time. She chose me as one of the few people to let in. She spoke to me about her parents, about her childhood, and how she felt as if her life was only conceived for one thing – to follow orders until she couldn't.

We always sat in my room; she'd lean against the wall, I'd sit on the floor and she'd ask what she could do to make herself a better leader. On the outside it may have looked like we hated one another but we really didn't – anything said in briefings or to do with an op was strictly professional, we understood each other. I could tell Jess her plan was utter shit and she herself was a lunatic, and she wouldn't take it personally. She could tell me I was a control freak, spoiled, selfish and I would take it with a pinch of salt. In short, we bounced off each other in a good way; I think that's why we were put in this team together.

'Grace Maria Aspin.' David sharply clicked his fingers in front of my face.

'Sorry.' I sighed.

He laughed briefly, sliding into the desk chair next to me at the nurses' station. The soft glow of the lights beaming off his skin, his blue eyes swimming in warmth. He was in his usual dark blue scrubs, a pen tucked into the pocket along with his small box of mints.

'I was worried I'd have to go full Italian to get your attention,' he joked.

'If you had to we'd be in trouble,' I said, forcing a smile.

The ward was unusually quiet, there was only one patient and he was only in with a minor concussion. I felt obsolete: last year at this time of night I'd have been running around like a headless chicken but now, I was stuck behind the nurses' desk. In all fairness, I could be studying but I wasn't going to stick my nose in a book when all I could think about was Jessica.

'Do you want to talk about it?' David asked gently, his hand slowly reaching for mine, but I pulled away.

'Which part?' I asked. 'The part where the entire operation went south, the part where Harkness wants us to join the cause or the part where Jessica's died?'

He sighed, leaning back, tugging on the back of his hair.

'Which one do you want to talk about?'

'I would say that phone call you threw in the mix, although I doubt you want to talk about that lapse of judgement.'

'It wasn't a lapse of judgement.'

'I beg to differ.'

The silence grew but even though we were only inches apart, it felt as if a chasm had opened between us. Right now, with everything going on, a divorce couldn't be on the table. I had a funeral to prepare for and an assessment. I had to take care of my team.

I'd managed to convince Nicola to let me back on the wards after hours, promising David would be there to supervise. I just couldn't be in the dorm house, not yet.

'Did you have any idea that something would go south on the op with Jess?' I asked, sharply changing the subject.

'No,' he said, fiddling with the stapler. 'Everything was clean, above board. Nicola said something about the team going rogue.'

Instead of continuing the conversation, I asked the question I'd been dreading to know the answer to.

'Have they recovered her body yet?'

'Yes, she got here around four this morning, the pathologist came in an hour later. Cause of death was –'

'It's fine, I'll look at the report.' I cut him off, my fingers flying to the keyboard.

I'd rather read it in a doctor's words than hear David's emotional splurges. I needed some of that Jessica-like coldness right now.

'Grace.' He seized my wrist and out of sheer instinct I flinched. Realising what he'd done, David nodded in apology, letting go. 'Just let me tell you the facts before you look at it.'

'Why?' I asked. 'I saw what happened, COD was probably multiple gunshot wounds.'

As the words came out my mouth, the sound of the bullets pounded in my chest. I couldn't remember what I saw but I could remember the sound. It's all I could remember. Making another grab for the keyboard I yanked it towards me, but the stoic look on David's face held steadfast.

'Grace, believe me, it's best if you don't know.'

What on earth was he talking about? I spun the monitor my way, logging in and clicking through the different folders until I came across the one I needed:

J.G. WINTERS

As the document opened David turned his back on me, but I was too busy skimming the report to give a toss. There wasn't anything out of the ordinary: multiple gunshot wounds to the chest, scrapes and scratches on her arm and a fractured wrist.

In my nightmare I'd envisioned her so cruelly, but if I were to see her body now it would make it real and the guilt would eat me alive.

'I don't see what you're so uptight about,' I told David.

'There's a second page.'

A second page? Surely that was just the pathologist's notes. As I scrolled through the document I read aloud.

'After initial examination the cause of death was blood loss from the heart, due to multiple gunshot wounds. It appeared that the victim had been shot five times before the final bullet was shot. After going over previous records and the victim's last visit, which showed an elevated 27ml of hCG . . .' I trailed off my eyes fluttering open and shut as a shaky breath passed my lips.

'I told you not to,' David said.

'She was pregnant.'

David took my arms, pulling me from my seat, trying to comfort me but his touch pricked my skin.

'You were her doctor and you didn't say a word.' My voice was unknown to me, it was low, barely audible to anyone else. 'It said her last visit, you knew before she died. You knew she was pregnant but you cleared her to work.' I shoved him as hard as I could but he barely stumbled. 'You knew and you didn't tell me!'

I let it out in that sentence, that scream I'd been holding inside but it wasn't loud, nor did it shake the earth. It was quiet, my voice breaking as my breath left me. I thought we were in this together. He wanted a divorce, he *wanted* to ask his wife for a divorce to be with me but then he keeps secrets like this?

'She told me not to,' he said but his voice was calm, his arms wrapping around me. 'She begged me not to tell anyone.'

'You cleared her.' My chest heaved. 'You cleared her to go.'

'She wasn't sure if she was going to keep it – the op wasn't marked as a potential threat.' His voice but a whisper. 'I'm sorry Grace, I'm so sorry.'

'How far along was she?'

'Two months.'

She was pregnant and hadn't told anyone. For a split second I assumed Chris knew, but if he had, he wouldn't have taken the job in Budapest. Nicola had to have called him – as far as I knew he'd been put down as her next of kin after James had to be taken off.

Where was she going to be buried? I had no idea where Willow's grave was – would they be put in the same cemetery? Would we be allowed to attend? Was she getting cremated? Even though Nicola explained it all earlier I wasn't really listening. How she'd managed to arrange it amongst everything going on I didn't know.

I never envied Quinn's job, all she had to look at were news reports. Being in the ward was one of the ways to avoid the outside world.

‘This stays between us,’ I told David, promptly pulling back. ‘Not a word to my team or Christopher.’

‘He has a right to know.’

If Jessica hadn’t said anything then neither would I. Perhaps he did have a right to know, but my team was unravelling – we were grieving and this knowledge didn’t make it any better.

RING. RING. RING.

David slipped his phone from his pocket and groaned. I didn’t even need to read the name on the phone to know it was Olivia.

‘You better go, she’ll be worried.’ I leaned back on the desk, staring at my shoes.

‘Can I at least –’

‘Your shift ended an hour ago, she’s concerned. I’ll leave when one of the nurses comes in.’

His warm palm pressed against my shoulder but I couldn’t bring myself to look at him. I was a walking lie, if I told him the truth then this entire façade would collapse. Had I condemned Jessica’s baby?

David’s warm lips gently pressed my temple, his hands rested on my shoulders, but I screwed my eyes shut until he pulled away, hearing his shoes disappearing down the stairwell.

How could I atone for what I’d done?

CHAPTER 9

Numinous

Inspired.

NAOMI JADE

Now, there were many things I was willing to do in order to stay with the Omega Team – however, playing along with this new team was not part of the plan. Even though I'd snuck back over to the dorm house, I was caught the next morning when I popped out to the courtyard to find Kayson.

'Are you just going to stand there all day daydreaming?' the girl I'd met yesterday called Eve asked.

'Depends,' I said.

'On what?'

'If you're still going to talk to me in that annoying accent of yours.'

'I'm from Glasgow.'

'Yeah . . . the Glaswegian accent irritates me.'

I was tired, aching, grieving and not in the mood to play this game. I'd had to sleep in their stupid dorm house the past couple of nights, since Nicola kept randomly showing up to check on me. They'd put me in the room next to the bathroom and while it was nice, it felt foreign. I may as well have been on a different planet.

'You're gonna have to get over them at some point,' she told me.

'Eve, has any of your team died?'

'No.'

'Then shut up.'

We were stood outside in the courtyard, the rest of Eve's team doing some sort of circuit workout with the music blaring. I'd had to borrow some clothes from Quinn and Lily that morning, under supervision of course. They were a little tight but once I started moving they'd probably stretch out. Even though the team had been welcoming, I'd heard the comments made under their breaths; if I heard one more about my team or that Jessica had it coming, I was going straight to Nicola.

The girls in front of me suddenly started running towards the school.

'Are you gonna stand about like a fucking statue or are you going to run?' Eve asked.

Fuck you Eve.

I took off, arms pumping by my side as I went after them, a breath leaving my lips every time my foot hit the ground. There were four girls ahead of me but once they pulled out of the small path, I overtook them before we got to the main entrance of the school. I heard them all murmuring about it behind me but I didn't take any notice – I had to be here but I didn't have to get on with them. I wasn't planning on making any friends, I wasn't going to be hanging around for long.

I didn't know what route the group was going but I was leading so they'd either follow or do their own thing. As I ran past the large doors I headed down the path that went round the opposite side of the building, passing the modern grey one with all the gym equipment in it. Surprisingly, I hadn't been in there myself. Kayson and Lily hadn't included it in the training programme they'd put me through the last few months.

There were a lot of people in there working out but not anyone I cared to see. When Nicola said 'assess', I thought she'd send the Runners to the gym – or maybe there was some other kind of test waiting for them.

'Naomi, slow down!' I heard Eve call from behind but I didn't even acknowledge her.

Running was one of the spaces where I could be left alone in my head, a space to think, a space to breathe.

As I turned again I was at the back of the institute. It seemed bigger now all the equipment had been removed. I'd trained a lot back here on the warmer days; Lily would bring out everything from a rotating arm that I had to jump over to a Samurai sword. Now it was an empty field and in the far distance a metal fence stood tall, rings of barbed wire at the top. Even though they could walk out the front door, it sat there, like a constant reminder.

I went to run straight down the field, since I could work out on my own, away from the team but felt a small firm hand tug me back. Eve stood there, a little annoyed.

'The next part of the route is round the back of the school, not down the field.'

'Eve, you know I'm good to work on my own.'

'We're a team, we do this together,' Eve said.

'You're not my team. Nicola might think you are but you're not. This is merely a formality.'

'Shouldn't you see a formality through?'

'Not when she keeps pestering me,' I stated, pulling my arm back.

'I knew Jess too, you're not the only one,' she snapped.

'Don't you think I know that?' I asked. 'I'm not stupid.'

'I never said you were,' she said, almost offended, backing up. 'Like it or not, you're stuck with us. Wouldn't it be better to make it easier on yourself?'

'I'm not staying with your team.'

'What are you going to do, secretly run away with them?' she scoffed.

Despite wanting to punch her face in, Eve had a good point. Nicola wasn't willing to let us out of her sight because she didn't trust us. How would she feel if we shattered that trust entirely?

As one final parting gift to Jessica, we bring hell to Harkness's door.

CHAPTER 10

Exanimate

Once but no longer alive.

GRACE ASPIN

I thought it would be raining. That's what funerals are like in all the movies: as the heroes approach the graveside the heavens open, with sheer anguish relentlessly battering down on them. As I stared out my window, watching as everyone else carried on as normal, the clouds sat innocently in the sky parted, the blue sky shining through.

I've been to a few funerals in my life, for family members I hardly knew. However, the one I wasn't able to attend was Willow's. I didn't even know where she was buried, if she was at all. We had succumb to Trojan then, thoughts and feelings for Willow more fleeting with every passing moment. I hadn't made the effort to look or even made a phone call to ask.

I hadn't forgotten about her but I wasn't anxious to remember.

A soft knock sounded at the door and Nicola slipped into my room, holding something in a long black bag. Body bag was my immediate thought.

'I brought this,' she said, and laid the bag on the bed, unzipping it.

Inside was a deep navy blazer, accompanied by a navy dress shirt, skirt and trousers. On the shoulders of the blazer was one black tab with a white stripe, while at the breast side pocket, there was a small blue tab as well as a green one.

'What are those for?' I asked, walking over to my bed, my fingers tracing the fabric.

'Honours, for your service. This is going to be the formal occasion uniform for Reign agents: all the other branches of the services have one, I thought you should have your own. The honours were added for your time in Brora, as well as stopping the bomb.'

'Then what's the tabs on the shoulders for?'

'For being a Reign student in the time of Daniel Harkness.'

As his name left her lips I couldn't help the shiver that ran up my spine or the hard swallow I had to force down. When I'd heard his voice in London I had convince myself he wasn't in the same building, that he wasn't hiding in the next room watching me but he could have been. Daniel was always going to be a part of me and I hated myself for it.

'What happened to wearing all black?' I asked, however Nicola didn't reply.

She herself didn't look like she'd been getting much sleep, the dark circles under her eyes more prominent than yesterday. She hovered awkwardly in the middle of the room, seeming unsure of whether to sit or leave.

'There's going to be a car to collect you at the main gates, it'll be ready to leave in twenty minutes. The rest of your team have been informed –'

'Did you get the flowers we ordered?' I cut her off, my eyes returning to the window.

'Yes, they arrived this morning.'

'I'd appreciate it if you could wait until we're at the graveside before giving them to me: the team and I would rather put them down ourselves.'

'Of course.'

'You can't wash it away,' I told her. She looked at me, confused, so I continued. 'You can pretend all you want that Harkness didn't control Reign, you can dress it up with new classes, new formal uniforms and brand-new rules, but we're still the same agents.'

'Grace, I don't know what you're talking about.'

'We were confined here, prisoners. You think just because you don't hit us every agent will melt in your hand?' I asked. 'What are you going to do when a student speaks out about the abuse?'

'This isn't the day to talk about it.'

'Shall I wait for ground to open up?' I yelled. 'There isn't going to be a good time to talk about it.'

KNOCK.

KNOCK.

Lily appeared at the door dressed in the new uniform that I'd already taking a disliking to: a blazer, dress shirt, long trousers and heels.

'Grace, come on,' she said, leaning against the door. 'Leave it for today.'

'Seriously?' I asked.

'We can conquer the world tomorrow,' she said to me pointedly. 'We have more important issues, like who's going to carry the coffin.'

I hadn't even thought about that.

'Is Chris coming?' I asked, but Nicola shook her head. 'Did you tell him?'

'He's unreachable.'

'This is outrageous,' I shot out, and Lily's eyebrows raised. 'I mean, come on.'

'There's nothing I can do, he's unreachable,' Nicola protested.

'You've had four days to call him and for all that time he's been unreachable? Did you even try to contact someone else in his team?'

'Grace, this isn't as easy as you make it out to be.'

'You know what –' I started but Lily swooped in, taking my shoulders.

'We'll meet you at the car Nic,' she said to her.

Nicola looked as if she was going to say something but gave up, marching out of the room.

'I think we need to take some deep breaths,' Lily said.

‘I think we need to stab her with that shoe of yours,’ I muttered, watching through the empty doorway.

‘That was someone else’s move,’ she said, a deep sigh trembling through me. ‘Today’s about Jessica, the world can go to shit on its own for a few hours.’

‘What if Chris finds out we had the funeral without him?’

‘If he’s unreachable he could be in a danger zone. Don’t think they’d want to bring home another body.’

I sighed heavily, trying to get it through my head that this was happening today.

‘We’ll carry the coffin,’ I decided. ‘The five of us.’

‘We need six.’

‘We’ll make do,’ I said. ‘She’d want us to do it.’

CHAPTER 11

Lacuna

A blank space, a missing part.

NAOMI JADE

The casket handle was rigid and heavy but I held on tight, as if it were your hand; your fingers interlocking with mine, your warm palm pressing on my skin. The wooden base rested on my shoulder, I imagined it was your arm slung around mine as you whispered nonsense in my ear. I strained my neck, the muscles tight, pressed my lips, closed my eyes and imagined. That was the saddest part of it all because all I could do now, was imagine you, Jess.

With each step, I imagined you were there beside me, in those ridiculously tall heels that everyone could hear from a mile away. As the casket was lifted from my shoulders and placed on the ground, it was as if your arm had slipped away and you were standing beside me.

As the casket was lowered into the ground and I stepped back, you were there with me. I imagined you wearing one of your old band T-shirts, a pair of jeans and combat boots. Despite being in control of my own imagination, the bruises and scars still appeared on your skin.

In that moment, it was just you and me. Everyone else had vanished and I couldn't care less. You stood not two feet away, sauntering up to me as you usually would, with that dickish smirk that you passed off as confidence. Why were you so confident? You had no reason to be. You led this team like it was nothing, you always had a plan.

Did you plan for this? Did you plan for your death? You couldn't have because there weren't any videos, there wasn't a letter, there wasn't even a fucking text. Did you know it was your last mission? How couldn't I have known that when I hugged you, it would be the last time?

I couldn't understand the people who begged for five more minutes to say goodbye; I wouldn't know where to begin. I was breathless, raw and trembling. If I had five minutes with you, I know I wouldn't say a word.

That's the worst part about loving you, Jess. When we were young you made it so easy to become attached and I don't know if I should hate you for it. You should have known something would go wrong, you should have stayed with us, you shouldn't have gone – you had to have known?

Should I still love you for being my friend? Should I still love you even though all I can feel is misery as I stand over your grave?

I hugged you for the last time almost two weeks before but a mere echo lingered; your arms pressing on my back, your nails tugging at my shirt and breath hot on my neck.

Someone passed me one of the roses we'd picked for you, a white rose. Thank God you didn't like lilies – not because they were funeral flowers but they were all out at the florists. We weren't allowed to put any pictures of you, Jess, given everything that was going on. I know Nicola told us to find a photo but it wasn't for anyone else to see, it was just for us.

I'd snuck home when my parents were out for twenty minutes, had to ransack through the cupboards but I found the photo album eventually. The photo I chose was one from a school dance: we both looked like babies, but it made me smile. The school prefects had convinced you to sing a rendition of some stupid song but you pulled me up too and said 'we're in this together'.

We weren't anymore though, were we?

CHAPTER 12

Anagapesis

No longer feeling affection for someone you once loved.

LILY CHAN

When the casket was lowered into the ground I took in a stiff breath, lifting my head high. I wasn't going to salute the coffin, Jess would say it looked stupid.

The funeral party was too small for my liking, there were probably only about fifteen people here, most of them other agents from Nicola's division or Reign.

A lone car sat at the edge of the cemetery. I half thought it was Chris, given the small American flag on the bonnet but it couldn't be, he was in Budapest.

Naomi placed her rose on the grave just as Grace had started to hand them out, a white rose. To be frank, we had no clue what her favourite fucking flower was, it was a complete guess. Besides, they were there purely for decoration, we had our own way of saying goodbye once everyone else had left. When Grace handed me my own rose I tossed it onto the first step of the little grave, shoving my hands in the blazer pockets.

Since this wasn't a religious funeral there wasn't a priest to say the last rites or whatever. I half thought Grace would have wanted to say something but instead, Nicola took her place at the side of the grave. She spouted some utter bullshit that wasn't true – how selfless and great Jess was, how she lived life to the full, did everything she could.

But she didn't live life to the full, she was nineteen. She also wasn't a good person, she was an asshole who shut us out whenever we got too close and when we didn't like something, she didn't care. She'd made Quinn cry more than once; when she sent the videos to Naomi's mum I saw it as an opportunity but Jessica just screamed at her, asked her how could she be so careless? That night in London Quinn told me everything.

As Nicola addressed the crowd I knew my team weren't listening, because everyone apart from Naomi knew it was horseshit. Jessica didn't care because if she did she wouldn't have jumped at the opportunity to work with MI6, she wouldn't have just left us.

I hated her. I'll never be the same person because of her.

She went on an op she wasn't ready for with a team who didn't even know her! Then she went and got herself killed. Why didn't she bring us with her? We could have protected her! But no, as always she went off on her own because that's the way she liked it.

Grace was barely holding it together, Naomi was a walking emotional time bomb, Quinn looked ready to fall over, and Kayson – well, fuck knows with him.

CHAPTER 13

Filipendulous

Hanging by a thread.

KAYSON ASHFORD

I needed a drink.

The hip flask was heavy in the pocket of my suit but I didn't think it was appropriate to neck it in the middle of Nicola's speech. I didn't know much about Nicola and Jessica's relationship, they seemed to get on well from what I saw. I'd gone back through the security footage with Quinn a few times – we did that when we were bored, looked through old videos to see if we could get any clues as to what Trojan might be planning next.

Naomi was busy training with Lily so we didn't want to burden her with more research and surveillance. What surprised me, though, was that there was nothing – there were no indications that any of this was going to happen. When Reign fell, did Harkness move all assets out of there? He must have, considering an entirely new management took over.

Even though Nicola was talking, out of the corner of my eye I saw Lily turn towards the gates of the cemetery and I soon saw why: a long black car with a small American flag on the front. That couldn't be Chris, he would stand with us.

I knew Luca was behind me so I leaned back, whispering in his ear to find out who it was. He tapped my shoulder and off he went.

For fuck's sake Jess, you really knew how to make us all feel like shit. You were a cold-hearted bitch but I loved you for it. When you told me you were taking a temporary job at MI6 I was happy for you because you'd been stuck in a destructive cycle your entire life and this was something new. Is that why you let your guard down? You didn't do as much research as you normally did for an op, you just kept saying everything was going to be OK and that you trusted Nicola.

You left Grace to fill your shoes, fine, she could do it, but Naomi is going to be sent to another team. Did you think that through? Not that she would go willingly, I've seen her train with them and let me tell you, she's not going down without a fight.

You asked me to protect her and that still remains my promise to you.

During the summer Lily and I trained her – you saw, I don't know why I'm saying that. We made sure she could protect herself, fight against the enemy but we didn't train her, to lose you. Even now I can see it on her face, she's holding back the tears. She hasn't cried yet, not over you. I half expected her to be one of the first.

I hope she doesn't bury herself in work like you did, I'll try to stop that. I hope she doesn't push her emotions down. I hope she doesn't lose herself in finding your killer, I'll explain to her how it won't work.

I hope she stays the same naive, clumsy and curious girl I met on the doorstep.

I fucking hope she doesn't end up like you.

CHAPTER 14

Meliorism

The belief that the world gets better.

QUINN EATON

That was all rather dreary, wasn't it? I tried to smile but everyone wore deadpan expressions. I remember we talked about it once, you'd wanted your funeral to be a party, with dancing and alcohol.

Well we've got one part of that covered, I've broken out the good tequila, the Mexican one you liked. Kayson and I spent half the morning trying to pour it into the hip flask – we couldn't find a funnel you see, so we had to make one out of paper, then that got really soggy so we had to switch to the ladle with that little spout bit at the side.

We all thought that should be our way of saying goodbye.

When Grace gave me the rose I immediately reached into my pocket and stuck a diamond earring in the centre. You stole it – wait, that sounds kinda bad – never mind, *we* stole it. I was on comms that day when we were training.

That jeweller probably never figured out where it went. I know you didn't wear a lot of jewellery but I thought you'd appreciate this.

There's a part of me that still can't get over that you're gone, it's different to Willow. Her bench is in a cemetery about twenty minutes away. Guess it just shows you that anyone in the ranks can fall, first a Carrier and now a Team Lead.

Death is weird isn't it? You reflect on your own life and everything just seems inadequate. I couldn't say for sure that I would have seen your stupid team abandoning you but surely you saw the warning signs? I pulled the records for the team – unfortunately they've all gone off the grid but don't worry, when they resurface I'll grab a few of them for a chat.

I gently tossed the rose in the grave and it landed on top of the coffin with a small thump. Everyone else had put theirs on the actual grave but I wanted a little bit of me in there with her. Despite everything, I didn't hate her or dislike her. She was my friend, one of my best.

In memory of Jess I had an earpiece in: it wasn't live or on a channel but I had Willow's playlist on quietly, it got me through a lot; losing Willow, and whenever I was feeling sad.

Jess, you and Willow weren't the best of friends but you did have some similar tastes in music. I remember this one song came on – it was about five minutes long, you and Willow were trying to cook dinner but you were banging your heads to the tune.

There are only three of us left now, Grace, Lily and me. Jess, if you're watching, please don't let it go down to one.

I hope you're happy in the afterlife or heaven or I don't know, I think you said something about liking the beach once. You and Willow are watching over us, you won't let anything happen, I know you two wouldn't. That's the proof I'm asking for, if there's a God up there. If we don't lose anyone else I swear I'll convert and go to church every Sunday, I'll even go to confessional. There has to be one cleared by security.

I know I should have been listening to Nicola but I've never liked funerals, I just wanted to go home.

'As a member of our security team she was . . .' Nicola trailed off, swallowing hard. 'She was dedicated to the job like her brother and from that, I believe we have a lot to be thankful for.'

CHAPTER 15

Dépaysement

When someone is taken out of their own familiar world and into a new one.

NICOLA RAMOS

'As a member of our security team she was . . . she was dedicated to the job like her brother and from that, I believe we have a lot to be thankful for.'

This was the second Winters funeral I'd arranged, attended and spoken at. The headstones were black, simple and clean. Jessica's was next to her brothers'; I'd come by early this morning to freshen the other two up.

I hadn't just known Jessica when she was an agent, I'd known her since she was two years old. I remember seeing her taste ice cream for the first time, I remember hugging her while her brothers chased their mother down the drive as she left for work. Then when she went to the Pyramid Delegates I barely saw her; even then she became a different person. Jess held herself differently after that.

We'd suspected for about a year that something was going on at Reign; it took long enough to get James inside that we thought it impossible to start pulling other agents out. As well as Jessica that day I managed to pull one of the senior agents from the programme, Megan Orr, she worked a cover in the city, the shop a front for handovers from other agents – for God's sake, now wasn't the time to be thinking about this.

A whole generation lay at my feet and I wanted nothing more than to go over to that car, drag the pair of them out and force them to look. I'd invited them to James's funeral but neither of them showed: why they came to this one I couldn't know for sure, perhaps the guilt had finally set in.

With a deep breath I wrapped up my speech and left the graveside, many following after me but not the Omega team. They stood there, tall and unmoving.

I observed them for a moment, not a word was exchanged between them as they stared at the open grave. The Omega Team were tricky, but they were the only fourth years who were available to me – the rest of them were being assessed internally. Soon I'd lose them too. What Lily pulled was unacceptable, the team had lost sight of the true mission objective. They'd been assessed over the last few days and I wasn't overly fond of the results. I needed to get a psychiatric evaluation on them all.

But for now I gave them some privacy, marching over to the black car and chapping on the window. Agent Harrison sat in the driver's seat and I smiled briefly.

‘Please inform Mr and Mrs Winters that they will have to wait until the graveside is clear before they approach. Then we’ll reconvene at Reign.’

‘Yes ma’am.’ He replied.

‘Thank you.’ A man said but I didn’t acknowledge him.

He was no better than her.

CHAPTER 16

Saudade

The love that remains.

NAOMI JADE

'Who wants to start?' Kayson asked, slipping the flask from his pocket.

'Me,' Quinn piped up, taking the hip flash and unscrewing the cap. 'Jess, I'm gonna miss you. I never thought that we'd make it work in the team but you were great.' She took a sharp swig of the flask but burst into a coughing fit, passing it to Lily.

'You OK?' I asked, a small smile breaking out as Lily rubbed her back.

'Tequila,' she said, in between breaths. 'Is really strong.'

Lily necked a good bit before toasting it to the grave.

'Jess, I respect you and everything you did but you were a pain in the arse and a real bitch.'

'Lily!' Quinn exclaimed hitting her on the arm. 'You can't say that about her.'

'What she gonna do?' Lily asked. 'She's dead.'

Kayson's deep laugh sounded from behind me and I couldn't help but share it. In all fairness, Jess would have found that quite funny.

Grace rolled her eyes, clicking her tongue but Lily just laughed, passing the flask to me. The sharp tang of tequila met my nose but I pushed past the burning thoughts and let the cool liquid slip down my throat.

'I knew you since high school,' I started. 'You were my best friend. When you went to Reign I tried to stay in touch but you pulled away – rightly so, I'm not worth getting punched over.'

Kayson's eyes flickered to mine for a moment, his hands rubbing my shoulders.

'There's so much that I had to say to you when you came back,' I said. 'I wanted to show you that I'd finally managed that move – the one where I can take down Lily and Kayson at the same time. Don't think they were really going full force though.'

Lily mused.

'Medium pace,' she told me.

'I wanted to show you the ideas for my room, since I was going to move into Willow's. I also wanted to see if I could beat you in a drinking competition, since you kicked my ass in high school.'

'High school?' Quinn asked.

'Yeah, in second or third year she could drink the seniors under the table.'

'You would only have been fifteen.'

'We're meant to be saying goodbye,' Grace cut in. 'Not how much of a bitch she was or that she had a drinking problem.'

'Or that she repressed her emotions,' Lily added.

'Or that she was scarily good with a gun,' Quinn said.

'What about that time she pinned Naomi to a wall?'

'Yeah, that was weird,' I muttered.

'She also dated an American,' Kayson sneered.

'Dear Lord,' Grace muttered, seemingly completely done.

I laughed a little as the team quietened.

'Goodbye Jess,' I said softly, passing the flask to Kayson.

But it wasn't goodbye, not yet, not until we'd poured the flask over your grave. You could linger in my imagination a little longer.

Kayson took three gulps, wiping his mouth with the back of his hand.

'I was only on your team for a short while but you were a great leader, you were dedicated to your role. Perhaps a little too much. Your request to have me transferred to the Omegas was accepted – officially a part of the team.'

'Since when?' Grace asked.

'This morning,' he answered. 'Jessica asked if I'd be willing to transfer after the harbour.'

Grace didn't say anything but it was clear by the look on her face she wasn't aware of this. Neither was I but I pulled Kayson a little closer then, it was going to be good having him around more. That way I wasn't sitting around waiting for him to come home from an op, at least I'd be with him.

I wondered why Jessica hadn't told us about Kayson's transfer, if anything I thought the team would be the first people to know.

'Fuck, now I need to see you more than once a day,' Lily grumbled.

'Lily, this is a holy place, I'd appreciate if you stopped swearing,' Grace said eloquently.

'Oh, bite me, Princess,' Lily snapped back. 'What is God gonna do? Strike me down?'

'You're unbelievable,' Grace muttered.

'Grace,' Kayson said, pushing the flask in her direction and I saw his point, this wasn't the place to start a fight.

She took it, only managing a small sip, begrudgingly swallowing.

'We joked a lot, you and me,' Grace said.

'Were we all sleeping when that happened?' Lily snorted, but a quick thwap to the head from Kayson shut her up. As much as I appreciated the jokes, Grace would want to do this properly.

She continued.

'Said that I wanted your job, you said you wanted mine. I'll be honest, I did,' she admitted. 'But not like this. I have no clue what I'm doing but I take comfort in the fact that you didn't either. It's not my right to judge you for what you've done or what you were, that's in God's hands. I hope you're able to find peace in death. I hope you're able to forgive me for what I did.' She paused. 'Forgive me for my actions.'

Grace took the rose at her side, the petals stained red with a single finger print as she tossed it into the grave. She grabbed a small handful of dirt from the pile, tossing it in.

'I won't utter his name but he's going to pay for what he did to you, to us. We'll make sure of it.'

'Speaking of,' I piped up. 'Since this is going to be the last team meeting Jess will attend, I have a proposition. Nicola said we can't leave the Scotland but to bring down Trojan we have to – all the big decisions are going to be made in London. No one will do open business here, not anymore.'

'What are you saying?' Lily asked.

'That we take the fight to them. They probably think we're going to hide after what happened. I say we go to London and finish the job.'

'That's insane!' Quinn exclaimed.

'Insanity got me here,' I told her.

'You want to avenge her?' Kayson asked me and I nodded.

'And James, Jacqueline, Willow – everyone who has been hurt by Trojan.'

'That's a tall order,' Grace said but she wasn't looking at me. 'Technically we'd be committing treason.'

'I've got nothing else going on at the moment,' I said.

She laughed but shook her head.

'It's risky.'

'So's crossing the road,' I retorted.

'We'll need new identities.'

'I was thinking of switching up mine anyway,' I said. 'Nicola wants to pretend this isn't happening, she wants to control us. I say we go to London and figure out who's pulling the strings. Starting with Lillian – she oversees all the government-run institutes, she has to know something.'

'How long will it take to get new IDs?' Lily asked Quinn. 'Passports and a driver's licence?'

'My contact can get them done in an hour, all she needs is the photos, probably throw in a getaway car for free,' Quinn rapidly shot back.

'How much can you take from the armoury without drawing any attention?' Grace asked and Kayson laughed.

'Enough.'

'What about the plane?' I asked.

'. . . I know a guy,' Lily said.

'Won't they just shoot us down?' Quinn asked. 'If we're unidentified then they'll shoot us. Nothing is getting in or out.'

'I know a guy,' she repeated.

'I'll pack the essentials,' Grace announced. 'The rest of you know what to do. We leave tonight.'

Here we go again.

CHAPTER 17

Residuum

Remaining parts.

GRACE ASPIN

'. . . I know a guy,' Lily said.

'Won't they just shoot us down?' Quinn asked worriedly. 'If we're unidentified then they'll shoot us. Nothing is getting in or out.'

'I know a guy,' she repeated.

Oh, of course she had a guy, I found it better not to ask questions with her.

'I'll pack the essentials,' I said, a small smile on my face. 'The rest of you know what to do. We leave tonight.'

With a final sigh I tipped the flask, splashing the rest of the tequila over the black glossy top.

'Goodbye.'

Even though Naomi had suggested it, I had been thinking the same thing – well, not the sneaking down to London part, but about avenging Jessica. Would that atone for what I'd done? If I brought her killer to justice?

We all headed back to the car at the far end of the cemetery, however as we did, the click of another car door sounded, the one sporting an American flag. A tall man stepped out dressed in black, his brown hair slicked back. He marched down the aisle of graves, a stony expression on his face. He carried a briefcase at his side and for a moment I panicked – what could be in there?

'He showed,' Kayson said breathlessly.

'Who?' Quinn asked.

'Jessica's father.'

A stunned silence hung in the air around us for a moment, until the piercing smack of heels broke the air. Emerging from the car this time was a slender woman, once again dressed in black. Her hair was the exact same colour as Jessica's but bolt straight instead of curly. Jessica and Charlotte were very similar, even in the way they held themselves.

'And mother,' I murmured in awe.

All of us stared like spectators at the zoo, witnessing a sight that Jessica had never seen. Her parents together. The wind picked up so as the pair chatted their words were lost; maybe it was best we didn't hear.

'Only took three of their kids dying for them to show,' Lily said, and this time I didn't move to correct her.

'I've never seen her dad,' Quinn whispered.

‘I’ll be back in a minute,’ I said quickly, reaching into my bag.

I knew Nicola had invited them so I’d brought a little something just in case, despite Kayson telling me they didn’t deserve it. There were a few questions but I ignored them and walked over to her parents, their conversation finally reaching my ears.

‘I found out from my secretary about James –’

‘You’re here now,’ Charlotte said.

‘Am I supposed to thank you for that?’ the man exclaimed.

‘I made sure our children could defend themselves, that they could protect this country.’

‘And where have they ended up Charlotte?’ I thought Jessica inherited her anger from her mother but it wasn’t, it was her father.

The way his eyebrows creased together and face blazed told me everything I needed to know. Charlotte hadn’t told him a thing, even after he left. He was more clueless than us.

‘You took our children away from me and forced them into –’

‘You were the one who couldn’t handle it!’ Charlotte screamed.

I glanced back at my team who were motionless; Quinn however, appeared curious. She wasn’t watching Charlotte – she was watching Jessica’s father. I soon saw why; the anger I’d witnessed before still lingered but monstrous tears lingered in his eyes.

As I lingered behind them, his lips quivered.

'My sons, my daughter.' His voice shaking. 'My daughter Charlotte, she was nineteen.'

'When you left she was no longer your daughter.'

'She was a kid, she didn't deserve this!'

I coughed before it could go any further.

Despite my curiosity, I knew this conversation was not for my ears. What was a bit peculiar though was that the man, who I now knew as Jessica's father, was American.

I pulled out a thick brown file from my satchel bag, gripping it tight.

'I apologise, but I'm unsure if I'll see you at Reign,' I said, holding out the file to them. 'This is Jessica's file, it dates back to her time in the Pyramid Delegates as well as some personal mission reports. I picked a few I think you would like.'

Charlotte took the file delicately but the man snatched it from her hands.

'Clayton!' she exclaimed, irritated.

'Pyramid Delegates, Reign – what else haven't you told me?' Clayton asked but Charlotte didn't reply, her piercing blue eyes fixed on me.

'Who are you?'

'Grace Aspin, the Second in Jess's team. I'll leave you with some privacy.'

I turned quickly, wanting to be out of there as soon as possible when Clayton called my name.

‘Thank you,’ he said, nodding. ‘I really appreciate this.’

‘It was no trouble at all,’ I replied, before marching back to the car, the team all sporting perplexed looks.

‘We need to look into Charlotte Winters,’ I informed them, opening the car door. ‘If Willow was right then we need as much intel as possible. She was a donor for Reign.’

‘What about Clayton?’ Kayson asked.

‘I think there’s more to the story than Charlotte told Jess, he’s clueless when it comes to the affairs of his children,’ I said.

Kayson’s phoned pinged.

‘Luca’s heading back to Reign to get more intel but he ran the plates, the big fuck-off car belongs to the CIA.’

‘The CIA?’ Quinn squeaked.

‘Her mum is MI6 while her dad is CIA.’ Lily laughed. ‘Talk about conflict of interest.’

‘Not to worry,’ I said. ‘We’ll be long gone before anyone figures out what we’re up to.’

I took one final glance to the pair at the grave, Clayton was knelt down, a small pink teddy bear in hand, head hung low. Charlotte however, stood there as rigid as a board. Surely she felt remorse? Or perhaps she was waiting for a private moment.

If Jessica was upset you’d never know; it was clear where she got that from.

‘Why did Nicola even invite them?’ Lily asked.

‘The same reasons that none of us will knock the living daylights out of them or say how they failed as parents. Decency and common courtesy,’ I told her.

‘I want to talk to them,’ Naomi blurted out.

As I watched Charlotte and Clayton at the grave I saw them for what they truly were; two parents who’d made terrible mistakes and now, stood at the graves of their three children. It’s always the parents that were meant to die first, that’s why the word orphan exists. However, after the last month I came to the horrifying realisation that eventually, a word would be created to encompass the pain of a parent losing a child.

I feared for the creation of that word, if at all.

‘No,’ I said softly. ‘No matter what, they’ve lost their daughter. We had our goodbye. Give them privacy to say theirs.’

CHAPTER 18

Eccedentesiast

Someone who hides pain behind a smile.

NAOMI JADE

Despite the bathroom being big enough, five of us in here made it a little cramped. I was actually surprised a fight over personal space hadn't broken out.

Grace said we needed to change our appearance: even though we'd be back in London we needed to keep a low profile and avoid any press shots with the Prime Minister. The best place to be was at his side, where we'd have direct access to Lillian Montague and hopefully, Charlotte Winters.

As Quinn was breaking out the hair dye, I sat on the bathroom floor cutting out semi-permanent tattoos for Kayson. Everyone had brought their own 'kits' and everything was laid out in organised chaos on the bathroom counter. Lily had already shaved the side of her head, slapped on lighter foundation and added fake snake bites to her lips so she was helping Quinn dye the back of her hair.

‘You’ll look older with brown hair,’ Lily commented.

‘That’s the point,’ Quinn replied, taking a make-up brush from the counter and with it, made her features harsher and more defined.

Grace had ditched her pristine jewellery on the counter and was shaving a small slit through her eyebrow, her eyes catching mine.

‘Naomi, are you alright?’

‘Course,’ I said, giving a small smile, handing the tattoos over to Kayson. ‘Just not a big fan of dying my hair.’

‘It’s not permanent,’ she said. ‘You’ll need to pop in some blue coloured contacts too.’

Kayson’s hand gently tugged me over to the bathroom counter, his fingers gripping my waist and sitting me in front of him, my ass teetering over the edge of the sink. In his hand was a little white contact box but as he unscrewed the caps he asked, ‘You ever worn contacts before?’

‘No,’ I admitted.

He stuck his finger in the solution, bringing out a blue contact.

‘Look up,’ he said.

As I did, his other hand caressed my jaw, his warm fingers pulling my skin taut as he placed the thing in my eye. It wasn’t as uncomfortable as I expected – it slipped about for a moment but then Kayson’s face came back into focus. Without even blinking he slipped the other one in.

‘How do I look?’ I asked.

‘You suit brown better,’ he said.

Well, thanks.

I spun round to face the mirror, my eyes now a crystal blue. It was weird for sure, but it was nothing compared to the bottle of black hair dye Grace was holding in her hand.

'Come on you, this needs to be done before we leave,' she said.

As I slipped off the counter, Grace shoved Kayson out the way, already grabbing strands of my hair.

'We're going to be able to do this, right?' I asked, a little nervous.

'If you were having doubts you should have mentioned something before I shaved half my hair off,' Lily said, wrapping the wire around the electric shaver.

'No,' I added quickly. 'Not the plan, just, do you think we'll be able to pull this off? Nicola's gonna hate us.'

'Well at the end of the day she doesn't get a choice, we're doing this whether she likes it or not. This team has conducted many successful operations before and this one isn't any different.' Grace paused. 'Well, it is a bit. We're committing treason, breaking into Her Majesty's Secret Service, hacking military grade databases and we're one member down.'

'Please tell me you're not gonna give pep talks,' Quinn piped up.

Grace laughed.

'It's going to be extremely difficult but we can do it. This is our chance to prove ourselves, our worth. Once we expose the corrupt agents, there's no way they'd let us go. They're not going to push us to the side, they're not going to split us up.'

'Oh yeah, did we tell you how the assessments went?' Lily asked, a finger in her eyeball as she slid a contact around. 'So after being told to run pointless laps around the training grounds and a mock operation, Nicola told me that after the funeral she wanted to split us all up, even though she'd just accepted Kayson's transfer. Said it was an emotional mistake.'

'Yes, she wanted to disband the whole team but we convinced her not to, said we'd compromise if we could stay together,' Grace grumbled.

I couldn't believe what I was hearing. It was bad enough she sent me away but to split everyone up? What did she think that would achieve?

'Apparently,' Lily started, going for the other contact, 'we're too dangerous working together. We're bad influences.'

Grace turned. 'No, she said you were a bad influence.'

'Which is a badge I wear with pride.' Lily smirked.

'Too dangerous?' I asked. 'She does realise she's running a school of assassins? Dangerous is literally in the name.'

I had to speak to Nicola later. Even though they'd compromised, I wanted to know what she thought splitting everyone up would do.

The dye was cold on my scalp but I let Grace do her work and took to watching everyone else. Quinn now had a small plastic shower cap on, her eyebrows processing the new colour while she covered up the small mole on her neck. Kayson had started applying the tattoos to his arms, creating a sleeve, and honestly – it was very, very attractive. I tried to look elsewhere but my eyes kept flitting back to him, especially when he applied one to his neck.

'Question,' Lily butted in. 'What car are we taking?'

'I thought we could grab one from the garage round the back, they're big enough,' Kayson said, peeling one of the tattoo stencils from his jaw.

'Those have trackers,' Grace said.

'I can disable it. When Nicola took over she replaced them all and let me tell you, they're terrible.' Quinn laughed. 'A five-year-old could do it.

I knew for a fact I'd never be able to disable a tracker in a month of Sundays, so I also knew that in Quinn's mind I have the technical capability of a five-year-old.

'We'll drive it for half an hour and then ditch it,' Kayson said. 'Besides, Nicola will be too busy with the funeral party to notice.'

'Who's driving?' Quinn asked.

'Well it's an automatic, so Naomi,' Kayson answered.

'Huh?' I stuttered.

'Lily and I will be busy loading the car, Quinn's on the computers and Grace can't drive.'

'You can learn in the next twenty minutes,' I shot out to her. 'It's not hard, foot on one pedal, hit the other one to brake. It's like Mario Cart.'

'Naomi.' Grace sat the bottle down, her fingers rubbing my shoulders. 'You're going to be fine.'

'No, I have seen enough action movies to know that this doesn't end well for me.'

Kayson laughed heartedly.

'No one is going to be chasing us.'

'Trojan went to extraordinary lengths to try and get you back, Nicola is gonna do the same. God, I hope she doesn't send Eve, she hates me.'

'Naomi,' Lily said, leaning back from the mirror. 'All you need to worry about is getting yourself and Quinn to the garage.'

'I'll get the keys,' Quinn said to me.

As the heavy shadows slid across the bathroom floor, the next few hours flew by. I hardly recognised Quinn as she pulled on a dark jacket, pulling her hair into a bun. I didn't think it was possible but she'd made her face look even skinnier, harsher lines around her cheeks and jaw, her lips now a dark maroon.

We'd all been issued burner phones and a grab bag for essential toiletries and a change of clothes. Everyone else had left the bathroom, running to and fro between bedrooms, getting on with their various jobs so it was just me and Quinn left. Never mind her, I barely recognised myself as I straightened my now-black hair.

'I'll meet you at the garage, I know we're meant to go together but I have to grab some things from the command room before we go,' Quinn said.

'Isn't the Carrier meant to come with you?' I prodded.

'Meant to, but the Technical Support isn't a child,' she snapped, heading out.

Lily appeared, watching after her for a moment. A smile flickered on her face when she saw me.

'Has Quinn taken the high road?' she asked, but at the sound of the door slamming, she smirked. 'I'll take that as a yes.'

'She wants to go on her own,' I said. 'I think she's as anxious as me.'

'She just doesn't like getting fussed over – she hated it when Willow did, it was like watching a kitten fight a dog.'

Lily looked like some kind of rock star with her shredded band T-shirt and knee-high boots, all that was missing was the guitar.

'Does she still think I'm trying to replace her?' I asked.

'What happened to that self-confidence Grace was telling me about?'

KNOCK.

KNOCK.

Downstairs the click of the door sounded, but we weren't expecting any visitors. Apart from Quinn, the rest of us were still in the dorm house but it was quiet, like everyone was wondering the same thing – who just walked in?

'Anyone home?' Nicola called, but no one responded.

That's when a second pair of feet shuffling across the wooden floor echoed from downstairs.

'They're probably at the reception in the hall, make yourself at home,' Nicola said quietly, before the door shut.

Lily and I exchanged looks – who the hell was she talking to?

I walked cautiously out of the bathroom to the top of the stairs. It couldn't have been Eve, she'd have started shouting by now. When I looked down I saw a woman standing at the bottom of the stairs; she was dressed formally, like she'd just walked out of a business meeting. Her hair was immaculate and when she spotted me, sported an equally perfect smile.

'Hi there, my names Clarice Chambers, is . . .' She trailed off reading the white paper in her hand, 'Miss Grace Aspin here?'

'She's busy,' I blurted. Technically she was, I wasn't lying.

'Right, it's just I've come to discuss the matter of Team Lead.'

'Grace is Team Lead.'

'I'd rather do it in private.' Her hand grasped the banister. 'It's a bit of a delicate matter.'

'Whatever you can say to her you can say to me,' I told her. 'She's busy, I'll pass on the message.'

Clarice or whatever her name was stayed quiet, and it was only then I realised that Grace and Kayson were standing outside her bedroom door and Lily was poking her head out the bathroom. I turned back to the woman, who'd started climbing the stairs, and quickly made my way down a few to cut her off. She stopped, clicking her tongue.

'Please, just go and fetch her for me,' she said but I didn't move, not when I saw the three suitcases at the door, all varying in size.

‘No,’ I said. ‘Tell me why you’re here, cause this isn’t a holiday destination.’

‘I’m your new Team Lead, so you better stop speaking to me like that,’ she demanded, and I nearly choked on my own spit.

‘We don’t need a new leader, thanks but no thanks,’ I said to her.

‘Oh I think you do, this team is a mess. You’re assassins –’

‘In case you haven’t noticed –’

‘Mindless assassins who are a hazard to society. For someone who’s meant to be amongst the more intelligent agents, you’re not very observant of your own incompetence.’

Did she just call me stupid?

A soft ping sounded from my phone, it was a text from Lily.

LILY: Found our distraction. The funeral party is in the main hall.

A smile formed on my lips.

‘That’s Grace, she’s in the main hall, I’ll take you,’ I said, trying to lead the way but the woman pushed ahead, taking point.

As the door closed behind me I heard a few whispers from upstairs, but Clarice was too far away to hear anything. Her walk was fast enough to be a run – who shoved a stick up her arse?

What the hell was Nicola thinking? She had to have known this wouldn’t go down well, and especially after the funeral – anyone with a brain would know that was a terrible idea.

'If you're going for the likeable approach, you missed,' I said, managing to keep up with Clarice, but it didn't stop her little power march.

'I'm not here for likeable. Your team refused to be split up so I'm here to get you in line.'

Good luck, I wanted to say, there was more chance of Lily putting on a frilly pink tutu and dancing to Ed Sheeran.

We quickly ascended the stairs to the Academy, passing the great big doors and reception. As Clarice found her way to the main hall and barged in on the quiet, solemn occasion, her apparent prowess quickly dwindled. Even though there were only a few people at the graveyard, there were far more in here: Reign students, a few agents I recognised from Nicola's division who had been coming in over the last few months, and the faculty. Thompson stood at the back of the room deep in conversation with a man beside him, who had to be only a year or two older than me. He had black skin and dark buzzed hair. I'd never seen him before, maybe it was someone Thompson knew?

Thomas Ames, who I'd been training with occasionally was chatting to Dr McKay but at our abrupt arrival, stopped. Even Jessica's parents, who stood to the side keeping to themselves, seemed shocked at our arrival.

Guess power walking everywhere wasn't always a good thing, Clarice.

'Is Grace Aspin here?' she asked, although as I came to stand beside her, any composure had left the building. She coughed a few times, trying to pull it back, but she wasn't doing herself any favours.

Dr McKay threw me a look, but I wasn't sure if it was at my newly acquired appearance or the fact that we both knew that I knew that Grace definitely wasn't there.

'I don't think so,' Thompson said, sipping his drink.

'I haven't seen her,' the man beside him said. 'She might have gone to the bathroom.'

Clarice slowly turned to me and I had to force myself not to shrivel back under her stare.

'You said she was here.'

OK, distraction time – how do I do that again?

What would I do? Jessica's voice floated around my head.

Well, you had a flair for the dramatics, you walked out of a blazing wall of bodies like something from a frickin nightmare. That was it, be dramatic, the centre of attention.

'Because you're already trying to replace Jessica!' I screamed and the idle chatter that had started again, came to an abrupt stop, everyone's attention turning to me.

Oh, I hated this.

The entire room of beady eyes was anxious to hear what I had to say – how could I play it? Angry or sad? What about a blubbering mess?

'She's barely in the ground and now you've just waltz in here, yelling at me –'

'Stop, that's not –'

‘You’re going to tell me I’m a liar?’ I asked. ‘Her parents are standing right there!’ I pointed to the pair who’d sat down their drinks, the bloodshot eyes of Clayton screwing shut.

‘I didn’t know –’

‘She was my best friend and now you think you can come in here, into our home and replace her? You call us reckless and incompetent but do you actually know the first thing about us? Do you know that Quinn has nightmares from what happened in Brora? That she wakes up screaming nearly every night?’

Dr McKay edged his way toward me but I didn’t stop – even though it was a pretence I felt real emotions bubble to the surface. I was angry. She’d walked in here and treated us like dirt because of what she’d heard. Clarice didn’t know the first thing about what Harkness had put them through.

Yes, Lily made a mistake but you couldn’t blame her, it’s what he created.

‘I’ll answer for you: no,’ I told her. ‘You judge us but you don’t know the first thing about our team.’

‘Is that true?’ Clayton asked, his voice cracking. ‘You’re replacing my daughter?’

Clarice stuttered.

‘It’s only temporary.’

‘She’s just been buried, couldn’t this wait until the morning?’ he asked.

'This team is dangerous, sir, immediate action had to be taken.'

'What?' I asked, playing the victim. 'We – we saved our government.' Here came the fake tears and snot. 'Harkness told us we were nothing, he told us we were weapons, we did what we were told because if we didn't he'd . . . are you going to do that?'

'Do what?'

'He waterboarded me.' Images of Lily flew across my eyes. 'He beat us, starved us.'

'Of course not!' she cried.

'You think we're monsters, don't you?'

'No!'

'She's just like him!' I screamed, backing away from her.

Dr McKay rushed towards me, gently tugging me towards the door.

Conversation erupted in the hall, students shouting at the top of their lungs while the majority of adults stood motionless. Well, that distraction worked a charm.

'Wait!' Clarice tried but the voice of Ames told me she wasn't getting close.

'Are you OK?' Dr McKay asked softly, as he took me out of the hall and round the corner, where I wiped away the tears and let out a little laugh.

'I see why Jessica enjoyed drama now, that was kinda fun.'

He froze solid for a moment before rolling his eyes.

'Is this the part where I pretend I don't know where you went and keep everyone in the hall?'

'If you could,' I told him sweetly.

He gave a quick nod.

'Keep an eye on Grace for me.'

I paused. That was a bit specific but maybe he was just a good friend. Grace did spend a lot of time with him.

'Sure, can you text Nicola as well, ask her for backup in the main hall?'

Without any questions, he gave me a small mock salute and headed back into the hall shutting the door behind him, the shrill sound of shouting silenced.

I texted Lily to let her know the distraction was well underway before speed-walking through the school and out the back door to the garage. I really hoped there wasn't a sports car waiting for me – I only knew how to drive a manual so switching to an automatic might be tricky.

The garage where the cars were kept was at the back left of the school. It almost looked like one of those airport hangers where they kept the planes. Thankfully, I didn't have to worry too much about security since Nicola would be too busy trying to figure out why half the school was screaming the place down.

There was a code pad on the door but luckily for me four numbers were slightly rubbed off. OK, so it was a four-digit thing – that still left a lot of combinations. OK, come on, think – what would rub off the numbers? Oil from the skin? That would mean you'd have the most oil on your fingers with the first key so that had to be the one with the least amount of writing left. OK, that was the number eight. The rest of the numbers all looked the same, this might take a while. What if –

'Naomi, see the green light at the top of the pad?' Quinn asked. 'That means it's already open, come on.'

She grabbed the slats at the side of the door and hauled it back, her little fingers shaking under the pressure.

Well . . . I would have figured it out eventually.

Quinn ran ahead to the far corner, her rucksack full to the brim, slapping her back like a ton of bricks. I followed her over to a black SUV as she clambered into the back. I reluctantly dived into the driver's seat, catching the keys from Quinn and starting the engine. It rumbled like an animal – one that I didn't think I'd be able to steer.

'How long till the others get here?' I asked, my knuckles turning white as I gripped the wheel.

'Shouldn't be too long now,' Quinn said, unzipping her bag and pulling out her laptop, probably starting to disable the tracker.

As I adjusted my feet on the pedals I looked back to her in the rear-view mirror.

'Quinn, I know I'm new and I know that there are certain ways that the Carrier and Techie are meant to act but if you find it too suffocating with me having to follow you around, just say. You trained here too. You can probably take care of yourself better than I ever could.'

She glanced up for a moment.

'Thank you, I appreciate that,' she said softly. 'Willow was all over me like a rash, I felt like a child.'

'She really cared about you,' I said to her.

'I know.' Quinn sighed, tugging on her oversized purple shirt. 'It was funny, at the time it wasn't but one night she literally carried me out of the mission.'

'I think that's taking the role of Carrier a little too literally,' I said. We both chuckled at that but as the boot opened and the sound of Kayson's gruff voice filtered through, we stopped.

He clambered into the back with Lily in tow, I noted the gun in Kayson's lap and the packed holsters on Lily's thighs. Were we expecting company? Or were we going to fire at our own?

'Where's Gracie?' Quinn asked.

'Take a guess,' Lily said, and Quinn rolled her eyes.

'Tracker offline?'

'Yip.'

'Naomi, drive up to the front entrance, Grace will be coming out there,' Lily told me.

I pressed the pedal and we jolted – Mary, Joseph and the wee baby, this thing could shoot off like a rocket! My foot slammed on the brake, my body lurching forward.

'Yes,' Kayson muttered. 'That's the brake.'

'I know that,' I shot back, before pulling off again, more gently this time.

I pulled the car round slowly to the front entrance but stopped just before the main stairs, switching the headlights off. I couldn't hear anything from inside but then I remembered this building didn't exactly have thin walls – I wasn't sitting in my grandma's scheme, where you could hear babies crying from a hundred feet away, amongst other things.

The small slaps of Grace's shoes crunched on the gravel before she dived in the front.

'Nicola knows. Drive.'

'What?' I asked.

'Well, considering the only one with black hair on the team is Lily and you're not Asian or a man, she picked up pretty quickly that something was going on.'

So my Oscar-winning performance was for nothing? I'll need to throw my speech down the drain.

Fuck's sake Naomi, drive! Jessica's voice shot through my head.

I pressed on the pedal but just as I did Nicola ran in front of the SUV, her eyes filled to the brim with worry.

‘Oh, that’s not good,’ Quinn said softly.

‘Please don’t do this,’ Nicola begged, head shaking as she slowly walked towards the SUV.

‘Floor it,’ Lily demanded.

‘I could hit Nicola,’ I said.

‘She’ll move.’

‘What if she doesn’t?’

‘Naomi drive!’ Lily yelled.

Shit – sorry, Nicola.

I pressed my foot to the floor and the SUV shot off, my eyes trained on Nicola, begging her to move out the way – she didn’t.

I was going to hit her.

At the last moment she dived out of the way, crashing onto the gravel and I tried not to look back, focusing on the black iron gates at the end of the drive. I heard the scratching of gravel hitting the side of the car as we barrelled towards the open gates.

I thought we’d done it but as blurs of bodies ran towards the car garage, I had an idea this wouldn’t be as easy at we’d planned.

‘We need to close the gates,’ Grace said. ‘Close them so they can’t follow. Quinn, tell me you can control them from here.’

‘I’ll need a few seconds,’ she said.

Quinn tapped away at her laptop as I started to slow down; there was a sharp corner at the end of the drive and if I went round it at speed we'd end up rolling onto the road.

'OK, they should be starting to close now.'

'Now?' I shrieked. 'I'm nowhere near the gate!'

I pushed my foot down again, the engine groaning louder and louder as we picked up speed towards the gate but as we got closer, the gap got smaller and smaller. I begged for the SUV to go faster but the gap was closing and we were still too far away.

'Can't you hold them open?' I asked.

'It's not like flicking a switch,' Quinn told me and I groaned.

With a deep breath I pressed the pedal to the floor – fuckin hell I've never driven this fast before. I fell back from the speed, Grace's arm hovering over my chest but I didn't let up. If we were committing to this, we were committing.

'We're not going to make it,' Grace whispered.

'Yes we are,' I told her.

Did I think we were going to make it? Absolutely fucking not but it's what Jessica would have said.

A car swerved into view behind us but as we neared the gate I focused ahead – the gate was closing and going straight through was the only option.

With a final push and a cry from Quinn we scraped through the gate, the iron scratching on the car's tail as it locked shut. I kept an eye on the car behind us, now forced to swerve to a stop. Well, that was that problem solved.

Wait – sharp left turn – shit, shit.

I swerved onto the main road, slamming on the breaks, the SUV rocking from side to side as we joined the rest of the traffic. A few car horns blared angrily but I was focused on pulling into the right lane. If my last driving instructor ever saw that she'd have a canary – being a getaway driver certainly wasn't covered on her course.

I wished I had some music going while I did that, it would have felt so much cooler and perhaps, less like my heart was ready to throw itself from my chest.

'Where are we heading?' I asked, a little breathless.

'Glasgow,' Grace said.

'That's at least an hour's drive, even at this time of night,' I said. 'They'll get those gates open and when they do I imagine Nicola isn't just going to use Reign to track us down.'

'You have Eve's number in the burner phone, give me it,' Grace said, holding out a hand.

'I do?' I asked, fishing it out of my pocket.

'I put it in for emergencies.'

'Since when do we call Eve in emergencies?'

'Well she can't call Dr McKay, that's a bit obvious,' Lily said.

I wondered what the hell Lily was on about. I got that Grace was close to the people she worked on the ward with but surely she wouldn't think of calling him. Dr McKay did ask me to look out for her but that doesn't mean they're . . .

My eyes caught Grace, her head bowed as she muttered to herself.

'No way – you're shagging the doctor?' I asked.

Her head snapped up.

'You don't need to make it sound so crude.'

'Sorry, you're sleeping with a doctor who, as far as I'm aware, has a wedding ring.'

Grace kept muttering to herself as she flipped open the burner phone and pressed dial. It rang for a few seconds before Eve's voice answered, blaring through the speaker.

'Hello?'

'Eve, it's Grace, I need you to listen to me –'

'What the hell are you all doing?' she asked. 'Nicola is losing it out here.'

'I need you to be our inside contact – we can only finish this if we know what's going on in Reign. Is Nicola sending more people after us?'

'She's sending Ames and some other staff. Thompson got sent to cover the cameras.'

'Quinn, we need a different route, get me one with minimal cameras,' Grace ordered.

‘They have a tracker in that car, there won’t be any point,’ Eve said.

‘I disabled the tracker but if Thompson’s looking for us we won’t have long. We’ll have to ditch the SUV,’ Quinn said.

Grumbling and distorted shouting gritted through the phone’s speaker.

‘I don’t know who Nicola is speaking to but she’s asking that all available units are to be sent after you,’ Eve told us.

‘She’s getting the police involved?’ I asked.

I wanted to pull off the main road but Quinn was busy on her laptop and I hadn’t the faintest clue what route she was planning.

‘Police, agents, you name it,’ Eve said. ‘Think about it, you can blow the lid on the entire security system and you’ve decided that the best solution is to go rogue.’

‘Tell me you wouldn’t have done the same if you had the chance,’ Grace said, and Eve fell quiet. ‘Eve please, we need you.’

‘Naomi, we’ve got a tail!’ Kayson yelled and my eyes shot to the mirror.

A black car was chasing us, gaining speed by the second.

‘Just don’t get yourself killed,’ Eve said before the dial tone rang.

The chatter silent as we all eyed the car behind.

‘I have a feeling a few tyres are going to be destroyed,’ Grace said and I caught the edge of a smirk from Kayson as he rolled down the window.

‘Yes ma’am,’ he said, loading the gun with a snap. ‘Tyres only?’

‘I’m sorry, you’re going to shoot the car?’ I asked, a little alarmed.

‘Tyres only,’ Grace replied, eyeing it up. ‘We need more time to switch. Naomi, whatever happens keep driving. Follow Quinn’s directions – do we have a route?’

‘Are we minimizing casualties or –’

‘Please tell me you’re not even gonna to think about that?’ My head snapped to Grace but she dismissed me.

‘Kayson, get that car under control, we need a route for when we disappear. Quinn. Get us off the radar. We can’t be exposed here any longer.’

I couldn’t believe this was happening, a bloody car chase! I kept my eye on the speed, keeping it steady – what if I had to swerve? Would Kayson be thrown out the window?

This was slightly faster than I was used to in my little Corsa.

The rev of the engine roared behind me and I tried to keep my cool, but I couldn’t help it – all the months of training hadn’t involved this!

‘Naomi, in about four miles you’re going to pull onto the slip road on the left,’ Quinn told me.

I made sure to keep clear of any cars as I swerved in and out the traffic – I was thankful that it wasn’t too busy and hoped that after this was all over, there wasn’t a seven-car pileup on the news.

‘Got it,’ I replied.

Since it was late at night and there weren’t too many cars there were large gaps along the different lanes but unfortunately for us, that meant the tail could easily follow.

‘On your mark,’ Kayson said, his hand resting on the open window.

‘Now,’ Grace ordered.

I wanted to watch Kayson as he slipped out the window, his feet still on the seat and knee resting on the ledge but I had to focus on the road. OK! Think about something else, like oh! That car ahead looks like my gran’s – OK, not the best thing to think about.

BANG.

BANG.

BANG.

My eyes flitted to the rear-view mirror but the car was swerving every hit.

‘Shit, it’s Ames,’ Lily muttered, leaning her head out the other window.

Oh great, he was so going to hate us after this.

‘The slip road is going to be visible soon!’ I shouted back, already seeing the signs.

‘Lily, can you see anyone in the passenger seat?’ Grace asked.

‘No.’

‘Kayson!’ Grace yelled. ‘Get the tyres and the passenger side!’

‘Grace, you can’t!’ I yelled back.

BANG.

BANG.

BANG.

The crunch of glass and metal reverberated through the car, the screeching of tyres ripping across the tarmac. I couldn't bear to look. Everyone around us swerved or careened into others, the jolts and crashes falling silent against the roar of the engine as I floored it, heading for the slip road, police sirens wailing in the background.

The rustle from Kayson as the window closed brought me a little comfort, but what stripped it away immediately was that he'd shot at the passenger side. What if there had been someone Lily couldn't see? He could have just killed someone! What about Ames?

'You said the fucking tyres,' I said, slowing down a little as we practically flew round the roundabout.

'There was no one in the passenger side,' Lily tried, but I didn't care.

'You don't know that for sure. This is the reason that in the police they need to wait before applying lethal force because then they'll know they've not just murdered an innocent guy!'

'It's Ames, he's done this stuff for years –'

'And what if this was his last?' I asked – the car went quiet. 'We're already committing treason and now we might have added murder to the list.'

After a couple minutes of less than smooth driving, we'd reached the outskirts of Edinburgh, trying to stay away from any main roads. The one thing I had to focus on was my breathing. I was angry for the second time tonight: they didn't have solid proof the passenger side was empty. We might have just killed someone and I was an accomplice.

‘Quinn, how long have we got before Thompson finds the car and the police start to catch up?’ Grace asked.

‘We’ve got minutes,’ Quinn said. ‘I’m hoping because he likes us that he’ll pretend he can’t find us for a while.’

‘Nicola is a hacker,’ I said. ‘I remember Kayson saying.’

‘That’s why she was brought into MI6,’ Kayson said. ‘If Thompson’s pretending, Nicola would know about it.’

‘We’ve got to ditch the car now,’ Grace said. ‘Quinn, give me a street with cars or a car park.’

‘There’s not one for another three minutes,’ she said, but I pressed my foot down once more. ‘Make that sixty seconds.’

When we arrived, Lily jumped out the car, running ahead into the small run-down housing estate.

Despite being against the clock and with an army of people chasing us, I couldn’t help but ask. ‘Since when have you been sleeping with Dr McKay?’ I said to Grace, with a little bit of sass. If they didn’t want to talk about what just happened then I was certainly bringing this up.

‘Naomi, we have bigger problems,’ Grace stated, looking around anxiously.

‘No come on, we’ve got time,’ I challenged.

‘Naomi,’ Kayson said, his voice a little deeper than usual as he tugged me away from Grace, slinging an arm on my shoulders. ‘Let’s talk about infidelities later, yeah?’

I had to resist the urge to push his arm away – he could have killed someone and he didn't even seem fazed. I reassured myself that he trusted Lily and so did I; she knew what she was doing. She wouldn't have given the all-clear if she wasn't certain.

Kayson was right, this wasn't the time, not when the police sounded like they were getting closer. A low grumble tore down the road, with Lily in the driver's seat of a large family car.

'Get in, losers, we don't have all night.'

I wanted to ask where the hell she got that and how she thought the family she stole it from were going to get to work tomorrow. The only good thing in this scenario was that I didn't have to drive, my hands were still shaking. Kayson had told me on our 'date' that he was a great driver, better than Tom Cruise apparently, so why couldn't he have started us off in the first place? If this happened again I was not going to be the designated driver.

We took off into the night, now going through a mix of main and back roads. It took just over an hour to get to Glasgow. With each police car that passed us we held our breath, but most of the time we weren't given a second glance. After listening to the police radio chatter, Quinn informed us they'd headed in a different direction which, while comforting, didn't mean we were out of the woods. We decided to stick to driving through a couple of neighbourhoods in the Gorbals before heading into town.

Eve had called a few times. Apparently Harkness and Nicola had the same ambitions – they were both willing to go to extraordinary lengths to get this team back. Apparently, police had been alerted and were going to be stationed at the closed border in case we tried to cross there. Good thing we weren't driving to England.

The family car pulled into one of the lanes just off Buchanan Street, and to say I was surprised to be here would have been an understatement. If anything, I thought this was one of the places we should avoid.

'Why here?' I asked, hopping out the car.

'This is where my contact works,' Quinn said, leading the way through the street.

'Isn't this a bit too public?'

'We have completely different profiles and besides, it'll be at least an hour before they think to look here,' Kayson said, his hand pushing on the small of my back. 'Come on.'

As we followed Quinn up the street and into one of the shops, I honestly felt as if I couldn't trust anyone. Not for any major philosophical reasons but because the only person in the shop Beauty Secrets was the woman Megan, I'd met a year ago. She'd tried to sell me an eyeliner before Katie dragged me out.

'You've got to be kidding me,' I muttered. 'Is everyone on this street working for some sort of government agency?'

'No,' Kayson laughed rubbing my shoulder, heading to the counter.

'Quinn, what have you done?' Megan asked, pulling the girl into a hug. 'Please tell me that's make-up and you've not been starving yourself.'

'It's make-up.'

'I really shouldn't have taught you how to do any of this,' she said, cupping her face, tugging her head in every direction.

'Megan,' Quinn said, through squished cheeks and lips. 'We're kind of in a hurry.'

'Right, sorry.' She darted behind the counter, handing over a packed envelope to Grace. 'That should be everything you need, including a car to get to the airstrip.'

'Thanks for this,' Quinn said.

'Hold up,' I said finally, once I'd had a look around.

This was a completely normal make-up shop, I'd been in it even before last year, there was nothing out of the ordinary about it. Everything told me it was a real make-up shop but I'd just witnessed the staff handing over an envelope with fake IDs and car keys.

'This whole place is a cover-up?'

'Is she new?' Megan asked but Grace shook her head.

'We should go.'

'Does Reign own this too?' I asked.

'Thankfully, not anymore,' Megan sighed.

Not anymore? I wanted to ask.

When I came here over a year ago, was this shop was under Reign management? What could they possibly be bringing through here? Weaponry? Money? The possibilities were endless. As Megan stood proudly at the counter

I noticed she still only had one nail painted: before, I'd admired it but now it just looked strange. Was it some sort of symbol to other agents that she worked for Reign? For Nicola?

RING. RING. RING.

The dulcet tones of the phone on the wall sounded but everyone was looking at it, as if it were a bomb ready to detonate.

'Does Nicola have access to the security cameras here?' Quinn asked but Megan shook her head, pulling the phone from the receiver.

'Hello?' she asked.

We all held our breath – they couldn't have found us already, it was far too soon. Kayson and Lily edged towards the door, ready to make a run for it, Grace reaching into the envelope for the car keys.

'No, I've not seen them.' Megan's eyes flickered to us. 'I've not heard anything either, it's quiet. Perhaps they headed up north where it's more secluded – yes I will let you know if I see them.' With that she put the phone back on the receiver 'You all need to get out of here, now.'

'Let's go,' Grace said, tossing the keys to Kayson.

'Megan, thank you again,' Quinn said quickly. 'If anyone asks about us –'

'Deny, deny, deny,' she smirked.

Grace grabbed my hand, pulling me along, but I couldn't help the thoughts running through my head. When she said that Reign was everywhere, that they were the government, I never thought for one second that it also included shops on the high street. What about churches or cafés? How far did this go? The theatre had to be one of them too, considering what happened that night, as well as the police, since Harkness had filled in as the head of Scotland Yard.

It made me sick to realise that so many aspects of my life had been controlled by that man and I didn't even know.

Where Reign got at least some of its funds from now started to make sense too – any income generated from these places must have gone directly to him. If I could get in contact with Eve then maybe she could figure out where some of the money was coming from.

Reign was seeded throughout the country, there were so many leads to chase, I just hoped we weren't too late.

* * *

Thankfully the getaway car wasn't an SUV or a supercar but a simple minivan. Lily was driving this time, Quinn in the back beside me. Kayson was on the floor sorting through the different weaponry. I prayed we'd never have to use it. I didn't want anyone else to die.

What Harkness had done was unforgivable but if I was given the gun and the opportunity, I honestly don't know if I could squeeze the trigger.

Grace told us to get some sleep while we could but I knew straight away my brain wouldn't allow it. The thoughts whirring round my head were at warp speed, with no way to slow them down. I wondered what Jess would be like in this situation: probably stonewalling and calm as a cucumber. She hated cucumber.

I texted my mum from the burner phone, telling her to keep her own hidden. It was the only way we'd be able to secure any updates from her. She then informed me that there hadn't been anything on the Reign Academy and politics was just as crazy as ever so nothing new there. Unfortunately, her journalist contacts were in the same position as her so there wasn't any information available that we didn't already know.

I honestly didn't know how long it was until we reached the airstrip: it felt like ten minutes, but it could have been three hours. One by one we got out the van and while I wasn't expecting to be waited on hand and foot with a first-class ticket, I did expect to see a plane.

It was only when I heard the sharp grumbling from the sky and saw small blinking lights that I realised, that was the plane.

'Is that a cargo plane?' Grace asked, squinting into the black sky.

'Business class was fully booked,' Lily mocked, clipping the font tabs of her rucksack over her chest. 'The plane is going to touch down and open up from the back, we run on and the plane takes off again. Nice and simple.

Simple – she's jinxed it now.

Tyres skidded on the runway as the plane touched down and I had to turn my head from the sheer force of the wind as it shot by us, slowly coming to a stop.

Lily led the way, charging to the plane: to my surprise the back door actually opened, scraping against the tarmac like a ramp. We ran as fast as we could but as my foot left the ground I could feel the plane start to move again. Shit!

'Find something to hold onto!' Lily shouted.

The plane was filled with crates all varying in size – there was barely enough standing room, never mind hold-on-for-your-life room. I scampered to the side, a red strap dangled from the ceiling and I made a jump to grab it, wrapping my wrist tightly, my other bracing against the boxes.

I'd lost sight of the rest of the team but that was the last thing on my mind as the door shut and the plane took off, my entire body slowly tipping back, feet dangling in the air. The whirring of the engines grew louder, the crates shaking from the vibrations. There was a window behind me but I wasn't inclined to look out of it. Sure, I didn't have a fear of heights but I might when I'm practically dangling by my wrist!

'Hang on!'

The cold metal shell rattled around us as we took off into the sky so as a green light flickered above my head and my feet were firmly back on the floor, I let out a sigh of relief. Didn't die – good job, Naomi.

Well, gotta say this team did like to keep things interesting. The others appeared one by one, some looking a little more shaken than others.

'Nothing like that to keep the adrenaline pumping,' Grace muttered, straightening her top out.

'Life wouldn't be any fun if I didn't keep you on your toes,' Lily smirked, grabbing a radio from the wall. 'Thanks, Simon!'

'Any time, love,' a voice echoed through the intercom. 'Welcome aboard.'

'I'm scared to ask, but why are we not getting shot of the sky?' Quinn asked.

'I'm a cargo plane carrying essentials for the hospitals, I have a special licence,' he answered. 'They know I'm in the air.'

'And how do you know him?' Grace asked Lily.

'We like the same clubs.'

She rolled her eyes.

'OK, everyone get some rest,' Grace ordered. 'I need to sit down.'

Thankfully, I was able to get some downtime going through the go bag that I'd been slinging around for the last hour or so. I wondered what Nicola was thinking: did she think we were going to London or did she just think we were making a run for it?

'Hey there,' Kayson said, sliding down to join me on the floor. 'Penny for your thoughts or whatever it is you British say?'

'Nicola,' I said simply.

'From what we pulled on the dual carriageway, she'll think we've gone rogue. Had enough of her pretty little regime,' Kayson told me. 'Besides, we never gave her any indication that we would head this way.'

'Indication?' I asked. 'You've been hanging round Grace too long.'

'Oh, shut up.' He laughed, playfully hitting my arm. 'We'll be fine. We have new profiles, new identities and a plan.'

'This plan is turning into a make-it-up-as-we-go-along plan,' I said.

He nodded.

'I never said it was a good one.'

For most of the plane ride I leaned my head on Kayson's shoulder, trying to get some shut-eye. I knew we'd only be on here for an hour or so but the adrenaline had left my body, I was exhausted. Talk about an eventful evening. As I slowly slipped in and out of sleep I felt Kayson's fingers running through my hair and while I was tired, I couldn't help the small smile that snuck onto my lips. In Kayson's arms I felt safe and warm.

Despite him shooting a car. I had to hope he hadn't seen anyone in the passenger side either. If he had would he still have taken the shot? I couldn't think like that. He was an honest guy, right?

A blaring horn rang through the intercom.

'I've got good news and bad news.' Well, that wasn't reassuring. 'Good news is that we're only a few miles outside of our agreed drop-off point, bad news is that we're going to have to abandon ship.'

Abandon ship? We're in a plane!

Lily grabbed a radio intercom.

'We don't have the equipment to jump.'

'We have three incoming bogeys, they're going to shoot this plane out of the sky.'

'You said this wouldn't happen,' Grace snapped but Lily rolled her eyes.

'How long have we got?' she asked.

'Three minutes, tops,' the pilot replied. 'There's parachutes back there.'

Never flying with this man again.

Kayson and Lily scrambled to the sides of the plane, grabbing multiple grey rucksack-looking things from underneath.

'We can't jump,' Quinn cried, making a grab for her own bag, holding it tightly to her chest.

Grace marched over, stuffing the envelope from Megan inside her go back, strapping it to her front.

'We don't have a choice,' she told her.

'Has anyone here ever actually jumped out of a plane?' I dared to ask, spinning my own bag round.

'I have,' Kayson piped up, strapping on his own parachute. 'I had to do it in Washington, don't worry it's not that difficult.'

That's easy for you to say, Mr Action Man! What raged my anxiety more was the fact that a chorus of 'no's rang out from the girls. Great, only one of us had ever jumped out of a plane. A red light blared this time, covering the entire cargo.

'You have to jump!' The pilot screamed.

Everyone scrambled like rats trying to put on the parachutes but when I went to grab for mine, there were none left.

'Kayson, I need a parachute,' I said but he threw a look to Lily, who shook her head.

Please tell me I wouldn't be tumbling to my death?

'You'll go with me,' he said, grabbing my arms with an iron grip, looking me dead in the face. 'This isn't like a tandem skydive, you'll need to wrap your legs around me.'

'OK.' It was the only thing I could say as he put goggles over my eyes.

Everyone else was prepped and ready to go but there was one problem: the door was still shut. Lily grabbed for the radio.

'We need the door!' she yelled.

Grace's eyes kept going down to her watch.

'Five.'

What?

'Four.' Her voice filled with dread.

Did she mean?

'Hold on!' the pilot screamed.

'Three.'

'Brace!' Kayson yelled, his arms wrapped around my body, throwing us both to the floor.

BOOM.

The sound deafened me as Kayson and I were thrown into the wall, heat blasting into my face like fire, but at the same time a sharp wind blew like a whistle and it wasn't until I looked up that I realised there were holes in the craft. Holes! A sharp ringing sound pierced my ears, every thud and crack dull like I was underwater.

Time to go.

'Get the door open!' Lily screamed into the radio but to me, her voice was still muffled.

I couldn't see anyone apart from Kayson, boxes had been thrown about, their contents spilled onto the floor. It was bandages and IV bags – Naomi get out the fucking plane!

'The left wing is gone!' I heard the crackle from the pilot.

'The door!'

A groaning sounded and the door slowly creaked open – it wasn't all the way down but Kayson didn't look like he was going to wait for it.

'Go, Go!' he yelled.

Lily, Quinn and Grace all bolted, running past us and jumping out the back. How could they be so fearless? Guess we didn't have much of a choice.

Kayson yanked both of us up and ran for the exit. As we got closer he wrapped his arm around my shoulder and, as instructed, I wrapped my legs around his waist, hiding my face and clinging onto him for dear life.

Then, we fell.

The ground and the sky were one as we tumbled through the air, the wind throttling through us but I kept my face firmly against Kayson's chest. How close were we to the ground? I knew we were spinning as my stomach lurched but I didn't dare to open my eyes.

'Hold on!' Kayson yelled.

Yeah, cause I wasn't doing that before!

BOOM.

That sound tore across the sky and once again a blazing heat burned my back.

'Oh shit –'

My arms were ripped from Kayson's, his voice now silent as my world went pitch black.

CHAPTER 19

Friable

Easily broken into pieces of reduced to nothing

GRACE ASPIN

I really should have practised this at some point.

As soon as my feet left the plane I was tumbling through the air, holding onto the straps of my parachute for dear life, the rucksack at my front pulling me down. I threw my arms and legs out trying to stabilize myself. When I did I saw Quinn and Lily beneath me – for never having done this before we were doing quite well.

I slapped my arms by my sides and headed down to meet them. Despite the goggles the wind was drying my eyes but I tried my best to keep them open. I wanted to shout to the team but it would be no use, there was no way we'd hear each other from this far away. We should have put in comms before we left.

BOOM.

A sound I wished I'd never have to hear again exploded from above. I flipped onto my back and saw the plane was gone, replaced with fire and smoke that filled the sky – but what terrified me the most was that Kayson and Naomi had been separated. Kayson was trying to grab onto a chain of debris while Naomi was falling aimlessly through the sky. She was unconscious. Oh Lord, please, no.

I wanted to help but there was no way I could get back up – it was called jumping out of a plane for a reason, you only went down.

I flipped back to my front, heading down towards Quinn and Lily. I tapped Lily on the shoulder pointing up the way; she held a thumbs-up and signed the letter K in sign language, before flying off in the opposite direction.

OK, she was taking care of Kayson, that meant Quinn and I would get Naomi. If she was hurt I'd only be able to see when we were on the ground, I wasn't pulling some *Grey's Anatomy*-level story up here.

The sky was growing darker so if we lost sight of Naomi, chances were we'd never see her again. Quinn grabbed my hand and we both flipped onto our backs, trying to figure out the best way to do this.

Only one of us had to catch Naomi; we'd better not miss. I looked to Quinn, signing in front to her, then pointed to myself, signing behind, before taking in a deep breath and leaning back. If I could grab Naomi from the front and Quinn could go from behind, we'd have a better chance of catching her.

I thought I'd gone too far but the sight of Naomi's jacket billowing above told me I hadn't, she was getting closer. I looked over to Quinn who was now in position, waiting for me to make a move. I held a hand up until she got closer but just as I did, I realised how close to the ground we were. Must have been only six hundred feet.

Not exactly ideal.

I slashed my hand down and we both headed straight for her. I grabbed onto her torso from behind as tightly as I could, Quinn at her front. Then we tumbled upside down through the air.

I moved to the top of Naomi, holding round her shoulders and Quinn let go, her eyes widening in horror as she looked down to the ground. I needed glasses sometimes but I could still make out little blobs on the ground.

Oh no.

Quinn went to pull her parachute but I held up a hand seeing that Lily and Kayson hadn't pulled theirs as they sailed through the air. I knew we were trying to get in under cover but we didn't have to wait until we could see cars before pulling the chute!

Quinn came to my side and I grabbed her neck, pulling her close.

'Wait for them!' I screamed over the air, pointing to Lily and Kayson before pushing her away.

We watched them carefully but the pair kept falling – honestly appearing to be enjoying this, though considering they had to dodge debris and shrapnel I couldn't see how.

We were getting closer.

Quinn's hands were firmly on the straps while I grabbed onto Naomi tight, wrapping my legs around her.

The ground was getting scarily close and I held my breath, preparing for the worst, when out of the corner of my eye I saw a black chute fly into the air. Without a second thought I yanked down on mine and a sharp tug jolted me up.

I let out a breath as we started to glide down. I'd secured my arms around Naomi's waist, her goggles had fallen off at some point but no matter. She had bigger problems, judging by the blood on my fingers. No, not again.

I landed with a thud onto my bottom, skidding across the wet field, only coming to a stop as the parachute landed in a heap behind us. Naomi lay limply in my arms and as soon as I got the parachute off, I gently placed her onto her back.

As Quinn landed beside me I shouted, 'I need a light!'

I cleared her hair from her face as I tried to get a look at what had been hit: it wasn't until a torch beam shone on her face that I saw she had a nasty cut on her head. Her pulse was still strong so she was definitely alive.

Thank the Lord.

I unclipped the bag from my front, grabbing what I could from it.

'Is she OK?' Kayson asked. 'She was hit by one of the wooden boxes.'

'She's unconscious,' I said, grabbing for the smelling salts.

'Well, I can see that,' he retorted.

'Again with the not helping.'

I stuck the smelling salts under Naomi's nose. It took about thirty seconds but eventually she shot up, coughing and spluttering.

'I've got you, Naomi, it's us, we've got you,' I said.

She grabbed onto my arms, her face pale with panic.

'Never,' she spluttered.

'What?' Lily asked.

'Never doing that again,' she finished.

BAM.

I grabbed Naomi and tumbled back out of the way as a large metal engine crashed into the dirt in front of us. My breath caught in my chest.

'I know I was like dead a second ago but can we go somewhere else, please?' Naomi asked.

'Let me look at you first,' I said but Kayson pressed a palm to my shoulder.

'We need to move,' he said.

'Kayson, I have to examine her,' I protested.

'Whoever blew that thing out of the sky will send people to check. I'm not comfortable sitting around.'

'We're only a few miles out,' Quinn said, her phone lighting up her face.

'See, Naomi, you'll be fine, nothing a brisk walk can't fix,' Kayson said.

‘Oh yeah, that’s exactly what I need,’ Naomi grumbled as she was helped up by Quinn, ‘A hike.’

‘Well, it’s either that or –’

‘We risk getting captured or being put on an exploding plane or chased down with guns, yes, yes, I know.’ Naomi waved Kayson off.

‘I’ll help you.’ He tried coming over to her but she shook her head, wincing in regret.

‘I’m not dead or decapitated, lead the way,’ she said.

You know, considering everything that had just happened, I think it went quite well.

* * *

After an hour or so of trekking through the pitch black we’d reached a main road, and after following it, found ourselves near the housing estate we’d stayed in before. Saul hadn’t mentioned anything about anyone else using it and it was secluded enough that we’d be safe here for the night.

‘How did someone know to shoot that out of the sky?’ Lily asked me quietly.

‘I don’t know,’ I said honestly.

‘Was it Trojan?’ she asked. ‘Nicola couldn’t have known so it couldn’t have been her.’

'I don't know how they knew we were on that plane,' I said to her, a little irritated. 'Like your friend said, it was carrying essentials for hospitals, why shoot that out of the sky unless they knew we were on it?'

'Harkness must be getting confused in his old age,' Lily mused. 'I thought he wanted us to join the ranks, not dead.'

'Who knows with that man, we just need to be careful,' I said. 'We'll stay in the safe house tonight and then move on. For all Harkness knows, we died in that plane crash.'

We broke in through the back gate, slipping across the garden, using the shadows as cover. There weren't any lights on inside the house, which meant it was either empty or someone was about to get a rude awakening. We kept our bags close and Kayson took the lead, unholstering his gun and entering the house, Lily following suit.

As we grouped behind them I stood rigid at the door while they swept downstairs first, then moved up. Naomi tried to push past but I held a firm hand to her chest.

'Not until we know it's safe,' I whispered.

She threw me a look but kept quiet, waiting.

'Clear!' Lily shouted.

'Clear!' Kayson shouted in return.

Quinn let out a sigh of relief but all Naomi managed was, 'I need a sit down and a cup of tea.'

The next hour or so passed quietly. Quinn set everything up tech-wise, going over the fake IDs and the security cameras around the estate as well as a rather quick call with Eve. Apparently Nicola was going out of her head with worry as her agents hadn't turned up anything so she'd brought some students in for questioning. We hadn't spoken to anyone else of this plan and I felt safe in the knowledge that even if other students knew, they wouldn't say a word. Quinn had managed to get in contact with Thompson, who'd been hiding us as much as he could from Nicola. She'd tracked us to the Gorbals but from there the trail went cold.

There was part of my mind that said she'd never figure out what our plans were, but the other part said that'd she'd put the pieces together eventually. Although as I pressed the call button, I prayed she wouldn't find out from him.

'Listen Ruta, I'm on my way home, it can wait until I get there,' Saul answered.

'This is Nightingale. Before you say anything, Nicola doesn't know we're here and I'd like to keep it that way. We're in the safe house. Ger here as soon as you can.'

He paused.

'What do you mean she doesn't know?' he asked.

'I'll tell you later. We're here to get to the bottom of this Saul, and given the state of our government and secret service, sometimes laws have to be broken.'

'And if I tell her?'

'Then we'll expose the security system and how it devolved powers to Scotland to create an institute which chemically subjugated and brainwashed hundreds of Scottish citizens.'

'You're Reign agents.' His voice was hushed. 'I don't have authorization to take you on, never mind when you've gone rogue and are now threatening to blackmail me.'

'Great, I'll see you soon,' I said, hanging up.

I tucked the burner phone into the back of my jeans, pressing my hands on the kitchen counter.

Naomi padded through with a tired smile.

'Quinn wouldn't let me go to bed until I came and saw you about this,' she said, pointing to the cut on her head.

I nodded, telling her to sit as I grabbed my rucksack from the door, pulling out my mini medical kit. The cut on her head wasn't deep or life threatening but it had to hurt. I pulled up a chair, slipped on some gloves and got to work.

'Do you like your job?' she asked randomly. 'Being a medic?'

I sighed.

'Yes, it's what I've wanted to do since I was a little girl.'

'You still kept it up even after Harkness . . .' She trailed off, but as I put the anti-bacterial wipe to her head, she winced.

'He governed with fear,' I said, swiping gently at the skin. 'My studies were an escape for me, it's the only thing I had, it's what kept me going. If I could help people recover after what he did to them then . . . I don't know, it made me feel better.'

I wanted to tell her how it really made me feel, I wanted to tell her that it eased the guilt of what I did. I'd lived with what I'd done to Willow for over a year but it still hadn't gotten any easier. No matter how many wounds I tended to or lives I saved, they didn't amount to anything.

'I haven't thanked you yet,' she said. 'For saving me.'

I pulled back.

'We're a team Naomi, we all care about you too much to let you fall to your death.'

'Even after what I said?' she asked. 'About you and Dr McKay?'

'You think that's the worst I've heard?' I laughed a little at that but my expression calmed, when I remembered why she'd gotten so angry.

I knew Lily wouldn't lie, I knew Kayson was a good shot. What we did was justified, a little dramatic but it got us away safely.

'I'd rather endure the name calling and whispers than being on my own,' I told her. 'It's one of the things I never understood about Jess – she wanted to go out on her own so often, a one-woman army.'

'Why do you think she took the job at MI6?' Naomi asked. I paused.

'I don't know,' I told her honestly, making a grab for the adhesive strips. 'Nicola offered it to her and she went, chasing a lead on Harkness.'

'But there wasn't even a brief, a case file, nothing. Or maybe there was, did you see it?'

'No,' I said. 'It was all done through Nicola, we never heard anything about it.'

'I thought she would have said something,' she admitted.

'You know Jess – closed book.' I laughed bitterly, pressing down the thin adhesive over the gash on her head. It was small enough that it didn't need a plaster: with some tape pressing the skin together, it should heal in a few days.

'You said you joked, at the grave,' Naomi said, and I pulled back. 'It's weird, I thought you hated her, wanted her job.'

I had to stifle a laugh at that.

'Our relationship wasn't exactly conventional,' I said. 'I didn't want her job, not really. The Second in Command is meant to question every decision the Team Lead makes and last year, she was making some risky ones.'

Naomi mused silently after that, leaning back in her chair as I tidied up, ripping the gloves off – when I did, blood caked every line, dripping off my fingers to the white tiled floor. Where did . . . no, please, not again.

'Grace?' I heard Naomi ask but her voice was muffled, a ringing boiling my ears.

I turned my palms over, blood pooling in the middle endlessly, the reflection in the pool showing me one face: Jessica's.

A firm grip grabbed my wrists and I let out a cry, yanking them back, but Naomi's eyes broke into mine.

'Grace, you're OK,' Naomi said, her voice calm. 'You're OK – I think you're having a panic attack.'

All I could see was her blood, it ran like a never-ending river.

'Grace, look at me,' she said forcefully. 'That's it, OK take a deep breath in.'

I sucked in as much air as possible, copying Naomi as she breathed out. With every shaky breath, she replaced it with a level one, with every whimper she gave me reassurance, so when I looked back down to my hands, they were clean. No blood in sight.

This couldn't keep happening, these weren't panic attacks, they were hallucinations. What would happen if the team found out?

'See, you're OK. Probably just all the adrenaline or something,' she said.

I barely managed a polite smile.

'Yeah,' I admitted weakly as she let go of my wrists.

'I didn't know you got panic attacks like that, must be from Harkness,' she said, drawing her own conclusion, and I wasn't inclined to correct her.

'Don't tell the others,' I demanded. 'You can't tell them.'

'Grace, they need to know. Quinn has nightmares, Lily probably has some trauma and so does Kayson. You guys went through hell – that doesn't just end now that Harkness is gone.'

‘He’s not gone,’ I said, packing my medical kit away.

‘No, he’s not.’ A darker voice spoke, and I spun round to see Saul standing there. ‘He’s hiding with his contacts in the British Parliament and we’re going to stop him.’

CHAPTER 20

Accismus

Feigning disinterest in something while actually desiring it.

NAOMI JADE

Of all the people I thought I'd be pleased to see, I'd never counted Saul as one of them. He stood in the doorway, arms crossed. He almost looked disappointed, whether it was in us or about Harkness I couldn't quite tell. Perhaps he was just tired. I knew I was.

'For someone who was adamant there weren't any corrupt officers, you've changed your tune,' I said to him.

He nodded.

'Umesh Acharya was interrogated but this morning, he managed to escape.'

'Where were you?' Grace asked, almost sceptically.

'With Alexander. Since you've been unreachable he's been trying to sort out his security team.'

'Unreachable?' I asked, confused.

It wasn't like we'd packed our bags and fled to Tortuga – even with everything going on, I think we would have been able to take a call from the Prime Minister.

'Miss Ramos kept telling me you were indisposed,' Saul said. 'That you'd been sent on another assignment and in the politest way possible, told me to fuck off.'

'What?' Grace asked, astonished.

'Yes, so you'll understand my surprise when I received your phone call,' he said, sitting down across from me at the table. 'You've gone rogue?'

'We want to know what's going on.'

'You've fled the institute that created you, I see why all the alarm bells are ringing,' Saul smirked.

'We know Harkness is here and that means the rest of his colleagues will be too,' Grace continued.

'You want to hunt them down?' Saul asked curiously.

It was then that I felt Grace's hand on my shoulder.

'Is that so hard to believe?' she asked him, to which he replied with a charming grin, his lips tugging tight around his teeth.

Footsteps thundered down the stairs as Kayson ran into the kitchen, his hair dripping wet, shirt damp and cargo shorts clinging to him. He had run straight from the shower?

'I leave for five minutes and the English invade?' he asked, immediately on the defence. 'What are you doing here?'

'I invited him,' Grace said. 'We need him to get us inside Thames House.'

'Technically you do, yes, and I can arrange a meeting with Alexander within the next hour. From there we can arrange security passes that match your new identities.'

'How do you know we've changed identities?' I asked.

'Well, you've changed your appearances – you've got wanna be death metal rock star with daddy issues.' Saul pointed to Kayson, then turned to me and Grace. 'And a pair of runaways.'

His eyes fell to Grace but she just shook her head.

'This time we need to be here incognito,' she said adamantly. 'No one else can know.'

'I can promise the utmost discretion. No one will know you're here except the Prime Minister and myself.'

'So you won't go running to tell your bosses that highly dangerous assassins have crossed the border?' I asked.

‘We run lots of spies, Naomi,’ Saul said. ‘Discretion is what I do. Besides, who would I tell them to look for? I don’t even know anyone’s name apart from yours.’

‘Let’s keep it that way,’ Kayson said, his voice deadpan.

‘Naomi, can you get Blackbird and Pilot?’ Grace asked me. ‘They need to be here for this.’

‘Sure.’ I stood, heading for the door but Saul grasped my wrist.

‘They suit you,’ he said gently.

‘What?’ I asked.

‘Your eyes.’

I smiled a little at that, thanking him before my hand slipped from his. What a gentleman he was! I forgot how nice compliments felt. It could have been concussion but I swear Saul winked at me.

As I headed upstairs I knew the girls were in the room at the end of the hall, since it was the only one closed. I’d truly recommend this safe house to anyone: the beds were really comfy and I got a decent night’s sleep the last time I was here – considering my best friend died that same day.

Now I was making dead friend jokes. I should see a therapist.

I flung the door open, mouth open to speak but it appeared, Lily had already beaten me to it as she was tongue-deep in Quinn’s clit.

‘Sorry!’ I cried, throwing my hands over my eyes, turning my back.

Well, I never thought I’d be seeing Quinn’s boobs any time soon but apparently, today was the day.

‘Can’t you knock?’ Lily asked, laughing.

‘Sorry I didn’t know you two were – well I didn’t expect – is everyone having sex but me?’

‘I’m sure we could arrange something, fire thong,’ Lily told me.

I mean I’d never tried it before, the idea had always intrigued me since girls didn’t exactly – no, stop it, not the time!

‘Grace needs you, Saul’s downstairs and he wants to arrange a meeting with the PM.’

‘Naomi, don’t tell anyone,’ Quinn said shakily, her voice breathy.

I whipped round to reassure her – OK, she was completely naked. I threw my eyes up trying to be considerate.

‘Quinn, honestly, I’m happy for you,’ I said.

‘Really?’ she asked. ‘Cause you’re not even looking at me.’

‘Quinn darling, you’re naked,’ Lily hummed and Quinn squealed.

‘How did you take my bra off?’ she asked. ‘I didn’t even feel you take my shirt off.’

‘OK, I’m going to go,’ I shot out, throwing my hands out to stop myself from walking into the doorframe. ‘I’ll tell Grace you’ll be five minutes.’

‘Don’t tell her!’ Quinn shouted after me.

‘I’ll say you’re washing your hair,’ I said, heading back down the stairs.

In fairness I could see one of the reasons Lily was attracted to her: Quinn did have nice boobs, amongst other exceptional qualities of course.

* * *

Once everyone had assembled in the living room, fully clothed, Saul took centre stage, pacing the room. Oh, so he was that kind of a man.

'I can have you with the PM tonight, then you can start your investigation. Nightingale, let me help.'

'All I'm saying is that it's dangerous,' she replied. 'Last time we had to run from this country and we can't afford to do the same again.'

'I will handle this with the utmost secrecy.'

Grace passed looks around the room, asking the silent question: did we want to do this?

'I'm fine to go alone,' she told Saul and immediately, he started tapping away at his phone.

'You're not going alone,' Kayson said. 'At least one Runner goes with you.'

'You're not going anywhere without me,' Quinn said. 'If I can get access to the security system wherever Alexander's being kept then we have eyes on who comes and goes. I also need to handle all the security passes as well as look into Lillian and Charlotte.'

'I'll go, we need someone to cover Pilot,' Lily stated.

Guess I'll just go fuck myself then.

'Why are you looking into Lillian?' Saul asked.

‘Like I said before, Saul.’ Grace turned. ‘It doesn’t hurt to look.’

‘Right, well, if you’re all going then that gives me time to go over strategy with Naomi,’ he said, his full attention now on me.

‘Strategy?’ Kayson asked, crossing his arms.

‘Yes, her role means she’s the person who goes about unseen, receives intel, records private conversations, yes?’ he asked. ‘There’s a reception tomorrow – she’s attending while the rest of you cover the building.’

‘Do I get any say in this?’ I asked.

‘Don’t you want to go?’ Saul asked.

‘Yes I do, just ask me next time,’ I said to him but as he smirked, I couldn’t help the grin that crawled up my face.

‘Be prepared to leave with whatever you need,’ he said, his gaze finally breaking from mine. ‘You can take the car I came in, I’ll send over the details to the driver.’

Grace nodded to the team, who all shot up and left the room, all except Kayson who lingered by the door.

‘You’re OK with this?’ he asked me, but his eyes kept flickering to Saul’s.

‘Yeah, I’ll be fine,’ I told him honestly.

His face was morphing like a storm as his gaze finally settled on Saul, his eyes brewing.

‘I’ll take my burner, call if you need anything.’

‘OK.’ I smiled.

‘I mean it, anything,’ his gaze softened for a moment as he turned to me with a kind smile. ‘If you need a second opinion, advice on hiding a body, or if you just need to talk to someone else.’

If the most Saul and I were going to do was sit around talking strategy then I didn’t see any harm in it. I didn’t trust Saul completely but he seemed like one of the good guys, caught up in this mess like us – wait, did Kayson say something about a body?

Before I could ask, quiet chatter broke out from behind him, the girls gathering all of their stuff together. Kayson threw me a charming smirk, holding his hand out for me to take. As our fingers brushed he pulled me into a tight hug, his fingers trailing up and down my back. He wasn’t wearing his usual cologne but his touch was warm, inviting and safe. I didn’t want to leave but as Grace shouted for him he gently pulled away, his hand tugging mine a little longer.

There was safety in his touch, something that over the past few weeks had become a luxury.

‘You better go, you don’t want to keep the driver waiting,’ Saul said, looking at his phone. ‘I’ve alerted the PM’s team, they’ll be waiting for you.’

Kayson’s lips pressed thinly into a grimace, at what though, I didn’t know. Then his hand slipped from mine and he disappeared through the door.

As the chatter of the team filtered outside and the sound of a car driving away revved through the complex, Saul let out a breathy laugh.

‘He likes you, doesn’t he?’ he asked.

'I don't know what you're talking about.' I replied, leaning back on the couch. 'We're friends.'

'He doesn't want to leave you alone with me.'

'I think you could be a little more understanding given the circumstances. We've just buried a close friend, we're not too keen on losing anyone else.'

Kayson and I were just friends and given what we'd just gone through, I think being a little more affectionate towards one another was a given. I couldn't lose anyone else, not after this.

'I apologise,' Saul said, sitting down.

'What's this strategy you want to talk about?'

'The meeting tomorrow brings the same people together as the last time, as well as political parties,' he said. 'Your team will be posing as politicians and security, walking around the building.'

'I thought Alexander wanted us in his personal security detail.'

'After what happened I've arranged agents of my own to look out for him. From the message he sent,' he said, staring at his phone. 'He's more interested in finding out how this happened.'

'Well, that's why we're here,' I told him. 'We've got a few links: Lillian Montague oversees all government-run institutes, which includes Reign by the sounds of it. Charlotte Winters is someone else: she had shares in Reign and wrote the legislation. They'll be who we look into first.'

‘Sounds like you have your starting point,’ Saul said, mindlessly loosening his cufflinks. ‘Before we go any further, I want to see how you fight – you may need to escape some, shall we call them, *uncomfortable* situations.’

‘I can fight just fine,’ I said defensively. ‘You’re here to talk strategy.’

‘Strategy that depends on your ability to fight.’

‘I’m from Reign, Saul, of course I can fight.’

Now, that statement may have been a bit of stretch, since throwing punches still felt a little alien to me but he seemed like the kind of guy who had been stuck in an office too long – luck could be on my side.

‘Then prove it.’ He stood, taking his jacket off and rolling up the sleeves of his white shirt, slipping off a silver-plated ring. ‘Well, then?’

‘I don’t need to prove myself to you,’ I scoffed.

‘You see, I would check your qualifications but after Nightingale informed me that your profile was false, I really don’t know anything about you.’

‘Not my problem.’

He grabbed my wrists, yanking me to my feet.

‘Who are you, Naomi?’ he asked, pulling me close, his voice deeper, his breath hot on my face, his eyes bearing down on mine.

The grip of his fingers intensified as he inched me closer, sending tingles through my arms but I didn’t let him make the next move. I threw my hands around before landing a solid kick to his chest.

He stumbled back, his hand smacking against the wall as he steadied himself.

'You don't like being pushed around,' he said. 'From the force of that kick, I take it you've been pushed around most of your life.'

'You don't know anything,' I said, going for the door but in the blink of an eye, he'd taken my wrist once more.

OK, he wanted to see how I fought – I'd show him.

I spun, throwing my fist to his cheek but Saul recovered quickly, jutting his elbow straight into my nose.

CRACK.

Blood gushed from my nose, covering the collar of my shirt as pain shot up through my head. Christ, what the hell was that for?

'You said Reign agents were made of tougher stuff, thought you'd see that one coming a mile away,' Saul said, casually fixing his sleeve.

'I've had one hell of a day,' I said, rubbing the sticky blood onto my jeans.

The pain vibrating through my sinuses pounded in my head – OK, perhaps this wasn't a great move since I'd just been hit with debris as I free-fell from a plane a few hours ago.

So what? I heard Jessica ask. *He wants a show, give him one.*

I may have one banger of a concussion but she had a point.

I spat the blood from my mouth but it wasn't all cool like you saw in the movies; a stringy glob dangled from my lip and I had to smear it all over the wrist of my shirt. Concussed and embarrassed, what a combo.

The condescending man in front of me wore a deceitfully charming grin but then I remembered what Lily had taught me, all those months ago. Hit a man where it hurts.

An old crappy vase sitting proudly on a table was within reach. I swiped it, throwing it at Saul but I wasn't trying to hit him, merely distract him. He caught the vase but I was already running, delivering a solid kick to his manhood. I grabbed the vase back, whacking him over the head, the thing shattering in my hands.

Saul fell to his knees but just as I was walking away he grabbed my ankle, yanking me down to the ground with a thud. Lily also mentioned never turning your back on your opponent – crap. He threw me onto my back but just as I was about to headbutt him – cause, fuck it – the unyielding tip of a blade pressed against my neck.

Where the hell had been hiding that?

'Tough but cocky,' Saul said, softly leaning up. 'You're quick, I'll give you that, but not smart.'

At that comment I felt a smirk slip onto my lips. I pushed myself up, the stinging edge of the knife cutting into my skin. Grace told me to get close to him and this was pretty close.

'Smart, no,' I echoed. 'However, you wouldn't have the guts to slit my throat, but me? I wouldn't have an issue taking that knife and slitting yours.'

It was a lie but even so, Saul grinned. His other hand pressing on my chest, slowly pushing me beneath him. His breath was hot but not laboured. The way he held the knife to my neck was almost tormenting, as if he was ready to cut deeper but then his thumb wiped the warm blood from my lips. Then inched deeper into my mouth, tenderly tugging the skin.

Was he going to kill me or kiss me?

His thick lips parted, his eyes boring into mine and as they did, I found myself relaxing as he leaned closer. All I could see was him.

'Do you have any idea what I want to do to you?' he asked, his voice dark and low in my ear.

A shaky breath passed my lips but I wasn't scared – what would he do? Every nerve was on fire as his fingers ran over my bare skin, fireworks sparking with every movement.

SNAP.

The blade cut at my bobble, my hair falling down my back. The man grinned, his once-stray thumb trailing round my neck.

'You should wear your hear down more often,' he whispered, before he gripped a handful of my hair and tugged.

A breath escaped me as his teeth started to nibble at my ear, but Saul's deep laugh sounded as pulled away.

'I'll be back later,' he said, then left the room.

What the hell? I – I didn't expect that. I'm not saying I didn't enjoy it but fuckin shit. The pain in my nose jolted through me once more and I groaned. I'd have to clean this up before anyone saw.

My fingers trailed over my lips, where his strong touch had been mere seconds ago. What would I tell the team? Could I tell them? What would Kayson say?

I must be the official secret-keeper of this team: Lily and Quinn had slept together, Grace had panics attack and now Saul had done . . .well that.

Fuck me. Why does this keep happening?

CHAPTER 21

Toska

A dull ache; spiritual anguish.

GRACE ASPIN

'Now under the circumstances I'd be inclined to call your boss, but I'm rather impressed with your little team,' Alexander said, sitting behind his strangely extravagant desk. 'Even though you've gone against orders it's for the right reasons and I appreciate your dedication.'

It'd taken a half-hour ride in the car but we'd eventually arrived at a large building, hidden away in the backstreets of London. It was a little too close to the capital for my liking, perhaps I'd mention that to Saul later.

It wasn't a safe house, more a kind of corporate building, hidden within an abandoned-looking building. When we'd arrived, the creaky door was flung open by men dressed in tactical gear – if I had to guess, I'd say there were SAS. They didn't look any of us in the eye as we headed down the death-inducing lift. It rattled like old chains and smelled of, well, urine. As we descended the men handed us clearance passes – level four? Wasn't that access all areas?

Huh, we really were going to be all over this.

Under different circumstances, I think Quinn would have been excited as the doors opened to reveal a sleek, modern set-up. We were underground clearly but monitors were set up on large desks and walls, all with security feeds, graphs and statistics running over them at a rapid rate. The room didn't have many lights, not that they were needed; all the light came from the tech set up around the room.

A man had led us through the technical paradise and into more business like corridors. We passed a few rooms before we landed our eyes on the Prime Minister, who stood behind the open door.

'We want to help you,' I said, hands clasped in front.

'From the message Saul sent I gathered as much,' he replied, shutting the door. 'He informed you that Daniel Harkness is hiding within government.'

'We plan to look into Charlotte Winters, she has shares in the Reign Institute so it gives her reason to harbour Harkness,' I said.

Now while I didn't have any proof of this, I wouldn't have put it past the woman.

'Really?' he asked.

'I apologise in advance, but Lillian Montague is also someone we plan to investigate – she oversees government-run institutes.'

'But Scotland designed Reign, that power was regrettably devolved to them.' Alexander told me. 'Lillian wouldn't have anything to do with it.'

'All the same, sir, there's no harm in looking into it.'

'Rightly so.' Alexander sighed tiredly. 'I'd give my left arm to figure out what's going on.'

Given my recent track record, perhaps I should be a little more understanding instead of seeing enemies everywhere. His former boss was torn apart and Alexander had been thrown in, expected to know all the answers.

'We'll get information to you as quickly as we can, sir,' I told him. 'Give us three days.'

'I'll give you two.'

'Deal,' I smirked. 'We'll need complete access to your systems.'

'Oh, I don't deal with any of that,' he said, rubbing his eyes.

'That's alright,' Quinn piped up, holding her rucksack a little tighter. 'Can you tell me where your support team is, the guys with all the computers?'

He smiled tiredly.

'Back down the hall you came, turn right at the big steel door,' he told her, but before she could leave, he called out. 'Bring back some coffee would you? They hoard all the good stuff in there.'

'I'll try,' she offered, heading out.

I turned to Lily but she didn't need an order, she was already halfway out the door.

'Wait!' Alexander called after her. 'I need you, you stay.'

The two girls paused in the hallway throwing confused looks to one another but I motioned to Kayson, who slipped to Quinn's side, leaving Lily trapesing back.

'Sir?' she asked, although from the look in her eyes she was anything but happy to call him that.

'Your skillset,' Alexander started, picking up a pen, 'is remarkable. I need another meeting with you. I want you at my side while the rest of your team root out the problematic officers.'

Lily's mouth opened to speak but nothing came out, her eyes locking with mine.

'We work as a team, and given how we've come to be here, I'd rather we weren't split up.' I said to him. 'It's protocol our team stays together.'

Was it protocol? No, absolutely not but I wasn't leaving Lily alone.

'I get that you're cautious, especially after what happened with Jessica-Grace.'

What? How did he know her name? I wasn't aware her name had been released – surely her file would have been classified. Even if it had been, he'd seen it. My face must have been telling, I'd let myself fall victim to another mistake. *Come on Grace, you're better than this.*

Alexander sighed.

'When I'd heard from Steven Melville that you'd be coming down here the day of the attacks I pulled the Omega files. A few days later I noticed one had been closed so it must have belonged to the agent you mentioned at the meeting. She was killed the same day as the Capital Attacks.'

I swallowed hard.

'Yes, she was.'

'I'm surprised you didn't throw Hyde out the window after what he said about her. If I'd gone through what you had, I would have.'

'After all we've been through, that this country's been through, petty conversations shouldn't result in violence,' I said.

'I think that was some light humour, Grace, ya know, to make this less serious.' Lily muttered, rolling her eyes.

'Oh right, I apologise,' I said, a little flustered.

Alexander waved me off.

'Don't worry about it, you've probably had a long day. In fact, why don't you go chase up the coffee. I need to talk to your colleague,' he said.

I looked to Lily, was she OK with this? The whole thing with this team was that Runners accompanied anyone who wasn't a Runner themselves. Of course she was capable of being there on her own but I wasn't sure if she was comfortable with it.

I mean, what's the worst that could happen? I wondered. She'd probably tell him to fuck off and shove whatever proposal up his ass.

'Sir, I'd rather stay,' I said.

'It's fine,' Lily said, hands moving to clasp behind her back. 'Go and find some coffee or preferably, whisky.'

‘I’m sure Ruta has some hidden around here,’ Alexander said with a smirk.

How was he being so calm about this? He was surprisingly easy going; perhaps he was just being kind.

‘Now that’s the kind of woman I want to work with,’ Lily said with a charming smile.

It took me aback; she’d been so against being a bodyguard to Alexander, which I presumed he was going to ask her about. Maybe she was just being polite – come on Grace, when is she ever polite?

‘I’ll leave you to it,’ I said.

‘I’m sure you’re aware of the reception tomorrow?’ Alexander shot out. ‘I expect to see you there.’

‘Wouldn’t miss it for the world,’ I replied, throwing one last nod to Lily before heading out.

Even as I left and the secret conversation began behind closed doors, the world still ticked by out here. Officials passed me, chattering about security protocol and budgets, while others talked about how shit it was that they had to miss Sharon’s hen party.

Some people really had to get their priorities straight.

‘Excuse me!’ I heard a familiar voice call from down the hall, it was Ruta. She rushed over, appearing to be running on pure adrenaline. ‘Hi, excuse me, sorry but I have to ask, did the Prime Minister say anything about his call with Lillian Montague?’

'Sorry, no,' I told her, and the woman sighed heavily. 'Why?'

I was thankful she didn't recognise me; her eyes flickered to the security pass I'd been given by the SAS before continuing.

'I need to get them both to sign these documents,' she said, flicking through them. 'Lillian was supposed to be here three hours ago.'

'Really?' I asked.

'She's famous for being late,' she told me.

'You wouldn't happen to know her well, would you?'

'Personally, no, but I handle her affairs occasionally.'

'Did she oversee the Reign Academy?'

Ruta paused, letting out a sigh.

'Yes, she did.' She took my arm gently, leading my down a corridor, keeping her voice quiet. 'She corresponded with Daniel Harkness frequently but according to her, she had no idea he was associated with Trojan.'

'She didn't?'

'That's the story she's selling,' Ruta said. 'I don't believe it for a minute. I've seen her accounts, there's a money trail set by him that she's been keeping a track of.'

'Have you told anyone?' I asked.

'Are you crazy?' she asked, pulling me to a stop, waiting for a couple of men in black to pass us by. 'I don't want to lose my head. I've heard she has underworld connections.'

'Underworld, as in black market?'

'As in drugs, organs, money, weaponry,' she said. 'There have been shipments of weapons through the catacombs under London but this all happened before the Capital Attacks, like –'

'Someone was preparing for it.' I cut her off. 'Why are you telling me this?'

'You can dye your hair but I know it's you. It's hard to forget a face, especially when you got up the courage to yell at Saul. Lillian may oversee things but I run this place. I know you're from Reign but I trust you more than anyone else here.'

'Don't say anything to anyone.'

'I keep secrets for a living.'

'You just told me one on Lillian.'

'I keep secrets for the good guys,' she retorted.

'Alexander should be done speaking to my colleague in a few minutes,' I smiled, 'if you want to ask him where she is.'

'I'll have more chance of talking with the Alpha Ground Team. You look tired, there's a couple of beds at the end of the hall if you want to take a break. I'll send your colleague that way when they're finished.'

'Actually,' I started, a thought coming to me, 'you wouldn't by any chance have a prayer room here?'

She stopped and I sighed – that was probably was the last thing on anyone's mind, but I needed a moment of clarity, even if it was just to stare at a wall.

She took my hand.

'This way,' she said and led me down the hall.

There was something about Ruta; even though we were walking through one of the most anxiety-ridden corridors in England, she had this perpetually calm nature. Her grip was soft and gentle.

We approached a room with tall glass doors, Ruta pushing them open. Compared to the corridor this room was dark but it wasn't cold or foreboding, it was comforting.

'I apologise, a couple of fuses have blown so it was safer to shut off the entire room, but I managed to find some candles.'

Ruta picked up few more candlesticks from a small box, setting them up at the darker side of the room.

There were rows of benches in the room and a table covered in a thick cloth underneath a window made of stained glass. However there wasn't any light coming through it, from what I could tell it had been bricked off.

As Ruta lit up the last few candles, I noticed a few prayer rugs in the corner.

'It's not much but it's clean,' she said. 'Luckily a bill was passed a few years ago that all underground facilities had to include rooms like this and they did their research; this room faces north.'

I smiled warmly, heading to the table, my fingers running over the smooth material.

'I would have gone to confessional when I was back home but I couldn't bring myself to,' I said.

'These are trying times, but I find it helpful when I take time in the day to myself,' Ruta said, standing beside me. 'I make the time to kneel before God, to be vulnerable.'

'Vulnerable,' I muttered. Something I wished I had the luxury of back home.

My eyes flitted to the mats in the corner a couple of times.

'Would you like to pray with me?' I asked, softly turning to her.

She smiled, nodding quickly, and took a mat from the corner. She slipped her shoes off and washed her hands, face, arms and feet in a small sink by the corner before joining me.

As she straightened the prayer mat, I knelt down before my own God and clasped my hands. I wanted to ask him so many questions: why this had been allowed to happen, why so many innocent people had to die. Why were Jessica and her child called to his side so soon?

As Ruta laid her hands down I closed my eyes. Yes, we believed in different Gods, we believed in different methods of prayer, but we were united through one thing: faith. I prayed for forgiveness; I prayed for his light and tender touch for those who'd lost their lives, as well as his healing hand to their family members.

The thing I prayed for the most, however, was his strength to continue on through me so I could walk down this treacherous path. I understood there were trials and tests for me ahead so I asked for his guiding hand to help me with the crucial decisions. So I could protect those I loved as well as those I hardly knew.

I honestly couldn't say how long we were there but when I opened my eyes Ruta was rolling up her mat and Kayson stood at the back, arms crossed.

'Bit of a fire hazard don't you think?' he asked.

'Well, as long as you keep your arms close to your body and don't touch the candles, I think we'll be just fine,' I said sarcastically, standing up. 'Why aren't you with Pilot?'

'She's with Blackbird, I managed to drag her away from the IT guys.'

'Good thing you did,' Ruta told him as she slipped her shoes back on. 'The coffee in there will keep you up for hours. It's surpassed industrial standards. We could give your team some if you're struggling,' she joked.

'I think a caffeine addiction is the last thing we need. Imagine Pilot wired on coffee.'

Quinn had always been a fan of green tea: every time she took a cup it was like she unlocked another part of her brain. I was genuinely curious what would happen if she had a cup of the IT guys' coffee. Maybe I could grab some on the way out, for emergencies.

'We better get back,' Kayson said, opening the door, and I nodded. 'Quinn found the trail connecting Charlotte, we've caught her red-handed profiting from Harkness, as well as signing off on papers that permit him to manipulate agents through substance abuse.'

‘That was fast,’ I said, a little concerned. This seemed too easy.

‘Substance abuse?’ Ruta asked.

‘Long story,’ I told her.

‘The CIA have been watching her for some time; it was just a case of putting what they had on her with what we did together,’ Kayson said.

‘Could Charlotte and Lillian be working together?’ Ruta asked, already going for the files in her hand.

‘It’s possible,’ I said.

‘We don’t have evidence but I’m going to say yes,’ Kayson said. ‘We’ll work on finding something on Lillian.’

‘Ruta told me there’s a money trail, connecting her to Harkness,’ I said.

‘I can send you what I have,’ Ruta said. She handed me a pen and I quickly scribbled down Quinn’s email.

‘We checked the security, the day we had to run from here. He wasn’t in the building,’ Kayson said. I only managed a stiff nod. Of course Harkness wasn’t there. ‘Let’s get out of here.’

I marched after him, and Ruta called after me. ‘Good luck.’

On the ride back, Lily was a little quieter than usual – even when I asked her about Alexander’s proposal, she waved it off. I really hoped she hadn’t sworn at the Prime Minister, but then again I hit an MI6 agent – things happened.

When we arrived at the safe house, Lily and Quinn headed upstairs – for sleep I hoped, while Kayson headed into the kitchen. Perhaps it wasn't the time to do a briefing, they hadn't had the easiest day. We'd be up first thing in the morning so everyone needed rest.

There was no sign of Saul so I'd ask Naomi what the pair of them came up with before giving her a final check over. I hoped she'd be able to get some shut-eye tonight.

I needed sleep, no matter how much I dreaded the thought.

CHAPTER 22

Sweven

A vision seen in sleep, a dream.

GRACE ASPIN

'You dug our graves.'

The blood on the floor clung to my fingers, creeping its way up my jeans. I couldn't stop it.

'You knew all along that we were working for Trojan, you knew the entire time but you didn't say a word.'

'He would have killed me.'

'He killed Willow.'

'I didn't know – Jess, please you've got to believe me. I didn't know he would do it,' I pleaded.

'Yes, you did.'

I felt his hand on the back of my neck holding me in front of Willow, her face peeking through the body bag. Her eyes snapped open, staring right at me, then with a snap her hands grabbed my chest and I couldn't help it – I screamed.

'Grace!' Kayson yelled – wait, what?

He sat over me on the bed, his hands pinning my wrists and it was only then I realised, I wasn't in the bowels of Reign. I was safe from him.

'It was just a nightmare,' he told me.

The cold wet tears lay dead on my face and I sucked in air like a child when crying to their mother.

'I'm OK. Must be catching them from Quinn,' I stuttered.

'Yeah, but I've never had to stop her from clawing at her own skin.' He let go, pointing to my chest.

I looked down to see red scratch marks all across my skin – how on earth had that happened? I must have done it in my sleep. I knew my nightmares were bad but I didn't think they'd bleed into reality.

'What was it about?' Kayson asked.

'What time is it?' I asked in return.

'Just after six.' He sighed. 'Come on, tell me.'

'Reign, Harkness – take your pick.'

I slipped out of bed, placing the duvet back as well as a pillow I'd managed to knock off. I needed to get this situation under control; we had evidence on Charlotte and Lillian. My main priority was the mission.

'Do you want to take some time out?' he asked.

I whipped round. 'Don't be ridiculous.'

'Grace, we all need time to process what happened, no one's gonna judge you if you want to sit one out.'

'Kayson, I'm the leader of this team, which means I dictate what we do. Now if you don't mind, I need to get dressed before this morning's briefing.'

I swiped for my hoodie, heading for the door, but Kayson grabbed my wrists, throwing me onto the bed.

'What use is a leader if she hasn't got her head straight?' he asked, closing the door.

'You're questioning me now?'

He laughed. 'You questioned Jess all the time.'

'You're not my Second, Kayson, you don't have the right to.'

'Oh yeah, cause I'm just some dumb Runner,' he snarked.

'You said it, not me.' I stalked towards him. 'Now get out of the way.'

'This isn't your head talking, this is Harkness, you're not thinking straight,' Kayson stated. 'We need to get more evidence on Lillian and Charlotte but you're all over the place. You were talking in your sleep, I doubt you've had more than two hours.'

I rolled my eyes, going for the door but he shoved me back, hard.

'Grace, you need to talk to someone about what happened to you. Harkness never got physical but he tore your mind apart.'

'No he didn't,' I spat. 'He works for Trojan, that's it.'

'I was there that night, I saw him drag you down to the morgue and that was just the first time,' Kayson said quietly and my whole body went rigid, my blood running cold. 'He made sure there wasn't a bruise on you but that day in the command room, I never understood why you didn't defend yourself.'

'What?'

'The day we had to get Quinn's mum to safety. Why didn't you tell us what Harkness did to you?'

'He never touched me. I wouldn't let him.' I shook my head.

'Why are you defending him?' he asked. 'He's wired your mind –'

'No he hasn't!' I screamed, my nostrils flaring angrily. 'He hasn't touched me, he hasn't set foot inside my mind because it is not his to control. Harkness never hit me, he saved me.'

Kayson's eyes were wide with bewilderment, his mouth agape.

'Oh, Grace . . .'

'He saved me!' I shouted. 'He saved me from the punishments and when I took the drugs, I couldn't feel anything. Even though I was losing myself it was bearable, I could live with what I'd done.'

With a cry I wiped away the tears, my fingers nearly ripping the hair from my head. Harkness kept me safe, he promised never to physically hurt me in exchange for my silence. I would tell him everything I could about our team but after Naomi arrived, I had to stop. I admit it! I was a mole, I was how

Harkness knew everything about the Omegas, I was the one feeding him the information on Jessica and Willow.

It was the reason I'd strangled the life out of Gabriel at the docks: if I took away his life then he couldn't hurt anyone else and neither could I.

I'd played God, I'd taken a life and I wasn't sorry. It made me feel good and if I had to live with that sin over my head for the rest of my life, then I would.

Despite prayer last night I didn't feel any better. I couldn't go on like this. Harkness put us in teams for a reason and they worked. We just had to go back to that. I had to go back to that.

'I'm arranging a flight for you back to Scotland.' This time Kayson's voice was firm, his face unreadable. 'You need to speak to a specialist because you're not fine. What he's done to you is sick, he didn't save you. You were his pet.'

I sucked in a breath, seeing the small glisten in his eyes. Was he going to cry?

'Runners are supposed to be soldiers,' I stated, feeling a cold composure wash over me. 'You want to talk to me about emotions – you bawled your eyes out like a newborn when we got back home.'

He inched towards me.

'Quinn and I watched the footage when Harkness broke through our comms; you were frozen. You're terrified of him.'

He needed to get back in line, I needed to show authority over him. I needed to be a leader. One that wasn't afraid of anyone.

'Don't you remember who gave you those scars?' I asked, my thumb running along the three thin scars on his forehead.

He reeled back, shaking his head, almost as he were remembering the day it happened. The day Harkness ordered me to cut Kayson. It was him or me.

'I'm trying to help you,' he begged.

'I never asked for it.'

I knew I had to lead this team, not the way I wanted but the way that worked. The way that kept us safe for years, was by Harkness's design. I needed strong people I could rely on – yes, Kayson was emotional so that needed to be corrected. My personal feelings needed to be corrected as well, they had to be pushed aside.

We would get the evidence we needed to bring in Lillian and Charlotte, then we'd go home and we could start again, like we were before. Nicola thought she could just brush over what happened, no fucking way.

'Now run the perimeter, I'll wake the rest of the house,' I said.

He pressed his lips together.

'Yes ma'am,' he replied through gritted teeth.

When we came to Reign we were children and the Academy shaped us into capable men and woman. Adults were strong, adults won wars. Harkness ruled by fear and it worked, therefore I'd lead by example.

No more crying, no more weakness – just brutal honesty and conviction.

* * *

After getting everything in my bag sorted and changing back into the clothes from yesterday, I made my way downstairs. Kayson was there but he didn't speak to me. I knew I was justified in my actions. The way that Harkness ran this team worked, we were efficient, and that's exactly what we needed to be again.

We didn't have the luxury of letting anger or sadness slip through, that's why the English security department failed to find the bomb. We were superior to them because we stopped ours and now, we were helping to clean up the mess that they made. They should be thanking us.

I was silenced all these years, never allowed to fight back or scream, so why should anyone else? We had a job to do, I had a team to lead.

'Are we ready?' I asked.

Lily was already sitting at the table going through the different weaponry they'd managed to smuggle out. It was a lot. Guns and magazines covered the table, loose ammo and knives lodged in between.

'Yes,' she replied flatly.

Had Kayson told her what I'd said?

'What did the PM want last night?'

‘Nothing important,’ Lily said, engrossed in the killing machine in front of her. ‘Wanted to know about Reign.’

‘What did you say?’

‘Nothing.’

I turned at that. I expected more – a profanity perhaps, something I’d later rein in. I thought she may be tired but even when starved, she’d crack jokes. I had to move on: Lily was a grown woman, if there was something wrong she would have made it known. God knows she moaned enough about it in the past.

‘Did he ask you to be his security?’ I asked.

‘No,’ she answered. ‘We spoke for a half hour, that was it.’

‘About?’

‘Confidential.’

What? Since when was anything amongst this team confidential?

‘I’m sorry?’ I asked.

‘Confidential,’ Kayson said, leaning back on the counter. ‘If we’re going by Harkness standards that means you shut your fucking mouth.’

Well, excuse me but in this team’s history nothing had ever been confidential. Especially to me.

‘Everything OK?’ Naomi asked, hand resting on the doorframe. She scanned the room, her eyes inevitably landing on mine.

‘Just tired,’ I answered her softly.

'Quinn will be down in a minute,' she said, but by the looks she was casting around the room, it was clear she didn't believe me.

I sat down at the small table across from Lily, trying my best to avoid Kayson's glare burning into my skull. I felt some guilt: the scars on his head were ones I inflicted but I had no choice. With the situation we found ourselves in, perhaps bringing it up wasn't the best move but it was the only one that appealed to me. I needed this team on top form – it was hardly my fault it was Harkness's methods.

'Today we infiltrate the reception, gather every piece of data we can about Lillian Montague and Charlotte Winters. I have an eyewitness who would testify against one; today we back them into a corner.'

'So what?' Naomi asked. 'We just break into different offices and see what we can find?'

'You're a ghost, Naomi,' I told her. 'You're breaking into the high priority offices with the passes the SAS gave us last night.'

It was then that Quinn teetered in the room, her eyes tired.

'Your mum's on the phone,' she said, pressing the speaker button. 'OK Carol, everyone can hear.'

As she spoke, Quinn rubbed tired fingers over her face, she barely looked like she'd slept at all.

'Naomi, are you alright?' Carol asked.

'Yeah mum, I'm fine. What have you got for us?'

'Well, the good part is that no major or independent news companies have published anything about Reign. Politics is politics, people screaming and shouting for change, the PM has announced he's making a speech later this evening about new restrictions,' Carol said.

'We're going to the reception this morning, he'll be there,' Naomi replied.

'Reception?'

'Everyone who's anyone will be there, all coming together to see if they can solve the problem,' I said. 'Keep an eye on the news for the announcement, he never mentioned it to us last night.'

'Mum,' Naomi shot out. 'There was a car crash in Edinburgh, was that on the news?'

'There was a plane crash I know but let me see, I'm not sure,' she mused. 'Yes, there was something about that.'

'Was anyone killed?'

'Yes, I think there were a couple of fatalities, but give me moment, I'll check.'

I couldn't look anyone in the eye. I had given Kayson the order. As I dared to look up Naomi's gaze burned into mine, her arms crossed. Yes, I gave the order but Kayson didn't have to follow it! He could have used his initiative for once.

'There was only one death, someone by the name of Thomas Ames.'

Dear God, we'd killed him, Kayson had shot him.

I leaned forward, catching Kayson turning his back, hands braced against his head. No, this – this wasn't supposed to happen.

'The bullet went through the passenger windshield but with the type of glass, it splintered, going all directions. Fragments going into his heart and head. Along with the crash, a large shard of glass went straight into his chest and he succumbed to his injuries on the scene.'

We'd gone rogue and killed a man. This wasn't looking good. Quinn grabbed for her laptop, scrolling through Interpol, MI6, CIA and the FBI but as I glanced over her shoulder, I realised our names weren't anywhere to be seen.

Was Nicola keeping this under wraps? She couldn't be if he'd been named in the press. Why wasn't she throwing us under the bus? Why wasn't there a warrant for our immediate arrest? We'd killed someone publicly.

'Hang up,' Kayson ordered grimly.

Quinn did as she was told and as the line went dead a chorus of profanities and heavy breaths erupted like a volcano.

'The glass splintered, that's fucking bullshit!'

'I swear, I didn't know, it was dark.'

'We train for that shit, Ashford!'

'We killed him! We fuckin killed him.'

'The glass couldn't have splintered, the glass sustained bullets in the past,' Lily muttered.

'Fuck!' Kayson roared. 'Fuck!' He threw his fist into the wall, pounding on it.

‘No!’ I shouted, quieting the room. ‘This wasn’t our fault, they pushed us and we ran. It was only a matter of time before someone else did the same.’

‘. . . Grace, what kind of messed up logic is that?’ Quinn asked me.

‘It was only a matter of time before someone else broke out, you were there Naomi, you didn’t agree with us being silenced. Where’s the justice?’

‘You’re saying killing Ames was justice?’ Kayson spat.

‘He was there with Harkness, he played a part in this.’ I pressed my hands on the table.

‘If you’re taking that approach, that means your precious Doctor McKay deserves to be shot too,’ Lily said.

‘He’s different, he helped, he was being held captive just like us,’ I stated. ‘But Ames, he was part of Harkness’s team. We have a mission objective, let’s get back to it.’

‘Grace, a man is dead on your order!’ Naomi exclaimed.

‘If you don’t like the operation I’m running, Naomi, then get out!’ I shouted right back. ‘But I’d be wary, you wouldn’t make it forty-eight hours alone.’

She stared at me in shock, her eyes wide, mouth gaping but she didn’t say anything.

‘That’s what I thought,’ I snapped. ‘Anyone else have an issue with it?’

My eyes scanned the room but everyone was looking at the floor, all except Kayson who stared right at me.

‘The tech guys told us the SAS are dropping off the radar like flies – we should join them.’

‘I’m not running from this,’ I stated.

‘We’re a fucking mess. You really think the five of us can take down Trojan?’

‘No, I don’t,’ I snapped back. ‘But it is better than sitting here and doing nothing! We can do something.’

‘Kill?’ Naomi asked, tilting her head. ‘Jessica wouldn’t want this.’

‘She is dead,’ I growled, walking towards her. ‘So we’re doing this my way.’

She didn’t say anything after that but the tension in the room was thick. I knew I was right, this was how I would lead this team and I didn’t have time for their antics. Jessica indulged them but I wouldn’t.

‘We don’t have another choice. We are going to expose leads to Trojan, the Secret Service are going to be indebted to us and we’ll be heroes,’ I told them with a smile, trying to reassure them. ‘We’re going to come out of this on top.’

‘Give me the briefing in the car, I think I need to go puke,’ Naomi said, completely disgusted as she left the room.

Quinn shuffled out after her, barely looking me in the eye and once Lily had packed the weaponry into bags, so did she. As Kayson brushed past me he grabbed my arm tighter than he ever had before. He leaned close, his lips practically brushing against my ear.

'If this is what you call Harkness saving you, Grace, he should have just put a bullet in your head.'

CHAPTER 23

Abditory

A hiding place.

NAOMI JADE

Grace had fuckin lost it.

In the car our leader, who totally wasn't having a psychotic breakdown, told me the rest of the team would attend the reception at the House of Lords and against Saul's plan, I was to go to what was left of the Houses of Parliament. According to Quinn, Lillian's office was safe from the blast so there should be something there for me to find.

Saul had met us at the reception of the building, one used by Thames House for functions such as this, so it would be well guarded. He'd handed over a change of clothes for everyone before heading inside himself, not waiting for the team to follow. Guess he wasn't aware of the new plan, considering I had a new formal suit in my hands.

As the rest of the team got out of the car, I grabbed Quinn's hand.

'Open comm lines as soon as you get inside,' I told her quietly. 'And if she . . . you know.'

Quinn bit her lip.

'We'll get her out of there.'

'Naomi, we gotta get inside,' Kayson butted in. 'If you need anything let us know and we'll get it to you.'

'You'll be busy here.'

'I don't care if you need to scream the place down, if you need help, inform us,' he said, slamming the car door, and I was off through the streets once more.

I hated this stupid car, I wanted to break the windows.

We arrived at the Houses of Parliament, and using the SAS pass, I was through without any questions. The hard-boiled glare on my face helped. I just used the face my dad pulled when I wasn't 'acting right'.

There were many things I was good at: I was a decent getaway driver, a slightly more than adequate chef, an alright investigator, but one of the things I wasn't good at was pretending I belonged – as well as picking this shitting lock.

Lillian's office may have been untouched but the lock on her door was a bloody nightmare. Apparently, this wasn't as easy as the movies made it out to be. It took me about ten minutes to get through, most of which was spent trying to remember what Lily told me that one time we broke into Thompson's office during the summer.

When the door opened with a heavy click, I walked inside.

'I'm in,' I said, tapping my ear.

'Great, we're set up here,' Quinn replied. 'Remember, anything goes sideways just get out. Harkness probably thinks we're dead but just in case, be prepared to leg it out the window.'

'Noted.'

The office was quite spacious and surprisingly tidy, the windows covered in sheets of plastic. A computer sat in the middle of the desk, which was comforting, as well as the filing cabinets that lined the wall and tall cupboard. Well at least I had loads to go through.

'I have Lillian,' Grace's voice floated through. 'I have her under control, if she leaves, Blackbird, it's onto you. There's no sign of Charlotte on my end.'

'I checked with the front desk, she's meant to be here but so far she's a no-show.'

'She might know we're onto her.'

'Or it could be because all her kids are dead,' Kayson said sharply. 'Maybe it's given her a fuckin reality check.'

Charlotte Winters was a woman I wanted to understand. How could she not come to James's funeral? How could she abandon her kids for work? Why was she only now realising that she could lose everything?

I darted over to the computer, whacking on a pair of gloves and got to work. I slid in the USB and let the programme hack its way into the network.

Thankfully this thing was password protected: if we'd needed retina or a voice command we'd have been screwed.

'OK, I'm in, Carrier 1,' Quinn said. 'Nightingale, I'm into Target One's computer and have control over the feed here at drop-off A. Working on drop-off B. Carrier 1, step away from the computer, see what you can find elsewhere.'

Different screens started popping up as Quinn hacked her little heart out, so I went to the filing cabinet. As I my fingers filed through refused bills, legislations and draft speeches I realised nothing here was of any importance. Nothing even remotely resembled Trojan – even the bank statements looked official and were signed off by three different people.

What if those three people worked for Trojan? No, stop it! Saul said this would happen, the paranoia and fear. I had to keep moving. As I got to the back of the drawer all that was left to look at were pens, post-it notes, a G-string and a blue vibrator.

The country's in crisis and she's getting it on – so fucking English. At least we'd have the class to have a bottle of Buckfast or whisky in there too.

Flinging the sliver of material back in the drawer I moved onto the others, but once again came up empty. Couldn't this woman make it easy?

'I feel like I'm looking in the wrong place,' I said.

'But it's her office, she must keep something there.'

'If she's part of Trojan then it would have been hidden, think about it. Until recently Trojan's files were hidden on the Academy server where no one would find them. Since Lillian is a part of this, she's probably smart enough not to leave stuff here.'

'I was afraid that might be the case,' Saul's voice scratched through. 'This is why I told you sending her there was a bad idea, there's nothing.'

'It was somewhere we had to cross off the list,' Grace retorted.

'Naomi, you have incoming, ten seconds. Hide,' Quinn said.

I gently closed the drawers, moving everything back to how it was, then ran to the cupboard, slipping inside. I pushed myself to the back wall and thankfully, there weren't any skeletons in here, just suits and jackets.

As the door to the office opened with a click, heavy footsteps followed. Two pairs of them.

'Pilot, we need facial recognition for Carrier 1,' Kayson ordered.

'I'm on it, I'm on it,' Quinn mumbled. 'His name is Conrad Hyde, he's the head of the Bank of England. He was in the emergency cabinet meeting with you. Weird, don't know what he's doing here.'

Suddenly, a new voice entered the room.

'You seriously think she'd keep it in this shithole?' The voice was gruff, older.

'I need to know what he's going to say,' the first man replied.

'The other man is Gareth Brixton,' Quinn told me. 'One of the chiefs of the Metropolitan Police Force.'

'I'm going over there, Carrier 1 stay put,' Kayson demanded.

'No, the PM is leaving for his announcement, go with him,' Saul fought back.

'To hell with him.'

'We can all have a good chat later about our political leanings but you need to protect him in case the worst happens. I'll go for her.'

Even though I was trapped in a cupboard, I knew that this team (despite the dysfunctional part) knew what they were doing. At least I hoped.

I knew Jessica wasn't the good guy but she wasn't the bad one either. Did that still apply to this team?

Get it together, listen in, Naomi, this could be important.

Gareth sounded like he was from a southern part of Scotland and by the accent, grew up working class. Sure, he could be a possible terrorist but he would be easier to approach. Hopefully.

As the team rattled on in my ear about their own op, I slinked over to the small crack in the door, peering out. Conrad was a tall, slender man in an expensive-looking suit, his hands frantic as he typed on the computer.

Shit – I'd left the memory stick.

Conrad was ranting and raving about Alexander's speech but my mind threw itself into overdrive. If he took that would they be able to trace it back to us? Had I just blown this entire mission? Grace was going to kill me, I knew I wasn't ready for this, how could I be?

It wasn't supposed to be difficult and I'd screwed it up.

I had to hope he didn't see the memory stick.

Gareth was wearing a cheap-looking suit and a long trench coat, struggling to hold the files in his hand as he fiddled with a walking cane in the other.

'You know Lillian, she won't be happy about this,' he said. 'We were meant to wait.'

'Wait for her?' Conrad asked. 'She doesn't have control of Trojan, you know that, he does and besides, she's too busy covering Charlotte's arse.'

'Yes and maybe if we'd waited, like she told us, we wouldn't be in this mess. You know as well as I do that Alexander's boss wasn't meant to die.'

'Neither was Alexander's wife but you don't hear him complaining,' Conrad muttered. 'There are always going to be casualties.'

'Human life is not –'

'Oh, save your speech for the camera.'

As Gareth walked around the room I pushed myself back to the wall of the cupboard, a hand falling to my comm and tapping it a few times.

'I can hear everything, don't worry. There's no death certificate for Alexander's wife but I'll keep looking. If Charlotte's definitely not here that means we only have one target to follow. Lillian's definitely Trojan but the good news is she doesn't control it.'

'Why is that good?' Lily asked.

'Because that means she isn't the dangerous one.'

‘I’ll go after Lillian, she seems to be the ringleader of these two and plant a bug on her. Naomi, stay in position until Saul gets there, once you’re out he’ll lead you back,’ Grace ordered.

I tapped the comm that would send a buzz through the system to acknowledge I understood, then kept as still as I could. I’d have to wait this one out.

At least Grace wasn’t losing it on an op, it could be going worse.

CHAPTER 24

Tacenda

Things better left unsaid.

GRACE ASPIN

Once Kayson arrived at the front desk I'd been able to get closer to Lillian – she was at the far end of the West Room, talking with some officials.

Dressed in a pencil skirt and shirt, I felt the part, I was in control. We'd get what we needed from Lillian, and she'd pay for what she did to this country.

'I've secured Pilot in the back room,' Kayson said.

'I've still got control of Lillian,' I said.

'They're gone,' Naomi whispered as I heard the click of a door. 'I'm going after Gareth.'

'You can't,' I said, quietly, passing by a few politicians who wandered the halls. 'Wait for Saul.'

'I have to try,' she said. 'He knows more than we heard. If Lillian is the ringleader then these guys are Trojan.'

‘We haven’t got evidence or confirmation – wait, Carrier 1.’ I pulled out my phone, pretending to be answering a call. ‘Wait for further instructions.’

‘He’s going to get away.’

‘Wait.’

‘No.’

I wanted to scream down the phone *you don’t disobey orders because you feel like it!* When she got back I’d – I . . . I’d think of something. She needed to be taught a lesson, if she wanted to do things her way then she should have left when she had the chance.

‘I’m inside,’ Saul said. ‘ETA three minutes Carrier One, I can cover her.’

‘Fine,’ I muttered. ‘Pull her out if needed.’

‘I’m not a kid.’

‘You’re certainly acting like one,’ I shot back.

This was getting ridiculous – I called the shots, not her. I thought Kayson or Lily would have taught her something about obedience over the summer? Or, I don’t know, her parents?

‘Nightingale, focus on Lillian,’ Kayson said.

As I made my way through the rooms, politely pushing past the crowds that had started to fill it up, Lillian laughed.

I’d give her something to laugh about.

Suddenly, the burner phone pinged, it was David.

DAVID: Tell me you didn’t shoot Tommy’s car.

I couldn't deal with this right now, I had a priority. The time for this pity talk could come later. He'd understand.

'Miss Montague.' I approached politely. 'There have been a few issues, would I be able to pull you away for a moment?'

'There are more important matters here that I need to attend to,' she replied, with an equally fake smile.

'It's to do with Mr Brixton and Conrad Hyde, ma'am.'

She pinched the bridge of her nose.

'The Metropolitan Police are going to be the death of me,' she said, and the men around her burst into laughter that I awkwardly had to share. I could never be a politician.

As I led her away from the group I couldn't help but smile as she took the lead: I slipped the bug in at the bottom, sticking it to the inside of her blazer. First contact. I could kill her but that would be wrong. We needed her.

'I've connected to the bug, it's now live Nightingale, good job,' Quinn said.

What was that phrase Jessica used to say? Showtime.

CHAPTER 25

Selcouth

Unfamiliar territory.

NAOMI JADE

To hell with Grace's orders – Gareth was a vital source of information and the only one I honestly felt able to approach. He was a little bigger in stature but by the look of the man, I'd be able to outrun him if needed, especially given he walked with a limp and cane.

Thankfully, Gareth and Conrad lacked Lily's keen eye and didn't bother taking the memory stick. I swiped the thing back into my pocket, running back down the corridors a few minutes after the pair had left and I was in the clear.

'Pilot, I need to know where Gareth is.'

'Carrier 1, wait for backup.'

'He's admitted associating with Lillian, they were going through her office, he could be another lead,' I said, trying to plead my case. 'He's going to get away.'

Quinn caved. 'He's heading for the car park round the back, take the stairs at the end of the hall all the way down.'

'You're a star.' I smiled, sprinting down the corridor.

'Carrier 1, I'll be with you in two minutes,' Saul said.

With Saul on the way, I jumped down the steps, my feet pounding and heart racing. I was right, I couldn't do this, but I had to try. Gareth had to be a lead to Trojan. I flung open the doors frantically looking for the man, spotting him a few cars down, lighting a cigarette.

'Excuse me!'

Of all the lines I could have come out with, I chose that one . . . wow.

His head snapped over and he rolled his eyes.

'I know,' he said, taking a puff of his cigarette. 'I'm moving the car, I'm going, I'm going!'

'I'm not the parking police.' I smiled, catching my breath. 'I just need to talk to you.'

'Listen, put it in a letter to your MP, I've got bigger things to worry about.'

'I know who you are, obviously, but I needed to talk to you about Lillian Montague,' I said, not too sure how to approach my next point. 'We need your help – we know she has connections to Trojan and, I bet, Daniel Harkness, who's hiding out in government.'

Come right out with it, well done Naomi, you spent days during the summer learning different tactics but you decide blunt and to the point. Wonderful.

'You've got to be kidding me,' I heard Quinn mutter in my ear.

'Carrier 1, ETA one minute,' Saul said hurriedly.

Gareth however, stopped dead, like he'd been frozen on the spot. It was only when his cigarette, now a stub, burned his fingers that he snapped out of it.

'I – I where did you hear that?'

'So she does have a connection with him, that you know about?'

'Why are you asking me?'

He was afraid, exhausted by the looks of it too. His hands were shaking like leaves and the bags under that man's eyes were dropping like melted wax.

'I want to get to the bottom of this. We need evidence to take Lillian down. If you testify against her –'

He laughed.

'Testify?' he asked. 'Take Lillian down?'

'It's not impossible. The walls are closing in aren't they?' I asked. 'Trojan attacked the capitals of Great Britain but now what?'

'Who are you?'

‘Someone who can help,’ I said. ‘You’re afraid and so am I but we can end this. Tell me why you were looking for Alexander’s speech.’

‘His – you were there?’ the man stuttered.

‘Please,’ I begged. ‘We don’t have a lot of time.’

‘Listen kid, you’d have better luck trying to get the PM to divulge the speech himself. But then, he’s inconsolable, he’s too worked up about the cat,’ he muttered bitterly.

‘The cat?’

‘Yeah, you’d think it would be his wife, but no . . . called it a stupid name too, Delilah, Daphne or something, apparently they were inseparable. Lived at Number Ten, that thing ate better than most of my force,’ he scoffed. ‘Talk about priorities.’

‘Alexander had a cat?’

‘Naomi,’ Quinn’s voice shuddered. ‘Willow’s parents had a cat called Daphne.’

I touched my ear.

‘I found the collar at Number Ten.’

‘She told me her mum and dad worked as politicians, but I never thought –’

‘Never thought to mention it?’ Lily muttered. ‘Great job, Pilot.

‘We’ve been busy in case you haven’t noticed, and she never told me who they were.’

‘I wonder why.’

‘She’s dead I didn’t think that –’

‘What, that she didn’t have a few skeletons in her closet?’

‘It’s not her fault,’ I said, defending her.

Who are you talking to?’ Gareth asked.

‘Gabriel told us it was her father who ordered the hit.’ Quinn trailed off. ‘Wait, MI6 has his DNA, cross-referencing now.’

I could barely let a breath past my lips until Quinn spoke again. Tell me we hadn’t been this stupid.

‘It’s a match,’ Quinn said. ‘Alexander Buchanan is Willow’s father. The Prime Minister of Great Britain is Trojan.’

CHAPTER 26

Aviothic

To fly away.

GRACE ASPIN

As I led Lillian away from the crowds and into the back offices, I could barely contain the gasp as I heard the news.

Alexander was Willow's father.

The chattering from the hall quietened as Lillian shut the door behind her, clearly irritated I'd pulled her out.

'What have Gareth and Conrad been saying?' she asked.

'Ma'am, I know this isn't protocol.' I felt as if Jessica was watching over me in that moment, since I came up with one of her completely stupid ideas. 'My name is Grace Aspin, I work for Daniel Harkness.'

'What the fuck are you doing?' Lily demanded but I didn't answer.

Lillian didn't freeze or appear shocked at all. In fact she studied me, her heels clicking on the rich wooden floor as she circled me.

'You can't be,' she mused.

'I'm on his side, my team were on our way back to London to tell him so when he blew up the plane. I was the only survivor,' I told her.

I knew this was one sure way of getting intel: if I worked on the inside I could act as a mole and send what I found to Nicola. It's not like I hadn't done it before.

She smiled, one of her hands fiddling with the strands of my hair.

'The only survivor?'

'Yes ma'am, I'm here to find Daniel Harkness but I've been unable to locate him.'

'My little Gracie has come back to me.'

I thought I was in control, I thought he was hiding in government, I thought – no. The harbinger of my nightmares slipped out from a false wall panel, the harrowing grin on his face growing as he headed straight for me.

'My little Gracie.' He grabbed my jaw and it took all my self-control not to flinch. 'Where's the rest of your team?'

'Dead.'

He tilted his head at that but let me go, his attention turning to Lillian.

'She can be useful.'

'She broke into the reception, Daniel,' Lillian said. 'Who knows who she brought with her.'

'My team are dead, ma'am.'

'Blackbird, get her out of there,' Kayson demanded in my ear.

'I can't leave Pilot,' she replied.

The woman laughed.

'You could be working for that Ramos girl,' she said. 'She may be your agent but I don't trust her.'

'That's the thing, Lillian,' Harkness said, wrapping an arm around me. 'Grace was different to the others, she didn't need NX14 to comply.'

'So she's a spineless brat?' she replied, unamused.

'She fed me intel on her own team. She was the perfect mole.'

No. Stop talking.

'Really?' Lillian asked, disinterested.

'How do you think we found out that idiot child of Alexander's was onto us?' Harkness asked.

I wanted to rip the comm from my ear but if I did, I'd throw the rest of my team in the firing line. It was too late, they'd already heard everything.

'Cut her channel,' Lily demanded, and I had to keep a straight face as the pair continued to talk. 'Pilot, cut her channel.'

No, don't leave me.

'Wait,' Naomi pleaded.

'I can't,' Quinn said, and I heard the quiver in her voice. 'She – oh my god. She sold us out.'

'Cut her channel now!'

Silence filled my ear. I was ready to scream – why did they have to find out? It wasn't like that! They were hearing it out of context, they didn't know the first thing that was going on. I didn't know what files Willow was looking at, she just used my pass so I went to explain. I didn't know – I didn't know he'd kill her. I fed him intel but it was reports, just like Jessica did, all I wanted was to be like her.

'She's medically trained, a little hesitant with a gun but I have a feeling, a really good feeling that if we gave her a team she'd be able to lead,' Harkness said, his lips kissing the side of my head.

I almost shrivelled away, even though the sensation was familiar.

I'd wanted a team that would operate like Harkness had ordered all those years ago. I'd thought that was how we would make it work.

Now I knew the only sure thing about his methods – you end up alone.

I'd imagine Quinn would wish for her mother at a time like this but I did not. I knew she would shame me for what I'd done, and rightly so. After the events of today I knew I could never go back to my family in Italy, I'd be better off disappearing from their lives forever. To escape the shame of it all I had to suffer the consequences of my own actions, but this time, I feared, it wouldn't be in private.

My family had their own underworld connections, they had their own influence but they wouldn't save me, they wouldn't come near me. They'd disowned me.

'Then you're just in time,' Lillian said, making a dash for the TV, flicking it on. 'His speech is being broadcast to the nation. Congratulations Grace, you've joined the winning side.'

CHAPTER 27

Nesta

Pure hope.

RUTA CHANDRA

The wind was cool as it blew against my skin and for the first time in weeks, I heard birds singing. The waves of reporters, however, weren't so pleasant. You'd think after years of doing this they would learn some manners but no, they stand like headless chickens, shoving their microphones and cameras into your face.

For once I was glad Lillian wasn't by Alexander's side. She'd never liked me, she only pretended to.

I thought about speaking out a lot, I thought about going straight to Alexander but he'd never listen. To him I was a glorified secretary, even though I helped oversee a lot of the businesses and organisations run throughout the UK. I'd seen the Reign Institute file being passed around, the majority of it was always blacked out. Lillian had to have done that, I couldn't think of anyone else who had the access.

As the Prime Minister approached the podium to address the crowds and those watching behind screens, an uproar grew in the cool air. Behind the reporters stood what I could only describe as an angry mob, holding signs and posters, calling for an election.

Yes, because that's what this country needed right now. More politics.

'Prime Minister!' one reporter shouted. 'When are you going to revisit the national aid charity that is single-handedly supporting those who lost their homes in the attacks?'

'Prime Minister!' another chimed in. 'When are you going to speak about Operation Red Dawn, leaks from the CIA have exposed sleeper agents!'

'I'm not here to talk about state business,' Alexander replied calmly into the microphone. 'I am here to talk about what is going on in this country. I am here to talk about the devastation that has ripped your children from your homes and families from their loved ones.'

I thought I'd get complacent after hearing him talk all these years – he raved in parliament for change. Always had – he'd been one I'd kept an eye on, since his former boss was quite the pushover. However, as he spoke with clarity and precision, I knew he meant every single word.

Despite suspecting Lillian, and apart from the occasional political scandal, all Alexander had ever done was fight for what was right. Most of his political endeavours over the years had been to help the poor and the working class. I was present when he convinced his boss to reduce the national tax and introduce a bursary for those who needed it.

'Times have changed and unfortunately we have become docile. We've relied on our national friends too heavily.'

'When are you going to address what happened in Estonia!' someone screamed.

Alexander continued.

'While we work to better our security system, restrictions will be put in place starting Monday next week. The people of this country are going to be restricted to their homes for a short period of time. The streets of this country will be empty, but they will become safer.'

The crowd roared again, like animals.

'These restrictions are to protect us!' Alexander shouted, slicing his hand through the air. 'There will be a curfew on Sunday night: everyone must be in their homes by ten o'clock at night, then remain there until the following Sunday.'

'You can't do this!' I heard someone cry.

'Within this period the civilian phone service will be down; only calls to the emergency services will be possible. This is so we can root out the bad weeds that have taken hold of our society, and I will personally see that every single one is eradicated.'

As the reporters' and crowd's aggression built like a wall, a man dressed in black with tattoos up his neck and jaw moved closer to the PM. Guess he had a new bodyguard.

'A national wage will be paid to every person of working age in this country, but all work apart from that involved in the emergency services is to be prohibited during this period of cleansing. We need to make Britain great again and in one week, I can promise work will be done by all to ensure we make a better future for the next generation.'

'What about us!'

'Yeah, what about us!'

'We need help now!'

'Please, don't be scared,' Alexander said, throwing his arms out. 'This one-week period will be short but the work my men carry out will be vital, to our survival. To ensure this curfew is kept, the police and military will be patrolling the streets. Anyone travelling without the appropriate reason will be fined and possibly arrested.'

'You can't do this!'

As the woman's voice screamed above the crowd, I noticed more and more police showing up but the thing that scared me, was the men in tactical gear behind them. Some had riot shields and all of them, had guns.

'To give you some peace of mind, the man behind one of the many attacks on our capital, who I can now name as former MI6 agent James Winters, was killed in the attacks on Estonia. We can all rest a little easier knowing that one of the men behind this has moved on. Which is why I ask, this Sunday, stay in your homes. If we sacrifice this short period of time, I promise you I will hunt down the others responsible and we will become great once more.

As the speech continued, I had faith that this world was going to become a better place. It had to.

CHAPTER 28

Viridity

Naive innocence.

NAOMI JADE

I knew Grace was going through a hard time and she'd lost a marble or two at some point, but this plan was insane!

'She fed me intel on her own team,' Harkness said. 'She's the perfect mole.'

What?

'Really?' Lillian asked.

'How do you think we found out that idiot child of Alexander's was onto us?'

No, no Grace wouldn't do that. She may be a bit selfish but she'd never sell the team out. What would she have to gain from it? Willow was also her teammate, they were friends, there was no way she'd give her up.

If she'd told Harkness about Willow then it would explain why she never wanted me in the Academy, then fast-forward, Jessica goes on an op and gets 'abandoned' by her team. Grace said it herself, they wouldn't leave her just because they didn't trust her. The first time we came to London it was a trap for us – how else would Harkness know we were there? When the plane was hit, had Grace told Harkness? No one else knew we were going, so it had to be someone else on the team. She couldn't have betrayed us, she wouldn't have . . .

'Cut her channel,' Lily ordered. 'Pilot, cut her channel.'

It was then that Gareth started running for his car and I had to bolt after him.

'Wait,' I pleaded.

'I can't,' Quinn said. 'She – oh my god. She sold us out.'

'Cut her channel and the bug now!'

Harkness and Lillian's voices dropped to nothing just as my hand slammed on Gareth's door, stopping him from getting inside.

'Gareth please, we can talk about this.'

'Gareth Brixton.' Saul's voice called from behind. 'We've never had the pleasure of being introduced.'

'You've got to be joking,' Gareth muttered. 'Was this a test? I didn't tell her anything.'

I turned, Saul was surrounded by men dressed in black, guns strapped to their sides, a black van behind him.

‘What?’ I asked Gareth, confused.

‘I’m afraid, Naomi, you’re a little smarter than I first thought,’ Saul said, walking towards me. ‘When I found out your name and asked about, I realised you were the one who broke into Reign in the first place. Then I saw how you fought, defensive, frantic – someone who certainly hadn’t been training for years.’

You’ve got to be kidding me – Nicola trusted Saul!

‘I need evac,’ I said, pressing my finger to my ear but only silence followed. ‘I need help.’

‘Oh, I’m afraid Quinn and Lily are a little busy right now,’ Saul said, shoving his hands into his pockets. ‘Kayson is with the Prime Minister, probably panicking that he can’t hear anyone either. I imagine there won’t be much of a welcome party when he gets back. It’ll be quite a shock.’

‘Saul, leave them out of this!’

‘Oh, such fire,’ he said, his lips swiping over his teeth. ‘I’d hold onto that, you’re going to need it.’

Gareth’s meaty hands grabbed mine, pressing me against the hood of his car, handcuffs snapping on my wrists.

‘I’m sorry,’ he whispered in my ear as the shadow of Saul’s men consumed my own.

I shifted my head so I could see him but I could only make out his silhouette through the blazing sun.

Even though I'd never been trained for it, I knew what was going to happen next – torture.

* * *

They hadn't drugged me, which was the only good thing to come out of this scenario. After being hooded and thrown in what I presumed was the van, we drove for an hour. One of the things Kayson taught me about kidnapping was to be alert at all times. Count the minutes, recognise the noises outside.

Apart from road traffic and roadworks however, there was nothing I recognised.

It was only when the van slowed for a final time and the tyres crunched on the road that I knew we had to be somewhere abandoned. What were they going to put me through? This thought became concrete when two men grabbed my arms and hauled me inside what I could only presume was some sort of warehouse. The smack of my trainers echoing as they dragged me through the building.

It took fifty-four steps before we stopped and a door screeched, then we walked another three steps and stopped again. This time it sounded like the door slid open, the metal crunching and scraping against the wall.

I was pushed another couple of steps before I was forced to sit down, my once-cuffed hands now strapped to what felt like a dentist's chair.

'You know, you really aren't that stupid,' Saul said as he ripped the bag from my head, the naked lightbulb blinding me for a moment.

'People keep saying that,' I muttered.

'According to Quinn's records, which we have access to now, you were quite close to uncovering a lot of things. You even managed to get a bug on Lillian Montague. Shame Charlotte didn't join us, she would of found this all quite the spectacle.'

'If you hurt Quinn I swear –'

'What?' Saul asked. 'What will you do?'

What could I do? My wrists and ankles were tied tight with leather straps; I didn't have a pin or even something to reach the buckles with. I didn't bother trying to rock back and forth, it would make me seem desperate, weak. I focused my breathing, looking around the room for anything I could use.

It was a small grey concrete room, old blood stains on the floor as well as used bandages. The door was red but unfortunately closed, and worse still, there were no windows.

'Escape?' Saul guessed. 'I know I said you weren't that stupid but come on, you've trained a few months and you think you can escape this?'

'I broke into Reign, a highly efficient and tactical institute run by terrorists, you might want to stop underestimating me.'

Saul nodded a little, opening the file that was tucked under his arm.

'Naomi Jade, nineteen this year, graduated school with decent exam results. Parents Carol and Charles. Your mother used to work for Thompson. Now isn't that something?'

What? He knew about them?

'You live on 35 Brigade Road, no siblings, only child. Well, that explains a lot.' The file shut with a snap.

'Leave my parents out of this,' I said through gritted teeth. 'They have nothing to do with it.'

'Not yet,' Saul said.

He walked over to a small tray in the corner, coming back with a pair of used bloody pliers. What was he planning to do with those? I felt myself fidget in the chair: I tried to stop but as he came closer I found it more difficult.

'What do you want?'

'Me?' Saul asked. 'Nothing but I think it'll be interesting for Harkness to see you alive, considering Grace told him you were dead. In fact, she said your whole team died in that explosion.'

He placed the pliers at the tip of my thumbnail, clamping down hard.

'But you nearly ruined everything, Naomi,' Saul said. 'There needs to be some retribution for that.'

RIP.

Sharp, jolting pain didn't even begin to describe the agony as I screamed blue murder, the air nipping and biting at my nail bed, blood spurting.

Every nerve feeling as if it was on fire but when Saul clamped the pliers on another nail, I begged.

'Stop. Harkness wants us on his side, he's not going to thank you for this!'

'Love, I'm just getting started.'

Six hours, that's how long Saul tortured me for.

With every slash, punch, cut and snap I focused on one thing, counting. Kayson had told me when the pain became so unbearable the human body would pass out and after the fourth hour, I wished for that release. I spent most of the time with my eyes shut because I knew seeing Saul taunt me with different weapons would make it worse. When he had me pinned to the ground in the safe house, when he nibbled my ear, it wasn't out of affection, it was out of ownership. He knew who I was the whole time and I'd played the fool.

The only hope I was given was when one of the guards told him that Lily, Quinn and Kayson had managed to escape.

Then the next round of questions began: where would the team go? Of course I knew, it was a registered hangar in the middle of a field. I knew the exact co-ordinates but my captor didn't. However, Saul did know that Grace's talk of joining their side was bullshit but what I didn't understand was why he hadn't told Harkness about her or the bug she'd planted on Lillian. The guards handed him the phone many a time but he didn't call anyone.

'Tell him,' I challenged, blood running into my eyes, the pain was almost so bad that I struggled to talk.

‘What?’ Saul asked, fixing his sleeve.

‘Tell Harkness the team is alive and they escaped,’ I said, but his eyes fell to the next instrument of pain on the table. ‘Unless you can’t.’

‘Can’t?’ Saul spat.

‘You hadn’t met Gareth before and if he’s high up, that means you’re not,’ I said, some of the pieces finally coming together. ‘You were given our team to advise by Nicola but she’s not Trojan, is she?’

‘Be quiet!’ Saul raged, grabbing my neck, but with all the strength I had, I leaned up into his hold.

His grip was tight but desperate – that meant I was getting somewhere.

‘You were given our team to make sure we didn’t dig deeper. That’s why you didn’t want us looking into Lillian, it’s how Umesh escaped custody.’

‘You don’t know anything.’

‘I know you’re going to die if you tell Harkness you lost his team,’ I spat right back. ‘Your one job was to keep us in the dark but you couldn’t even do that.’

‘You’re not the one in control here!’

‘And neither are you.’

CHAPTER 29

Orphic

Beyond ordinary understanding.

NAOMI JADE

I must have fallen asleep, I must have been dreaming, I must have gone mad.

'You know, for someone who was too scared to speak up most of her life, I'm impressed.' I craned my eyes open, a blurry figure swinging on a chair's rear legs. 'I really enjoyed the part where you figured it all out, his face was priceless.'

Even though the dark voice chilled me to my core, I knew she couldn't be real, even as her fiery hair came into focus.

Her head tilting, a sharp smile greeting me.

'Wakey, wakey, did you have a good sleep?'

'You're not real,' I grumbled.

'Oh, charmer,' she mocked. 'Not even a hello, just "you're not real". After everything, I thought I'd at least get a "fucking hell you're looking good for a dead girl, Jess".'

'You can't be here,' I said, knowing I couldn't trust my own mind right now.

'No, you can't trust your own mind,' Jessica repeated – how did she know what I was going to say? 'Oh, don't look so surprised. Your subconscious is in overdrive. A nasty hit on the head after falling from a plane and six hours of torture. I'm surprised you haven't started singing yet.'

'And after all that, I get stuck with you?'

'Hey, you're the one talking to yourself.'

As I looked the woman up and down, there was part of me that was glad to see her, even if it was my mind's idea of a cruel joke.

'Why you?' I asked, feeling my head loll back.

'Because I am the only one who'd get you out of this alive,' she said, slyly standing, her fingers trailing over the arm of her chair.

'You're a figment of my imagination,' I said but even as the truth left my lips, I didn't want to believe it.

What I would give to have her back, but she wasn't real.

It was the little things that gave her away; the wicked grin on her face and the way she was toying with me. Jessica wouldn't do that, if she was here she would help.

'Oh, for fuck's sake Naomi, stop psychoanalysing yourself,' Jessica groaned. 'You're tied to a chair and won't give up information to a desperate man – how long do you think he's going to let you live?'

'I won't give up this team.' My voice garbled as tears built in my eyes.

‘You want to die a hero is that it?’ she asked me, a bitterness in her voice as she slid closer. ‘The body does different things when you’re taken hostage, everyone deals with it differently. Until you’ve been in an environment like it, there’s no telling what you’d do. If you want to survive then you have to give Saul something.’

‘I won’t tell him anything.’ I shook my head but the dizziness washed over me again, the crusty dry blood falling from the cracks of my eyes.

‘Don’t you want to live?’

‘I can’t give them up.’

‘Then give him something else, you need to be smart.’

‘But I’m not smart!’ I screamed. ‘I don’t know anything, I don’t know what I’m meant to do, I was never trained like you. I don’t know anything!’

‘Oh right, well there we are then, I’ll just shut up.’ Jessica crossed her arms.

‘What?’

‘If you’re going to throw yourself a pity party then please, be my guest.’

‘Why are you being like this?’

‘What? Honest?’

‘I don’t know what to do, help me!’ I begged, my lip trembling.

Jessica marched over, her hands slamming either side of my shoulders with a smack, her breath cold on my face.

'Am I supposed to say poor you, poor Naomi?' she asked, her face dangerously close. 'Helpless, defenceless Naomi who would rather die than give up her team. She was so innocent, so pure.'

'But I don't –'

'Shut the fuck up,' she snapped. 'You're alone in this room, which means you have time to work so we can't waste it on tears or your fucking insecurities. No, you are not smart and no, you haven't been trained for this but what you can do, is think.'

I gasped in air but the dryness of it made a cough rupture from within. It wracked my body, my ribs screaming in agony, my hands balled into fists.

'You may not have been trained but you've been surrounded by assassins for months, you've picked things up,' Jessica told me, diving straight from anger to boredom apparently. God my subconscious was weird.

'Like what?' I asked.

She rolled her eyes.

'Saul is interrogating you, he wants information, but you haven't said one word. Now you're talking to yourself and quite frankly, losing it, but he hasn't come back. What does that tell you?'

'He popped out for a coffee, I don't know!'

'Listen,' she snapped.

I stared at her for a moment, until the quietness of the room sunk in. I could hear the wind as it whistled through gaps under the door. I couldn't hear any traffic but more importantly, I couldn't hear anyone on the other side of the door.

'There's no one outside.'

'You counted your steps, you know the route out of here,' she said. 'You didn't divert at all, you just kept going straight which means it'll be the exact same on the way out.'

'What if there's someone waiting? Outside of this building?'

'Then you're going to have to fight,' she answered. 'He uncovered your real identity and underestimated you.'

'But if Saul is as desperate as you said, he'll come back.'

'Then why are you still strapped to the chair?'

I tried to wiggle my way out, the sweat on my hand helping a little but it kept getting stuck.

'Pull. You only need one free to get the rest.'

The constricting leather tugged and burned at my skin. I thought of using my own blood to make it easier, but I'd fallen asleep. The once free flowing blood now dry and crusted.

'Weak points,' Jessica said.

I looked to the straps, they were tight but not without fault: on the left-hand side there was a tear. I sucked in a breath and pushed against it, balling my hand into a fist. The pressure against my skin made me want to stop but I couldn't – would I break my wrist? I had to try and get out of here. With a satisfying rip it tore just enough for me to wiggle my hand out.

‘Good,’ she said as I went to work freeing my hands and feet from the straps.

I managed to get to my feet and headed for the door, pushing past the aching and sheer pain. I listened for a moment before sliding it open, holding back a grimace. I was right, there was no one on the other side. I crossed a small room, pressing my ear to the next door; it was old and weathered; every single sound would come through but not a breath could be heard.

I opened the door and immediately made a run for it, counting each step. Suddenly, two men ran for me – they’d been standing guard at the exit I could only glimpse for a moment. I made a grab for one, jabbing my heel into his knee, then threw my elbow into his face, then headed for the other one, punching him on the nose.

I kicked my leg out behind, hearing the first man coming back for round two. The glint of their guns caught my eye but my main objective was to be so quick they couldn’t get to them.

I threw punches and kicks, one after the other, not slowing down for a moment even though fatigue was hitting me like a brick wall. I had to keep going, otherwise I’d be subjected to more torture. That I now knew I wouldn’t survive.

Desperate men do desperate things, rash things but I was no man.

I kept myself focused, taking one target at a time. When one was tumbling back I turned to the other. Blood spurted but not one bullet was fired as I managed to knock the two men out, sending them to the floor.

Saul had called my fighting style frantic but I believed it was just a game of survival. Strike fast and get out before anyone could hurt you again.

I eagerly headed for the door, keeping to the walls; I spotted the van outside still sitting on the cracked and broken road but when Saul came into view, I sighed.

He was a desperate man; time to appeal to his better nature.

I edged out of the door, holding my hands in surrender.

'Saul!' The man's head shot up, his eyes wide in fear as he shakily reached for his gun. 'Don't! Please, let me explain what Harkness is doing.'

'I can't, you know I can't. You can't be allowed to live.'

'Yes I can, and so can you. I was right before wasn't I?' I asked. 'If Harkness finds out you lost the team, it won't end pretty.'

'He'll kill me, yes,' the man muttered, his fingers still resting on the gun.

'We can protect you,' I said.

He scoffed. 'You couldn't even protect yourselves.'

'We can do better, we can help you.'

'Join the losing side? I don't think so,' he said.

'The right side, the side that doesn't care if you've made mistakes.' I edged towards him, hands still raised. 'You were coerced by Harkness, weren't you?'

'It doesn't matter.'

'Yes, it does. You matter. What did he do?' I dared to ask. 'What does he have on you?'

'Naomi, you can't fix this, it's too late. They've got the government in their pocket.'

'It's never too late,' I told him. 'If you come with me I can help, this team can help.'

'You can't do anything,' he said. 'Harkness will come for me.'

'Not if you tell him everything is under control,' I told him. 'Tell him that we're dead, that there's no sign of us.'

Instead of the holstered gun, his hand reached into his pocket. I appealed to my own better nature, I had to trust *human nature* for a moment. I lowered my hands, taking more cautious steps towards him. I had to show Saul I wasn't afraid of him.

'You're better than Harkness,' I said. 'Sure, you plied a couple of nails but you were scared, right?'

The man wasn't trembling, he was as solid as a stone but his eyes gave him away.

'You've been looking for a way out, that's probably why you've been close to Nicola?' I asked.

'How could you possibly think that?'

'I know people,' I stated. 'Harkness is doing the same thing that he did to Reign – he holds something over you and rules through fear. You probably have a family, friends. You could have killed me with that knife in the safe house but you didn't. You could have saved yourself the trouble but you didn't.'

'It wasn't the right time.'

'Now is the right time and I'm still breathing.'

My shoes softly hit the ground as I reached the man.

'You're scared of Harkness I know, but make the call.'

He hesitated, and as his hand pulled out his pocket, I thought of running, I thought of throwing a punch and snatching his gun but instead, he pulled out a phone and shakily dialled a number.

I didn't let out a breath of relief, this was far from over. I made sure to watch, memorising it. We could use that later. The phone rang for a couple of seconds before he answered.

'Jackson, what have you got?'

I eyed the man in front of me – he could ruin this whole thing with a simple word. If he told Harkness Grace's story was bullshit, he would kill her. Then he'd probably kill me. Saul mentioned that agents had this poise about them, the constant paranoia, the mistrust. I didn't trust him but I had to appear like I did. If he thought I trusted him then he wouldn't shoot me.

'Grace Aspin's story checks out, she must have fled before the team got there that night. My own team have surveyed the scene again, there's nothing. No signs of any other survivors.'

I wanted to sigh in relief but knew this was far from over.

'Any bodies?'

‘There’s nothing. Grace is clean.’

The phone line went dead.

‘Welcome to the losing side,’ I said.

‘If he finds out I betrayed him, he’ll kill me.’

‘Don’t worry, there will be a line.’

I ripped his gun from his holster and bashed his head, sending him tumbling to the ground with a thud.

Like I said, I didn’t trust him and like he said, I wasn’t stupid.

I grabbed his arms and hauled him into the unlocked truck, sliding over to the driver’s seat and starting the engine. These guys were idiots for leaving the keys in the van, perhaps they thought they’d have to make a quick getaway.

As I gripped the steering wheel, the fiery sensation returned in my fingers, each nerve screaming as I applied pressure.

Jessica wasn’t here anymore, I couldn’t see her, but I knew I had to keep going. It’s what she would have wanted. I also felt she’d be proud of me for smacking him over the head and in all honesty, I’d always wanted to do that.

CHAPTER 30

Wicked

Morally wrong.

GRACE ASPIN

'You need to go back to the safe house and collect your things,' Lillian told me. 'Then you'll hide out here until its safe for you to go.'

Half an hour later there was still no word from the team and I'd committed to working with Harkness. The idea made me want to throw up. I felt disgusted that I'd been forced to join his side, since I knew my team weren't coming back for me.

When I left I'd go straight to the meetup outside of town – I had to explain my side of the story. They had no idea what he did to me and they'd never understand. They probably thought I was the bad guy, that I was a traitor.

I knew I wasn't, that's all that mattered.

‘Yes ma’am,’ I replied obediently, then headed out.

As I left the reception I looked for my team but none of them were at their posts. They’d most likely fled. In all the years I’d been a part of this team they’d never cut the channel: one of the rules we prided ourselves on was never abandoning each other.

Now, even after we knew there were always two sides to the story, they still left me. For all they knew Harkness could be lying – I could tell them so but everything fitted too perfectly.

This team wanted justice, someone to blame and now that responsibility, had fallen to me. I understood you now, Jess, the leader is always the one to blame.

I felt angry that they left me but I carried on. Harkness had awoken something in me that I hadn’t felt for a long time. When his lips pressed my temple anger fired through my veins like a disease because Kayson was right, I was his obedient Grace. I’d forced my team into a situation, I’d screamed and yelled to get them to comply – it wasn’t my fault! It was how I was raised in his fucked-up institute.

Ames deserved it, his death was justice. He was a part of Harkness’s team – so what if he was young? He was old enough to suffer the consequences. The Academy made me into an assassin and then taught me how to make peace with it; my actions weren’t my fault. They made me think I was nothing but when Harkness saved me, I felt like something.

I felt as if we didn't have a choice, we had to get the leads to Trojan, and now I knew we'd worked alongside them the entire time.

I wanted to cry but it would be a waste; I wanted to scream but it would be for nothing so I focused on the anger, the rage, because anything was better than the inferno of guilt burning in my chest.

It took me a while but when I reached the designated hangar, the wind whistled through the air carrying the sound of my footsteps. As I turned the corner I tried to hold back a flinch as Lily held a gun straight at my head, the barrel pressing against my skin.

'Step back.'

'Lily.'

'I will shoot,' she warned.

'Wait!' Quinn's quiet voice wailed.

It was only then that I noticed Kayson's looming figure a few steps away, standing protectively in front of Quinn. She stepped out; her eyes were red from tears but her form was solid, strong.

I knew she'd be OK, I knew she was tough.

'Did you give Willow up?' Lily asked.

'No.'

'Did you tell Harkness we were on that plane?'

'No.'

'Did you tell Harkness where to find Jessica?'

'No.'

'Are we really going to believe this bullshit?' Lily sneered, her stare locked with mine. 'She's lying.'

'I'm not lying.'

'You've been lying since the moment I met you. You said your name was Grace but it can't be, I bet that's a lie too.'

'I swear it's not.' I tried to push her hands from the gun but she moved her finger to the trigger.

I threw my hands up in surrender.

'I didn't know he was going to kill Willow, I saw she'd stolen my pass to look for files so I told him about it, I said she was curious. I tried to convince him that she wasn't poking around. The next night he cuffed me to his desk, forced me to tell him everything.'

'He didn't force you, he didn't touch you!' Lily shouted.

'Yes he did!' The tears rose in my eyes but I didn't let them fall, I honed in on the anger. 'He kissed me and he touched me and he promised me that I would be safe if I gave into him.'

The heavy thud of Kayson's boots sounded on the floor as he tugged Quinn behind him.

'I saw her that night, he dragged her by her shirt to the morgue,' Kayson said. 'That's what you've been keeping to yourself all this time Grace?' he asked.

'Tell me you wouldn't have done the same,' I asked Lily. 'I had no choice.'

'You could have resisted.'

'Could you?' I pushed. 'If it was you he tied to the table like a dog? Could you be the one he didn't leave any marks on?'

'It doesn't matter, you betrayed us.'

'He beat you, Lily, he beat you into submission but that didn't work for me so he had a new tactic. I can see it now. I can see it all but I promise you, I am not a traitor. I swear my life on it, I swear to you before God I didn't betray this team.'

'God doesn't have a say in what I do,' Lily told me but Kayson's hands gently moved the gun to the floor.

'We cannot be like Harkness,' he said to her. 'We have to be better.'

'She killed Willow.'

'Indirectly perhaps, and she will face the consequences, but they will be decided by Nicola, not you,' he told her.

With a frustrated groan Lily pulled away from Kayson, taking Quinn by the arm, moving to the back of the hangar.

My lips parted to thank Kayson but he shook his head.

'What happened to honesty?' he asked.

'Kayson I couldn't have told you –'

'Not about what he did, I'm talking about Willow,' he said. 'I told you it was how we'd stay together.'

'You wouldn't have understood,' was all I could get out.

'You never gave me the chance.'

I wanted what he did to me to remain private, it was the one thing I had control over, it was the only thing I had control over. Now even that had been taken from me.

'They think I'm at the safe house collecting my things, we need to go back to Scotland, show Nicola what we have,' I said.

'I am not going anywhere with you.' Lily stated. 'You haven't even noticed have you?'

'Noticed what?'

'Naomi isn't here!' Her voice boomed.

I hadn't – wait no, no she wasn't here. Where was she?

'What happened?' I asked.

'We don't know. After you left, Kayson had to cover the Prime Minister but on the way back a group of armed men attacked him, he barely escaped alive. Then Quinn and I were ambushed, her ribs are covered in bruises. Now we don't have access to cameras, internet, phones – anything. We have nothing.'

Kayson didn't look exhausted or frail, he appeared tall and strong. However, he had a gash to his arm and neck, it looked like he really had dodged a bullet. Bruises had started to form on his skin and blood stained his knuckles and wrists. Lily was covered up for the most part – I could only begin to imagine what lurked under there.

'That's not possible.' My voice a whisper.

‘Are you awake now, Grace?’ Lily asked. ‘Are you awake to the hell you’ve dragged us into?’

I was going to apologise, I wanted to tell them how sorry I was, I wanted to tell them how I thought I was in control and that I was doing the right thing.

‘Hell? It’s a bit chilly for that.’ Naomi said.

I spun round to see her standing tall behind me, dried blood cracked on her face and hands, most of it coming from her fingers and nose, a gun at her side. She’d been tortured – instinct picked away at me, ready to reach for my medic’s bag but it wasn’t there. I had nothing.

The need to help her was strong but Kayson beat me to it, pulling her into his embrace; she flinched a little but her fingers fiddled with the back of his shirt.

‘I’m OK,’ she said.

‘Who did this to you?’ he asked. ‘Who did this?’

‘He’s on our side now, he was trapped just like you were.’

‘Who did this?’ Kayson said, his voice almost a growl.

‘Me.’ Saul’s once charming voice now pathetic and weak.

I could describe the look on Kayson’s face in many ways but it was a simple expression: his eyes narrowed, his fists clenched and then he took a deep breath. He looked ready to kill Saul, slowly and painfully.

He gently moved away from Naomi despite her protests, grabbed Saul and threw him across the tarmac like something inhuman.

'You did that?' he asked. 'You took her?'

'I didn't have a choice.' he pleaded.

'That's all I hear!' For the first time, I witnessed Kayson let go of everything he'd ever held inside, every emotion slipping through his grasp. 'That's all I've heard from you two. I didn't have a choice, it wasn't my fault, well who's fault is it?'

He spun around to face us all.

'If we blame each other then we will lose each other,' he said. 'We will lose everyone we ever cared about. What Harkness did to us, to me, it doesn't just stop because he left Reign. He's tortured minds for decades but now we have chance, a small, significant chance to change it. Alexander is ready to launch laws that restrict the public, that confine us for a week while they rewrite this country in their image. We have to stop them.'

'I'm sorry, I sent you with Alexander so you could be photographed,' Saul admitted. 'Trojan wanted a better visual of you Kayson.'

Naomi's hand pressed against Kayson's back but he pulled away, yanking Saul to his feet by the grip on his shirt.

'Trojan can take me to hell for all I care but Naomi – she chose to bring you to us, she chose to keep you safe.'

'He called Harkness, he kept to Grace's story, as far as anyone knows she was the only survivor of that crash. He's on our side now,' Naomi said, but she didn't move to intervene, her body starting to shake, adrenaline finally wearing off.

‘If you touch her again I will kill you, do you understand?’

‘I won’t, I swear.’

‘You’ll wish Harkness had gotten to you first,’ Kayson growled, tossing him to the ground.

Kayson trudged over, gently pulling Naomi back to us.

‘So, do we have a plan or are we making one?’

‘We need to go back to Scotland,’ I repeated.

Naomi shook her head.

‘Gareth Brixton, Metropolitan Police, we grab him and take him back to Scotland along with Saul, then we expose what’s happened before the restrictions kick in.’

‘What?’

‘You’re suggesting we kidnap this guy?’ Lily asked. ‘I’m not doing anything with her involved.’ She spat on the ground at my feet.

‘We’ve all made mistakes. We need her to get us inside. They think you’re coming right back?’ Kayson asked.

‘Yes.’ I replied. ‘They’re expecting me.’

‘Then Grace and Saul will distract Lillian, and Conrad if he’s around to cause any trouble. I’ll grab Gareth and then we’ll get out of there,’ Kayson said.

‘So we –’ I tried, but Kayson cut me off.

‘I’m taking Team Lead,’ Kayson stated. ‘We all go by my orders. Understood?’

What? Since when did he want the job? I couldn't put up much of a fight or the team would probably leave me in the dust. Would they ever trust me again? Even after I explained my side of the story? How could they? They'd never understand.

'Are you sure?' Lily asked. 'The first one died and the second went fuckin insane.'

How dare she! She didn't know the first thing about my situation and yet she stood there and judged me. What about her? She wasn't exactly a shining example.

'Enough!' Kayson's hand sliced through the air. 'Grace and Saul, get Lillian, Harkness, anyone who's an asset. Get them out of the way. Keep them distracted long enough so we can grab Gareth.'

'What happens after we get him?' I asked. 'We don't have a way across the border.'

'I could ask another one of my friends,' Lily offered.

'I am not flying with your friends again,' Naomi said.

'We'll contact Nicola and ask for immediate extraction,' Kayson said, before glancing to Saul. 'I'll leave you to organise that.'

'We're really going to trust them on their own?' Lily asked, eyeing me and Saul up. 'Harkness will be there.'

'We have to,' Kayson said, and as his gaze landed on me, there was something I noticed about him.

After everything we'd been through, he still trusted me. If the situation was different I would have told him he was an idiot for trusting someone like me, given the evidence, but as he stood there, pleading that I wouldn't make a run for it, I truly saw his darkest fear. Being alone.

We'd lost so much these past few weeks, for his sake I couldn't add myself to the list.

'Gareth might have made a run for it,' Naomi said. 'He looked terrified.'

'I can fix that,' Saul said, cautiously making his way towards us. 'I can get him back in the building, he's under the impression that he can trust me.'

'Grace and Saul, we'll give you a ten-minute head start, which also gives Gareth time to get back in the building. Comms are down so we have no way of communicating. Saul, we'll use your phone as the primary contact. I'll text you the exit point once you're on the road.' Kayson took out his phone, quickly grabbing the other's number. 'When you're in, update, when you've got them under control, update. When we're clear of the building, I'll let you know.'

'What do I do?' Quinn asked.

'You're staying in the car,' Kayson said.

'What? No, no way I'm helping.'

'If they know who we really are then we're never safe. The minimal people only. Naomi, you're taking point of Quinn.'

'I'm not staying in the car either,' Naomi stated, clearly offended.

'You're injured and these guys are professionals – you've not trained long enough,' he said, shaking his head. 'As soon as Gareth is in the building, I'll go and Lily will follow.'

I expected Naomi to fight against the order but she just bit her lip and moved aside. Kayson let out a small sigh of relief before he checked the watch on his wrist.

'You two need to get moving,' he said.

Without needing to be told twice, Saul headed back for the van – I didn't move.

I was right, I couldn't lead this team. Harkness was wrong, I wasn't worth saving. Quinn must of felt useless but I felt obsolete.

'Grace?' Kayson asked.

I tried to take a breath but it was like my body had simply stopped. I held my head high despite the tremoring in my chin and the quiver in my lip.

He'd taken over – Kayson had only just transferred to this team but he'd already overthrown me as Team Lead.

When I came here I thought fists would fly. Yes, Lily held a gun to my head but that wasn't exactly alarming. She'd pull the trigger without a second thought, that's how Runners worked, but it was me. Despite everything I knew she wouldn't shoot me.

If it were me there'd be blood, I heard Jessica say. *If you hadn't given Willow up I'd still be alive.*

‘No you wouldn’t,’ I muttered under my breath, but Kayson’s fingers on my chin made my voice fall quiet.

‘As soon as this is over, you’re being dismissed from duty and submitting yourself for psychiatric evaluation,’ he ordered. ‘OK?’

I didn’t even fight him, I didn’t even mumble, I just nodded and headed for the van. As I opened the door however, I saw Jessica’s figure. She wasn’t covered in blood but her face was sour.

‘You failed, Grace,’ she said. ‘Perhaps you weren’t cut out to be my Second after all. Look at you, removed from active duty and admitted to the psychiatrists – how the mighty fall.’ She smiled.

I got in the van, slamming the door shut, and as we took off towards the city I had to convince myself that wasn’t Jessica, not really. She’d be empathetic, she’d understand. Would she though?

Could I trust my own mind?

I had to call David.

CHAPTER 31

Foresee

To predict.

NAOMI JADE

After they'd left we waited, and it was truly the longest ten minutes of my life. I'd sat down and started to clean the blood off with some emergency wipes Quinn had stashed in her pocket.

I could barely believe the situation I'd found myself in – Saul had known who we were all along, as well as my parents. He'd been the perfect mole.

When I heard about Grace I wasn't surprised – well I was, but in a way she reminded me of Jess. She did what she had to do to survive, although my once-solid trust was now crumbling to pieces. If she was telling the truth and she didn't tell Harkness about the plane, then who did?

'Hey,' Lily said, shaking my shoulder. 'Time to go.'

'Right,' I mumbled as she pulled me up.

'Are you OK?' she asked. 'Being tortured isn't exactly a walk in the park, especially when you're not used to it.'

'I didn't give you up if that's what you mean,' I said, rubbing my arm, trying my best not to look at my barren nail beds, they probably looked disgusting.

'It's not,' she said. 'It can be tough, especially with Grace pulling what she did. You have point of Quinn but take the time to relax. You're both staying in the car.'

'I have a feeling Quinn would be better at defending me.' I laughed, but then Lily pressed a gun into my hand.

'This time, if you need it, don't forget to use it,' she told me. 'At the harbour you completely forgot about it. The gun is an extension of you and this type of weapon is easy to use. Point, shoot.'

'If I'm staying in the car I don't see why I need it.'

'For emergencies.'

'You two!' Kayson yelled. 'Let's move it. I know we still have the SAS passes to get in, but I don't want to waste any more time.'

'God, he's bossy,' Lily smirked.

The car that waited for us was a family car; it would blend right in to central London. Lily, Quinn and I piled in the back while Kayson started the engine.

Here we go again, again.

I understood now why Saul said all agents had this constant distrust about them – they were thrown into situations like this. As much as I tried to hold onto that faith in others, that I'd pulled out from Saul a mere hour ago, I felt it slipping.

How could you trust someone when all they did was lie?

That was Grace's fault: she confused being correct and justice as one and the same.

As we pulled up at the reception building once more that day, I looped my arm around Quinn's and after Saul's text, saying Trojan were distracted and Gareth was in the building, the Runners headed in.

A small bit of me was relieved I wasn't going in, since the pain pulsing from my wounds and bruises still came in waves. However, I was worried for them all because now I knew the inevitable – at least one person was going to die.

I knew it to be true because it was in their nature.

CHAPTER 32

Graceless

Lacking elegance or charm.

GRACE ASPIN

'Life is a funny thing, everyone always comes back to the same place,' Daniel remarked. 'Just like you came back to me.'

His hand grazed my hip but I kept a stony expression, focusing on the anger that fuelled my being.

'I don't apologise often, you know that. I am sorry for the loss of your team but you have to understand, this was your fault. You made me do it.' His voice was kind but his words were like venom.

Kayson's words flooded my head, helping me to understand that Harkness had destroyed my mind. A couple of months ago, if he had told me it was my fault I would have believed him. I'd spend a night in his office and then it would be forgotten, with no bruises to serve as a reminder.

'I understand,' I replied, nodding firmly.

'You always were good, my little Gracie,' he smiled. 'I'll give you a team, don't worry, there's just a couple of things we need to deal with first.'

His warm breath left a stench in the air but I focused on his shoes and the soft thud they made across the floor. I could pretend I was someone else, somewhere else and nothing could hurt me. Especially him, he could never hurt me again.

'What's this vital information?' Lillian asked, seeming rather impatient as she stared out of the window.

Alexander was still responding to the press so thankfully he wasn't in the room, but Conrad was looking me up and down like some prize pig. I didn't falter under his stare; I'd faced far worse than some sleazy bank manager. Saul had gotten in because he had vital information, although what information he held I wasn't sure.

'It's about Operation Red Dawn.'

What on earth was that about?

Harkness turned on his heel, as did everyone else in the room.

'I don't have much but I know one of the people involved, is Nicola Ramos,' Saul said, hands clasped behind his back.

'What's the objective?' Harkness asked.

'No clue but it has something to do with her.'

'I'll need you to go back to Scotland with Grace,' he replied. 'You'll report back to me. Grace, you'll take him and convince Nicola he's been your confidant the entire time. I may have lost Reign but I will not remain clueless.'

'Yes sir. I'll arrange a flight back.' Saul nodded.

'What should I do?' I asked.

'You're my agent, my perfect Grace.' Harkness smiled. 'You'll go back to Reign, act accordingly and then, if necessary, once Nicola has served her use, you'll kill her.'

Kill her? I didn't like the woman much but I couldn't kill her. No – as far as this room is aware you've switched sides Grace, you need to play along.

'Yes, sir,' I replied.

'Now get out,' Conrad snapped.

'Sir, if I may –' Saul tried but he barely got a sentence out, before Conrad jumped back in.

'You may not, I don't need agents. Daniel, there are bigger things at stake now – they can't be here for the new legislation, we have more people arriving this evening. Charlotte's gone off grid with that CIA bastard. Get them out of here.'

'There's no evidence she's with Clayton,' Lillian said. 'None at all, her daughters just died Conrad.'

'She's went straight to the Pentagon, mark my words.'

'Conrad's right you need to leave,' Harkness said to us. 'Saul and Grace, get to work. I'll expect an update weekly with what you've found.'

That was it? We were being thrown out already? I expected some big showdown or a fight, but we'd been dismissed within five minutes. That couldn't have given Kayson enough time to grab Gareth – I had to come up with something else, but I had nothing to offer them.

What could I do?

I didn't have time to think about it because gunfire thundered from outside the door, followed by screams and yells. Was that my team or had something far more sinister occurred?

'What the hell is that?' Conrad asked.

Harkness immediately went for his phone but the locked door behind us started to rattle and shake. This wasn't part of the plan – Kayson wasn't meant to come for me.

'Are people rioting?' Lillian asked, backing away from the door.

I locked eyes with Saul before looking over to the false wall Harkness had slipped from earlier, the wallpaper peeling at the edges of the door. If they were distracted we could make a run for it but if we did, would that expose our real agenda?

'If you want that intel we need to get out of here,' Saul said hurriedly, already looking a little tense.

'So do we!' Conrad shrieked. 'Have those idiots broken in? I knew that speech would cause a riot.'

I wanted to say that it wasn't a riot, it had to be my team. It was the glorious sound of my team at work.

'You came through the false wall sir, is there a way out?' I asked formally.

Harkness drummed his fingers on the desk.

'Yes, it's a straight corridor all the way, takes you out through the hidden door at the back,' he said.

‘Saul, we’d better get going,’ I said, rushing for the false door and shoving Saul ahead.

I contemplated my next move: I could reveal to him that I was a liar, I could tell him everything.

I could humiliate him.

However, with a firm nod from him I knew my best play was to remain silent and play along. The only person who would feel better if I revealed my true agenda was me, I had to think of the team. We didn’t need a repeat of the Edinburgh chase, we needed a clean getaway.

Blessed are the meek and blessed are those who suffer for the cause.

I sucked in a breath before running down the corridor after Saul, hoping to reach the light at the end of the tunnel.

CHAPTER 33

Morals

A lesson that can be derived from a story or experience.

KAYSON ASHFORD

BANG.

BANG.

BANG.

It was fucked up but the sound of bullets always brought me comfort. In the past it had provided me security; bullets had kept me safe.

Can't wait to see the look on the psychiatrist's face when I tell them that.

We'd grabbed a skittish Gareth from the back of the reception building but as soon as the guards caught on, the rounds had started flying. Lily was covering me as I dragged Gareth behind me, gaining ground with every step.

'If you give up now they'll let you live!' Gareth pleaded but I bit my tongue, continuing on.

The safety on my gun was off but I couldn't get Naomi's face out of my head. The anger that brewed on her face when I'd shot Ames haunted me. This wasn't her world, I got that but maybe she had a point. To us, it had become second nature but to her this was all still fresh. Perhaps –

BANG.

OK, now wasn't the time to revisit my morals.

'Lily, go!' I shouted over the racket. I didn't care for codenames, our window for escape was getting smaller and smaller.

Lily sprinting across the room, filled with politicians glued to the floors and dead guards who, unfortunately, had been at the receiving end of her gun. I followed her lead, dragging a snivelling Gareth with me, limping from what I could only presume was an old war injury.

Muzzle flashes nearly blinded me as more men charged into the building, a lot of them heading for where I presumed Grace and Saul were. The good thing was they'd be going there to protect them, the bad thing was that it would make it almost impossible for us to get to them.

I could kill them all, I could kill them all on sight and no one would give two shits. These people had ruined countless lives, taken innocent lives and destroyed my own. I couldn't let my anger fester, I had to be better than him.

The exit was almost in sight, the cool air failing to comfort me as three men came straight for me. I recognised them – they were the ones who nearly had my head earlier. Their grins were vicious, their guns hostile.

BANG.

BANG.

BANG.

Lily had swooped in front of me, killing them stone dead, head shots.

She grabbed Gareth's other arm and charged out of the building, heading straight for the car.

'This is going to be all over the bloody news,' I muttered as we ran round the side of the building, Lily tossing Gareth in the back of the car with the girls.

The car was still intact so fortunately nothing had happened while I was gone, this first op as Team Lead wasn't going horribly. Which was a first.

I dived into the driver's seat, Lily slipping in the back, immediately pointing a gun to the man's head. Something ticked me off about Lily, the way she swooped in – it was like she was on the drugs from the Academy.

Lily was a weapon, no doubt about it but after what happened, I thought she'd hesitate. Believe me, I was glad she didn't, but I thought there'd be something. I had to remind myself that people coped in different ways and Lily for the most part, had been filled with anger and lust.

I didn't know the relationship she and Quinn had, but I pitied Quinn, she'd break her heart. There was a reason Lily never had any stable relationships. They just weren't meant for a person like her.

A frantic Saul slammed on the window before jumping in beside me, followed by Grace, whose slight breakdown had apparently disappeared.

I'd need to book that psychiatric consultation when we got back.

'Drive!' she said.

This was how an operation should run, quick, straight to the point, in and out. I'd petition Nicola to become the permanent Team Leader when we got back – we couldn't carry on with Grace in charge.

CHAPTER 34

Falsity

Lies.

NAOMI JADE

The extraction plan had gone almost too smoothly. After everything, I'd thought something would have gone wrong but it hadn't.

Since I wasn't part of the extraction team I didn't know how many people had died. I'd heard gunshots but wasn't sure if any of them were fatal. No one had blood on them as far as I could see. Maybe this time it was just injuries.

I muttered a couple of curses under my breath – I'd been down this road before and had been proven wrong time and time again.

Of course people had died, I had to find a way to be OK with that.

When we'd first come to London the flight was chaotic but now, apart from the occasional murmur and grumble of the engine, there was only silence.

Kayson sat at the front of the plane, Lily at his side, presumably texting an update to Nicola, while Quinn for the one hundredth time was trying to get something out of Grace; she hadn't spoken a word since she'd gotten in the car.

This wasn't looking good, Nicola wasn't going to be happy. Would she bring up the man Lily had murdered again? Would she bring up the past? Would she bring up what we did and what happened today?

Was she going to split us up?

Saul was handcuffed to one of the chairs at the back along with Gareth – I had no idea where the cuffs had come from. Saul seemed to be contemplating a lot, I could practically see every thought buzzing about his head at once. Would Nicola arrest him or use him?

A couple of hours later we were in an SUV sitting at the front doors of the Academy and honestly, I was shitting myself. Nicola stood at the bottom of the steps, a scowl marking her lips as we all hopped out. She had a couple of healing scars on her head, from where I didn't know, but in true Nicola fashion, was still wearing shoes that could poke someone's eye out.

'You have some nerve,' Nicola said to Grace but she didn't respond, lingering behind Kayson.

'We have evidence that Trojan has infiltrated government, including recorded conversations that Quinn saved in the cloud as well as witnesses,' he said proudly.

'What?'

I shoved Saul out the van – that was a little emotionally motivated I'll admit – grabbing his cuffed hands and leading him to Nicola. Followed by Lily and Gareth. The poor man must have been exhausted because he'd been mumbling all sorts of nonsense on the ride over.

'Saul Jackson, Harkness's mole in MI6 as well as Gareth Brixton, a man high up within Trojan. We would have grabbed Ruta to testify against Lillian, but time was cut short,' Kayson said with a smirk. 'Now before you get all high horse, I'm going to grab a drink. These two can go to the meeting rooms. They've agreed to help so you shouldn't face too much of a struggle.'

It was only then I noted the silent conversation going on between Nicola and Saul: looks of betrayal, anger and disgust thrown between them.

'What happened to you?' Nicola asked me. I probably didn't look red-carpet ready.

'He did,' I said, motioning to Saul. 'I'm going to head to the medical wing, see if they have anything for when your nail gets ripped from your finger.'

I felt Saul's gaze burning into the back of my head but I didn't care enough to look back. He was someone I sympathised with, someone I thought was just like us.

Again, I was wrong.

'Stop,' Nicola ordered. 'Omega Team go to the dorm house, I'll send a medic and debrief you there.'

The crunching of feet on the gravel pounded towards us and Eve, amongst a few others surrounded us, all looking like they'd seen a ghost.

'All of you go back inside!' Nicola yelled, before she turned to us. 'I'll escort the pair of them myself.'

'But we need to be there when you interrogate them,' I tried.

'Do not push it,' she warned me. 'Get inside, now.'

I looked to Kayson – if he'd fight this so would I, but he didn't. He slipped off his jacket, giving Nicola a mock salute before heading off in the direction of the dorm house. I didn't move myself until Quinn and Lily took my arms, pulling me the same way.

The creak of the tall doors groaned through the grounds and when the troubled look of Grace's met mine, I knew exactly who had walked out the door.

'Grace?' Dr McKay asked but as he ran down the stairs, Nicola grabbed his arm.

'There are patients on that ward, I suggest you either return to them or help me with these two.'

'Nicola, I need five minutes.'

'I don't care what you need. Until I say so you are to stay away from Miss Aspin, or I'll report you myself for unproper relations with a student,' Nicola stated.

A quiet murmur broke out amongst the crowd as the words left Nicola's mouth – even Grace herself gasped.

'This ends today,' Nicola said. 'All of it, the lies, the deceit. It ends now.'

Even though I didn't know the full story myself, I knew rumours would start amongst the students. Well, Grace – you've got a shitstorm coming your way.

Dr McKay, tight-lipped and silent, grabbed Gareth and hauled him up the stairs but suddenly, the man broke out into cries.

'Wait, she has to say goodbye, wait please,' Gareth wailed.

What was he on about?

'Get inside,' David grumbled.

'No! She made a phone call in Thames House, we'd been watching her, she made a call to her mother.'

What the fuck was he talking about?

'It was just as insurance, just in case but then we thought she'd died in the explosion,' Gareth said slowly, turning to face me. 'If you leave now you might get a chance to say goodbye.'

No, please no.

Saul knew my parents' names, he knew my address and that meant Trojan did too. Without thinking, and disregarding Kayson I ran to the SUV, turning the key and speeding back off down the drive.

Grabbing the burner from my pocket I dialled my mum's number but all the bastard thing did was ring.

‘No, no, no,’ I pleaded, tears brimming as I reached the road. ‘Come on, pick up.’

I tried my dad, the same result. Please no, Grace believed in God, right and God wouldn’t have my parents killed, God wouldn’t let that happen because I didn’t deserve that. I hadn’t done anything to deserve that! I’d fought with this team, I’d saved my country and I’d escaped a terrorist’s interrogation.

My parents had to be alive, they had to be.

CHAPTER 35

Backstabbing

Betrayal in a traitorous manner.

GRACE ASPIN

'Naomi!' I yelled as she drove off in the SUV, going to run after her but I knew it would be hopeless.

I barely saw Kayson grab Saul from Nicola, pinning him against the wall.

'What have you done?'

'I haven't done anything, I swear.'

'You told him we were alive,' Kayson growled. 'You told him, how?'

'You took my phone before the plane!'

'So it was Grace?' Lily asked, and I laughed bitterly.

'No, it wasn't me!' I practically screamed. 'I wouldn't sell you out!'

'You had no problem doing it with Willow.'

'That's not what happened!'

How was this possible? If Trojan had Naomi's parents then they had to know the rest of the team were alive, but they let us go anyway. How did they know?

As I looked around the team I came up short: there were only so many of us, but I knew none of us could have done this. There had to be some sort of bug on the plane.

There couldn't be a traitor.

When the revving of an engine sounded I thought Naomi had come back but when I looked down the drive, five armoured jeeps were heading straight for us.

'Nicola?' I asked, a little worried.

'I didn't call them.'

I made a grab for Eve, pulling her back as the armoured cars ground to a halt and from the back a swarm of armed police, flooding the courtyard. Guns clicking and raised to fire. What on earth was going on?

Amongst the guards I spotted a pair of shiny formal shoes that unfortunately I had seen before, along with the dark black hair.

'Grace Maria Aspin, Quinn Tyna Eaton, Lily Chan and Kayson Ashford – I'm arresting you on account of treason against the Crown, the murders of British intelligence agents, the unlawful arrest of Umesh Acharya and the murder of Thomas Ames,' Chris Barnes said, hands clasped behind his back.

'Chris, what are you doing?' Kayson asked, throwing his hands in the air.

'My job. Sorry Nic,' he said, looking to Nicola. 'Her too, arrest her.'

'Chris, you can't do this. Chris!' Nicola tried, but men grabbed her, releasing Saul and throwing her in the back of one of the vans.

Had the time finally arrived? Was this my penance? After everything, Christopher had missed the funeral – I thought I'd get a chance to tell him myself and I still might, from behind bars.

'Let's go!' Chris said, heading back to the van. 'If anyone gets in the way bring them too!'

I ran forward but as I did red dots appeared on my chest and I found myself, throwing up my arms.

How did we get here?

I heard Quinn screaming but I couldn't bring myself to look at her, the tears of my anger finally falling, relenting after all this time.

'Stop!' I begged. 'Stop, Chris please wait!'

He appeared to be in charge but I had a feeling it was Trojan behind this. Why else would they let us come back here? They wanted to humiliate us. I didn't expect Chris to listen to me but with the wave of his hand, my feet rested on the gravel. I wanted to ask if he knew who he was working for but if Nicola didn't, then either he didn't or he'd known all this time.

It was then that I got a glimpse of where everyone was. Quinn was already halfway in the back of the van but her top was ripped exposing the blotchy bruising on her ribs. Kayson had been pinned to the ground by three men, pulling him in all directions; the purple bruising, cuts and slashes crushed into the gravel like salt in a wound. Lily had been thrashing so much that her jacket had fallen to the ground, leaving her in a vest top.

There wasn't a mark on her. If Kayson had barely survived getting out of the reception and Quinn was covered in bruises, how did she get out without a scratch?

There was a traitor among us but it couldn't be her – in the beginning she was so supportive of me, she helped wherever she could. We smiled, laughed and I completely trusted her. She wouldn't do this, not to us, not to me.

'Who were you texting?' I asked Lily. 'On the plane, you sent a message to someone. Who?'

'What?' she asked.

'How is it that he knew our every move?' I asked, begging to be corrected. 'How did he know we were in London in the first place? How did he know the plane we were on?'

'Because you told him,' she snarled.

'No.' I shook my head. 'You did.'

I thought my voice had been carried away on the wind but as the smile curled on Lily's face, I had my answer. Lily was the one who killed without hesitation, she was the one to reassure Kayson he could take the shot at Ames, she was the one that convinced us Jessica worked for Trojan. When she was locked in the cells, unable to defend herself, Lily was the one that convinced us she was a double agent. It was Lily all along.

She was the traitor.

This entire time I'd been fearful of Harkness, when I should have been terrified of what he'd created. When he fled Reign I thought he'd come back, I just didn't expect him to hide behind my friend. Perhaps in the meeting with Alexander she'd been subjugated to NX14, the drug they'd been using for years. Maybe she didn't know what she was doing. She wouldn't do this to me.

The guards holding her arms let her go without a care, and she laughed, grabbing for her gun. However, like Lily I knew the taste of those drugs. They didn't do this. Did Harkness have something on her?

Why did she look like she was enjoying this?

'It was a bullet to the head, wasn't it?' Lily asked. 'You said that to Naomi the day she broke in, that her mother would get a bullet to the head.'

'Lily what are you doing?' Quinn cried.

BANG.

Blinding pain shot through my torso, my knees giving way but the brutal hold of the guards didn't let up, clenching my arms.

'Grace!' David shouted. 'For fuck's sake Chris, let me help her!'

But as Lily stalked past Chris, he hung his head in shame. Then, like an animal, she crept towards me. Holstering the gun at her side with a wicked grin that I'd only ever seen on one other face.

'Where's your God now?'

CHAPTER 36

Cadaver

A corpse.

NAOMI JADE

From weaving in and out of cars to calling everyone I knew to see if they'd heard from my parents, I'd never driven faster.

I shot down the road, slamming on the brakes as I came to my parents' drive and ran as fast as I could, gun in hand.

If he hurt my parents I swear I would kill him.

I threw open the door.

'Mum! I shouted. 'Dad!'

Suddenly my foot slipped and I crashed onto my back, my head thumping on the hardwood floor. What the hell was that?

I looked to my shoe and saw a thin layer of red covering the sole. I'd slipped on blood.

I scrambled to my knees, following the trail but as it led me to the kitchen I wished I'd never come back.

My mum lay dead on the floor, her throat slit, her phone mere inches from her hand alight with missed calls. A few feet away my dad lay in a pool of his own blood, face down.

'No!' I cried, reaching for them.

This couldn't be happening, I had kept Reign and my parents separate, I had made sure they used burner phones.

I had done everything and it still wasn't enough.

I screamed, I cried, a pain wrenching through my chest like no other. I wished I was numb like before. Anything was better than this.

BAM.

The door to the house burst open and I was hoisted into the air, handcuffs clenching into my wrists.

'Mum!' I screamed as I was dragged out through the door. 'Dad! Don't touch them!'

Before I knew it I was thrown into the back of a cold metal van, my gun taken. Lily said I should have used it. I should have trusted her, trusted myself.

Trojan had killed my parents.

There had to be a pulse, my dad had to be alive, he had to – he had to give me a lecture about being reckless and how my friends were bad influences.

He couldn't be gone! How could they do that to them? They hadn't done anything!

I'd been good my whole life – I didn't deserve this! They didn't deserve to die.

With a slam the van doors shut and I finally saw I was left with one guard, armed but young-looking. They kept underestimating me.

I wasn't going to throw away Lily's advice again.

I waited until the van started moving then kicked him in the face, giving me time to jump back and swing my arms round. He tried to grab me but I didn't give him a chance, shooting down, grabbing his gun.

I pointed it at his chest and pulled the trigger.

BANG.

I was right, he was young, probably only a couple years older than me. His lips shook as he cried in pain like the bastard he was. For all I knew he slit my mother's throat.

BANG.

BANG.

BANG.

I kept going, emptying the entire clip into the man.

Everyone underestimated me, everyone thought they could lie to me. These men had taken my parents from me, they'd taken the people that had raised me. I hadn't crossed a line, this was justice.

Acknowledgments

Now, I've written these before but that doesn't mean writing them a second time is any easier. I had to comb through my brain to make sure I didn't forget anyone who was involved in the creation of this book.

I wanted to thank my editor Sam Firth who went through this manuscript with a fine-tooth comb, pointing out that I had repeatedly used words that didn't make sense. I mean in my head they did, but not by literary standards.

Once again I wanted to thank Ziyanda for the amazing character art that she created for this second book, especially since I gave her a bit of a challenge!

I wanted to say thanks to my family and friends, to whom this book is dedicated, for their repeated support throughout this entire process.

A special thank you also goes out to Kris Scott and Rory Meechan, as well as all the crew and cast involved in the short film, inspired by this series. They brought my little brainstorm to life in a hotel event room in Ayr, and I am forever grateful.

Emery Hale is a young Scotland based author, who has longed to put her stories onto the page. Ones filled with danger, love, betrayal and blood. When she's not writing she's an avid filmmaker and hopes to get her shorts in the next TV and film festivals.

CONNECT WITH EMERY ON:

Website: the_slate_universe.myshopify.com

Instagram: official_slate

TikTok: emery_hale3

YouTube: www.youtube.com/emeryhale

Printed in Great Britain
by Amazon

21469130R00231